WHEN THE
STORM
BREAKS

WHEN THE STORM BREAKS

A NOVEL

BONNIE LEON

Revell

Grand Rapids, Michigan

Published by Fleming H. Revell
a division of Baker Publishing Group
P.O. Box 6287, Grand Rapids, MI 49516-6287

Printed in the United States of America

Library of Congress Cataloging-in-Publication Data
Leon, Bonnie.
    When the storm breaks : a novel / Bonnie Leon.
        p.   cm. — (The Queensland chronicles ; bk. 3)
        ISBN 0-8007-5898-6 (pbk.)
        1. Pioneers—Fiction. 2. Queensland—Fiction. 3. Americans—
    Australia—Fiction. I. Title.
    PS3562.E533W465 2006
    813'.54—dc22   2005026198

Scripture is taken from the King James Version of the Bible.

Acknowledgments

Writing friends are a unique bunch. We're sometimes brutally honest with each other, but we also encourage and build up one another. Thank you to my writing partners.

I'd especially like to thank Ann Shorey, one of my writing chums. You came to the rescue when my back was against the wall. I couldn't have finished this book without you. Your creativity and encouragement were exactly what I needed.

Throughout this series I've sought the advice of "horse people," and Debbie Note was one of those people. Horses are part of who you are. Your insights were a great help to me. Thanks so much. I owe you.

And again, I must thank Kelley Meyne. You are amazing. I'm grateful for your skill and your attention to detail. Having an editor who works hard and whom I can trust is a comfort to me.

1

March 7, 1874

Rebecca hefted a large branch onto a pile of burning debris. Using the back of her hand, she brushed hair away from her face and glanced around at the blackened earth. It was all so sad, everything lost in a matter of minutes. Memories of the hungry fire that had devoured her home rolled through her mind. She could feel the heat, smell the smoke, and taste the powerlessness. Rebecca's heart raced, and she felt the familiar tightening in her stomach.

She tried to shut out the images, but the terror became real. Again Rebecca felt the anguish of searching for Joseph and Callie—searching and praying.

"That's the last of it," Daniel said. "At least for today." He rested an arm across Rebecca's shoulders. "I'd say we've made good progress."

Rebecca blinked back tears and tried to focus on Daniel. "What? What did you say?"

"We're done for today."

"It's still early."

"Right. But I've got to go to town. And I don't want you working too hard."

"We've still so much left to do." Rebecca studied a pile of rubble that had once been a cabin. "And I was hoping we could have a chat this afternoon."

"We will. When I get back." Daniel looked more closely at Rebecca. "You all right, luv?"

"Fine. Just tired." She leaned against her husband. "It's disheartening—burning what's already been burned, things we held dear."

"Right. But I keep thinking about Joseph and you and Mum. We could have lost so much more." He hugged her. "I'm thankful for our lives." His eyes scanned the charred earth where their home had stood and the wreckage that had been the barn. "God will see to us."

"I know you're right." Rebecca sighed. The more work she did, the more she felt the weight of all that had been lost. Each passing day, believing and trusting became more difficult.

Willa joined the couple, Joseph in tow. "He's right about what?"

"That God will take care of us." Rebecca couldn't keep from looking at the ruins of the once grand house. Her insides churned. What could God do now?

"Don't look so forlorn, dear. It will all be put right." Willa looked at Daniel. "Isn't that right, son?"

"Absolutely."

Rebecca studied Daniel. His words were optimistic, but she could see the weariness in the set of his shoulders and the worry in his eyes. And she knew that her news would only make life more difficult for him.

"Don't have all the details worked out yet." Daniel smiled. "But I'm going to speak to Charles Oxley about a loan. Planned on going into town today."

"Don't get your hopes up," Rebecca said in a snide tone. "He may very well be the stingiest banker ever."

"He's careful with the bank's money, but he's always done right by us. I'm sure we'll be able to work out something." Daniel glanced at a row of tents. Their sides expanded and collapsed in the breeze as if they were breathing. "It's time we started building a new house. And a barn too. Need to get the barn up right away. The corral will do for now, but I don't like the horses being unprotected.

"I better be on my way." He kissed Rebecca. "I'll be back in time for dinner." He glanced at Lily, who was bent over a pot suspended above a cooking fire. "Glad to have you back, Lily. Even your outdoor cooking is grand."

Lily offered him an open smile. "Do the best I can, Mr. Thornton."

Daniel lifted his hat and repositioned it on his head, then walked toward the corral.

🖅

Daniel scuffed the toe of his boot on the back of his pant leg, then took off his hat and walked into the Thornton Creek Bank. The small room smelled of dust and ink. A woman stood at the only clerk's window. When she'd finished her transaction, she turned and walked toward the front door, nodding at Daniel as she moved past him.

"G'day," he said to her and then stepped up to the window. "Morning, Mr. Oxley. Fine day, eh?"

"Right fine. What can I do for you, Daniel?" He peered out from beneath heavy eyebrows.

"Well, as you know, we've been hard done by with the drought and the fire. I was hoping to have a word with you about a loan." Daniel's heart hammered against his ribs. As Rebecca had said, Mr. Oxley hadn't been the most generous man in Thornton Creek. In fact, he had a reputation for being tough in business.

The banker stared at Daniel, then glanced at the door as if hoping someone would walk in. No one did. "Right, then. Well, why don't you come in 'ere and we'll talk." He opened a waist-high swinging door that led to the back half of the room. Sitting at a cherrywood desk, he motioned for Daniel to sit in a wooden chair.

Daniel settled on the chair. He felt awkward and didn't know what to do with his hands or his feet. He'd never been in a situation like this before.

"Might as well get right to it, then. Like I said, with times the way they are, and with the fire, I'm in need of funds. There's a lot of rebuilding to do."

"You lost everything?" Mr. Oxley picked up a pen and took a piece of paper out of a tray on his desk.

"Right. Pretty much."

"Including the house and the main barn?"

"Right."

Mr. Oxley dipped the pen in ink and scratched a note on the paper. "And what about the servants' quarters? Did they go as well?"

"Right." Inwardly Daniel squirmed. He had very few assets.

"What about the stock? How many head do you have?"

"Well, can't say for sure," Daniel hedged. "Before the fire, drought and sickness took a good number of them."

"So you'd say the herd is quite depleted?"

Daniel nodded.

Mr. Oxley added more notes. Setting down the pen, he turned his chair so he faced Daniel. "So what do you have in the way of assets?"

Daniel thought. He'd been trying to come up with something, but there just wasn't much left. "Well, we've the cattle, of course. As I said, they're a bit down—not much feed to be had. But they'll come back, given time. And we've several horses, a fine stallion and some good solid mares." Daniel studied his knuckles. They were red and rough. "I've got the land. It's worth a fair bit." He held out his hands. "And I've a strong back and hands that know how to work."

Mr. Oxley glanced at what he'd jotted down. He rested his elbow on the desk and rubbed his forehead before looking up and meeting Daniel's eyes. "I'd like to help you, Daniel, but with things the way they are, I just can't make deals willy-nilly. I'll need some good solid collateral, and the land's not enough. Not without water."

"You know it'll come. Droughts begin and they end. This one will too."

"Some have been known to stay a good long while though." Mr. Oxley's eyebrows peaked. "I just can't do it, lad. Sorry." He stood abruptly and held out his hand to shake Daniel's. "I wish you luck."

Daniel withheld his hand. "Just like that? You cast me aside with no thought? I've been 'ere my whole life, and my father before me. It was my grandfather who settled and built Douloo, and part of the town too. We've given this bank a lot over the years."

"I know that. And it pains me to turn you down." A man stepped through the door. Mr. Oxley tipped his head at the customer. "I'd like to help you, Daniel, but it's not possible."

Daniel pushed his hat onto his head. "Didn't figure you'd fail me. My father did business 'ere a good many years."

"True, but your father would have been the first to tell me how important it is to be a good businessman first and then a friend. The heart's important, but too much heart and a man will be out of business." He glanced at the customer. "I'll be right with you."

Lowering his voice, Mr. Oxley said, "I know of a man in Brisbane who . . . assists folks from time to time. Name's Robert Marshal. He's from America and runs an import business. Over the years he's built up a pile of money, and sometimes he helps people out of sticky situations." He grabbed the pen and a piece of paper and wrote down the man's name and address. Handing it to Daniel, he whispered, "Keep this to yourself."

Daniel stared at the paper.

"He might be able to lend a hand."

Daniel knew Marshal probably wasn't the type of man he'd normally do business with. "Will you vouch for him?"

Mr. Oxley didn't respond for a long moment. Then, his voice tight, he said, "No." He grabbed the paper he'd handed Daniel. "Never mind. Sorry I said anything." He crumpled the note and tossed it into the wastebasket.

Daniel's eyes followed it to the basket.

"'Ey, I 'aven't got all day," the man standing at the counter said.

"Right. Coming." Mr. Oxley hurried to the clerk's window.

Daniel studied the crumpled paper lying amid the trash. It most likely belonged there. On impulse he grabbed it and shoved it into his front pocket. Without another word he strode out of the bank.

𝕯

When Daniel arrived home, he immediately went to the tent that had been a house to him and Rebecca since the fire. He took out the paper with the name and address, set it on a table, and smoothed out the wrinkles. Staring at the name, he said, "Robert Marshal." It sounded familiar. He set the note in the bottom box of a stack of boxes.

The door flap was pushed aside, and Rebecca walked in. She mopped her neck with a handkerchief. "My, it's hot. I thought March meant cooler temperatures."

Daniel felt as if he'd been caught in wrongdoing, but he managed a smile. "You know the weather has a mind of its own, luv."

Rebecca sat on a straight-backed chair loaned to her by Cambria's mother. She pressed her hands together in her lap. "I was just hoping it would be cool. Oh, I miss the shade of the veranda." She looked at Daniel. "Did Mr. Oxley give you a loan?"

Daniel straightened a pile of papers lying on the boxes. "No," he said without looking up.

"No?" She sighed. "I'm not surprised. He never has been the sympathetic type."

"He's a businessman. And he's got to think about himself. If he handed out money to every bloke who came by, he'd be out of business in no time."

"That may be so, but there are situations that call for more consideration. Where would he be without the Thorntons? Your family has contributed so much to this town and to the bank."

"That's what I told him." Daniel sat on a cot, and pressing his elbows against his thighs, he put his face in his hands.

"What are we going to do?"

Letting out a slow breath, Daniel looked up. "He gave me the name of a man in Brisbane. I'm thinking about contacting him."

"Brisbane? Why all the way to Brisbane?"

"There's not a lot of money in these parts, and Brisbane's a big city. Plus, the weather is more moderate there, and I'm sure it's holding up better in this drought than we are."

"What do you know about the man? What's his name?"

"Robert Marshal. He's an American."

"Really? That's good, right?"

"Right." Daniel stood and walked to the doorway. Gazing out, his heart felt heavy. He ought to be grateful for all God had already done, but fear of what could happen had laid hold of him. He needed money. He glanced at Rebecca, guilt intensifying. He wasn't being honest with her.

"Is Mr. Marshal a banker?"

"No. He owns an import company. Think he supplies goods to all of Queensland."

"If he's not a bank, why would he loan money to people he doesn't know?"

"As an investment. He charges interest on the loans and makes a bit for his trouble. The wealthy have to find something to do with their money."

"I suppose." Rebecca thought a moment. "I'd feel better if you went to a bank."

"Me too, but I don't think a bank will give us a loan. We're in a bad spot right now, and the weather's not getting any better. Don't figure the money supply will loosen up until after the drought breaks. And we didn't just lose buildings to the fire; we lost just about everything—supplies, livestock, equipment."

Rebecca nodded. "You must do as you see fit. But I don't feel good about borrowing from someone we don't know."

"I haven't made up my mind yet. I'm still praying on it."

Rebecca folded her hands in her lap and sat quietly for a few moments. When she looked up, she was smiling in such a way that Daniel knew she had something important to say. "I've been waiting for you to get home. I have something to tell you."

Daniel waited. When Rebecca didn't say anything, he asked, "What is it, luv?"

She pressed the palms of her hands together. "We're going to have another baby."

Energy pulsed through Daniel. "A baby? Really? When?"

"I think possibly in September. I haven't seen the doctor yet." She smiled. "Chavive is due to foal the middle of September. How exceptional; we'll both be having little ones at nearly the same time."

Daniel wasn't sure he felt good about a baby. The timing was bad. But he knew Rebecca needed him to be pleased. "That's wonderful news," he said, crossing to Rebecca and kneeling in front of her. He took her hands in his and kissed the tops of them. "I thought you looked a bit tired. You're working too hard."

"I'm fine, really. And there's so much to be done."

"Yes, well, you've got to think of the baby now."

"I know this doesn't seem like a good time for a baby, but maybe that's just what we need. A new life to think about."

"Right," Daniel said, his need for financing becoming even more urgent. He knew he had to speak to Marshal. Without a loan, he could lose Douloo.

Rebecca grasped Daniel's hands. "It will be wonderful having another child. Do you think the house will be finished by September?"

"Yes. Maybe even before then. I'll hire a crew. We'll get it up straightaway." He sounded confident, but inside he was afraid. He needed money if he wanted to hire workers. And materials for a house weren't free. He'd have to get a loan. Daniel stood. "I'm going to speak to Mr. Marshal. Figure the sooner the better. I'll pack and be off to Brisbane tomorrow."

Rebecca pushed out of the chair. Resting a hand on Daniel's arm, she said, "Do be careful. And don't make any hasty decisions."

Unable to meet Rebecca's eyes, Daniel said, "No worries, luv. Mr. Oxley recommended Robert Marshal."

2

Willa hugged Daniel. "I had Lily make you some sandwiches to eat on the stage. I think she put in a treat or two as well." She smiled, her blue eyes warming as she gazed at her son.

"Thanks, Mum. I'm sure it'll be better than what I can get at the coach stops. Course, the Sullivans usually serve up a fine meal."

"By the time you make their station, the food will be gone."

Rebecca held young Joseph in her arms. Daniel took his son and hefted him into the air above his head, and the youngster laughed and grabbed at his father's nose. "You be a good lad. Don't give your mum any trouble, now."

"Good." Joseph grinned.

"He's a sweet boy." Willa smoothed the youngster's blond hair. "Course, he's a Thornton, so now and again there's some vinegar in him." She grinned. "But he's a lamb most of the time."

Daniel planted a kiss on the boy's cheek and set him on the ground. Turning to Rebecca, he said, "I s'pose I ought to be off, then."

"I suppose so." Rebecca glanced at the waiting wagon. "Why are you taking the wagon instead of the surrey?"

"Woodman's got supplies to pick up."

Rebecca nodded.

"Is something troubling you, Rebecca? What is it?"

"I'm fine. I'm just going to miss you is all."

"I'll be home before you know it."

Rebecca didn't reply.

Daniel studied her, sensing uneasiness. "I know you well enough. There's more going on inside your head."

Rebecca grasped Daniel's hand. "I must admit to feeling a bit anxious about this trip." She leaned in close. "I wish you weren't going."

"This is no different from all the other trips I've made to Brisbane. Everything will be fine."

"Of course. I'm sure you're right. I'm being silly."

"No worries."

Rebecca frowned. "But this isn't the same. It's about saving Douloo. I wish I were going with you."

"Best you stay put, luv. The traveling wouldn't sit well with you right now."

Rebecca rested a hand on her stomach. "I have been a bit queasy."

"I'll tell the driver to hurry so I can get home to you." He kissed her and started toward the wagon. Woodman sat on the seat, reins in hand.

Rebecca walked alongside her husband. When they reached the wagon, she stood in front of him. "Are you sure this is the right thing to do?"

"Is there another choice?"

"If we're patient, God may provide a way. Perhaps we should wait."

"I can't wait. If the Lord was going to do something, he would have done it." Daniel cupped the back of Rebecca's head in his hand. "What if this is his answer?"

"I hope you're right and it is."

Daniel dropped a kiss on her forehead. "I love you," he said and climbed up beside Woodman.

As the wagon moved forward, Daniel smiled at Rebecca and waved to his mother and Joseph. He maintained his façade of confidence, but inside he felt as uneasy as Rebecca did. He didn't like doing business with people he didn't know, especially when the one who suggested the person couldn't commend him. It spoke of a dubious reputation. Yet what choice did he have? It was Marshal or nothing.

𝕯

Willa moved to her tent with Joseph skipping along beside her.

Heart heavy, Rebecca watched until the wagon had rolled out of sight. *Why am I so troubled?* She walked to Willa's tent. Perhaps her mother-in-law could offer insight.

Willa took a cloth out of a wicker basket and dusted a table. "I dare say, the dust never relents."

Joseph grabbed a rag out of the basket and started dusting a box his grandmother had been using as a nightstand.

Rebecca smiled at his devotion and sat on the only chair in the small quarters. Her stomach was queasy. She ought to be resting. "I think I'll lie down for a bit."

Willa stopped dusting and looked at Rebecca. "You all right, dear? You look a bit peaked."

"I'm fine. It's just my stomach."

"Oh, I'm sorry, dear. I was hoping you'd have an easier time of it with this one."

"I am, actually. I'm not feeling nearly as sick as I did with Joseph."

"Good." Willa returned to her dusting.

Rebecca remained where she was. She needed to talk with someone about her fears.

"Daniel's going to borrow the money from that man."

Willa straightened. "I'm sure he'll do whatever's best for all of us."

Rebecca compressed her lips. "I have a bad feeling about it all. I . . . I don't want him borrowing from someone we don't know."

"I understand, dear. I wish Mr. Oxley had been more cooperative, but sometimes circumstances are such that we have no option but to step out into unfamiliar places."

"I know that's true." Rebecca pressed a hand against her stomach. She was feeling quite ill. "But I'm certain this isn't a good idea. I don't know why I know, but I do."

Tucking her dusting cloth into her belt, Willa moved to Rebecca. "Then we'll have to pray and just see what God does."

Rebecca nodded. "I have been praying—ever since Daniel told me he planned to go to Brisbane. And I still have no peace."

Concern touched Willa's eyes, and then she smiled. "I trust that Daniel will do the right thing."

"Of course," Rebecca said, but her unease remained.

✲

Stiff from days of travel, Daniel sat on a straight-backed chair and pulled on his dress boots. Walking to the bureau, he looked in the mirror and straightened his necktie and smoothed his waistcoat. Then he retrieved his suit jacket from the closet and pulled it on.

Returning to the mirror, he looked at his reflection. Holding out his hand, he said, "Good to meet you, Mr. Marshal." He tried another greeting. "Pleasure to meet you, sir." Searching for another acknowledgment, he finally decided he was being foolish and pulled out his pocket watch. "Eight thirty. No time for breakfast." He didn't mind. His stomach was unsettled.

Daniel walked out of the room and hurried down the stairs to the first floor of the hotel. Approaching the front desk, he smiled at a tall, skinny clerk. "G'day to you."

"It's a fine day, all right."

"I've an appointment this morning, and I was wondering if you might give me directions. I'm hoping to walk. Been riding too much the last few days."

"Right. Where is it yer wanting to go?"

"I'm supposed to meet with Robert Marshal of Marshal Imports. His office is on George Street."

"That's not too far, only a few blocks. You head toward the river, straight down from 'ere. George Street is one up from the quay. The businesses down there have their names posted. You shouldn't have any trouble finding it."

"Right, then. Thank you." Daniel walked toward the door, his steps quieted by a multicolored rug whose brightness had been muted by time and the many footfalls of travelers. Opening the front door, he stepped onto the sidewalk, then headed toward the river.

Daniel breathed deeply. The air smelled clean, without a hint of dust. He liked Brisbane. The streets were lined with a variety of businesses, but the buildings didn't tower over the roads the way they did in some cities. Most were no more than a couple of stories tall. Brisbane was just city enough for Daniel.

He approached a grand cathedral and stopped to study it. St. Stephen's Cathedral, so the cabbie had said. It was made of pale stone and had an impressive arched window of stained glass in the front, which was pressed in on both sides by imposing spires. Daniel wondered what Sunday services were like in such a church. It must be a far cry from what he was used to in Thornton Creek.

He continued. He turned onto George Street and made his way down the lane, reading the names of businesses posted above the doorsteps. A cart carrying ice lumbered past. Daniel stopped to take a calming breath. In spite of the cooler temperatures, he felt hot. Sweat trickled down his neck, and he tugged at his collar. It would feel good to get back into everyday clothes.

He moved on and finally came upon a block building with a sign hanging above the front entry that read "Marshal Imports." Daniel stared at the billboard. It was large, and the yellow on black color seemed abrasive.

Well, this is it. I've got to convince Mr. Marshal to loan me the money I need. In his mind Daniel reviewed the positive aspects of Douloo. He tugged at his waistcoat to straighten it and brushed a piece of dust from his jacket. "It'll be fine," he told himself, but he wasn't convinced.

Glancing up the street, he watched as a young man dashed across the dirt-packed road in front of the ice wagon. "'Ey, watch where yer goin'," the driver yelled. The young man waved him off, then strode down the street toward the Brisbane River.

Daniel took a steadying breath and reached for the door. Before he could grasp the knob, the door opened. A large man, very red in the face, hustled out and tromped down the street. Thinking the man looked angry, Daniel watched him for a moment, then caught the door and stepped inside. It felt cooler than outdoors. The room smelled of stale cigars and of something else. Was it licorice?

Daniel let the door close and walked toward a desk where a petite, dark-eyed woman sat. Her fingers rapidly walked over the keys of a typewriter. She didn't look up but kept working. The keys *tat-tat-tat*-ed while Daniel stood. When the woman didn't acknowledge him, Daniel cleared his throat.

"I'll be right with ya," the woman said and kept typing.

21

Finally her fingers stopped their rhythmic prancing, and she laid her hands in her lap and looked at Daniel. "G'day."

"That looks like a first-rate typewriter."

"The best. It's a Remington. Quite grand." She smiled. "Ya must be Daniel Thornton."

"That I am. I have an appointment with Mr. Marshal."

"He's waiting for you." The woman pushed back her chair and stood. "This way, please." Taking short, quick steps, she moved toward a long hallway.

As they walked down the corridor, Daniel had a sense of being swallowed up by the building. It was much larger than it had looked from the front. He considered turning around and leaving but knew he had no choice but to follow the young woman.

She stopped in front of a heavy wooden door and knocked. From inside a brusque voice called, "Come in. Come in."

The secretary turned an ornate bronze doorknob, and the door swung open. Stepping inside a large office, she said, "Mr. Thornton is 'ere ta see ya, sir."

A boxy-looking man stood. He didn't look pleased.

The woman moved past Daniel and disappeared down the hall. Daniel sucked in a lungful of air and stepped into the room.

He'd never seen such a sizable office. Everything about it was large— an oversized desk and chair sat in the center, three huge armchairs were scattered informally, a straight-backed chair perched against the wall near the door, and an enormous oaken bookcase took up much of the opposite wall. Everything was so big, Daniel felt small.

"So you found me. I hope you didn't have any trouble."

"No. None. I'm staying just up the street." Daniel offered his hand, but Marshal didn't seem to notice. Daniel's hand hung uncomfortably in the air. Finally he tucked it into his pocket.

Marshal wasn't a large man, maybe five feet ten inches. He

looked square in build, and his brown hair was thin. He was balding so badly in front that his forehead appeared overly large. The man's eyes were small, and his lids seemed half closed. He studied Daniel.

"Have a seat." He waited for Daniel to sit before he dropped into the extra-large desk chair. Lifting a crystal candy dish, he offered it to Daniel. "Licorice?"

"No. Don't like it much."

"I can't get enough of it." Marshal took a piece and stuck it in his mouth, then poured himself a glass of water from a pitcher sitting on the desk. "You thirsty?"

"No. I'm fine."

Marshal set the pitcher down. Pushing his candy into his cheek, he sipped the water. "So your wire said you have a cattle station west of here, on the flats."

"Right. A fine station too. My grandfather bought the land and built a first-rate house and put together a fine mob of cattle."

"A cattleman?" Marshal lifted his right eyebrow. "Thought most folks out west of Toowoomba raised sheep."

"Most. But not all. The cattle business is a good one."

Marshal nodded. "And now . . . there's a drought. And you're in trouble?"

The idea of talking about his hardships with a stranger didn't set well with Daniel, but he had no choice. "Right. There's been a drought. Looks like Brisbane has been spared though."

"One of the benefits of living on this side of the Great Dividing Range."

Silence settled over the men. Finally Marshal said, "Go on. You were telling me about the troubles you've had."

"Right. Well, there's the drought, and then we had a fire. The fire hit us hard." Daniel wanted to get on to what was good about Douloo. "The station usually has plenty of water and good grasslands. It's one of the best producing stations in all of Queensland and has been for a good long while."

"I'm not interested in what it was. I want to know what it is. How many cattle do you have?"

"We're down a bit. Got hit by red water, and then . . ."

"Right—the drought and the fire." Marshal leaned back in his chair. Unconsciously he stuck his licorice out on his tongue, then sucked it back into his mouth. "How many head you have right now, today?"

"Maybe five hundred."

"Not much of a station. What else you have?" When Daniel didn't answer right away, Marshal continued in an annoyed tone, "Livestock, house, barns, you know . . . what might you have that would be considered valuable?"

"Everything burned. But we have some fine horses . . ."

"And what is it exactly that you want from me?" Marshal eyed him contemptuously.

Daniel wanted to get up and walk out, but he didn't dare. He had to have the money. "I need a loan to get the station back on its feet."

"Ah, money. And just how much do you think you'll need?"

"I'll have to replenish the herds, and we've got to rebuild . . ."

The door opened, and a young man walked into the room. "Oh, sorry. Didn't know you—"

"No. Come in," Marshal said. "The other boys too."

The man glanced over his shoulder. "Boss wants us all."

He stepped into the room, followed by two other young men. Dressed in work clothes and in need of a bath, they were obviously not Marshal's partners. More likely roustabouts.

"I'd like to introduce Daniel Thornton, boys. He'll be doing business with us."

Daniel felt his hopes rise at Marshal's reference to their

24

doing business. That sounded like someone who'd decided to loan him the money.

The men stared at Daniel. "This is Jack," Marshal said. The tallest of the three nodded. "Luke." The man brushed long blond hair off his forehead and sneered as he nodded at Daniel. "And Wade." Wade seemed a bit less surly than the other two and nearly smiled.

"They help me run my business. Good blokes. They're tough when they need to be though. If we have any trouble, they take care of it."

Daniel wondered what kind of trouble. "Good to meet you," he said.

The three didn't respond but stood sullenly just inside the door.

Daniel looked from them to Marshal. His stomach felt as if he'd swallowed rocks. He knew he ought to leave and forget he'd ever heard of Robert Marshal. His brain said go, but his need held him there. Douloo depended on this man.

"I've been watching you, and I can see you're an honest sort. I'm good at that, figuring people out." Marshal chewed on his piece of licorice, and the odor of it intensified. "Everyone comes up against hard times. And I like to help the ones I know really need it and are good to their word." He smiled, but the gesture didn't touch his eyes. "I've decided to give you a loan. I'd hate to see you lose that station of yours, especially since it came from your grandfather."

"That would be grand," Daniel sputtered.

"I'll have the papers drawn up and sent to you. I expect payments to be made on time and in the amount agreed upon. Understood?"

"Yes and no. We haven't decided on the amount or the terms."

"Not a problem. You come by tomorrow morning, and we can go over those details. I'll see to it that Margaret has the contract ready by the time you get here."

25

"What would you consider as collateral for the loan?" Daniel asked.

"Why, the station, of course. That's all you have that's of any value."

"I can't risk the station."

"I'm the one taking the risk. Am I right to assume that if not for me you would lose the place?"

Daniel didn't like Marshal, and he hated needing him. "I'll be back tomorrow." He replaced his hat and started out the door. He glanced at the three men lined up against the wall and knew that when he walked out of this room, he should keep walking and never return. But he also knew he'd be back in the morning.

3

Rebecca rode Chavive to the makeshift corral and dismounted.

"I'll see to 'er," Woodman said, taking hold of the halter.

"Thank you, but I'd like to brush her myself." Rebecca patted the mare's neck. "I could use help with the saddle though."

"Roight." Woodman uncinched the saddle and hefted it off the horse's back. "She's lookin' fine, mum." He set the saddle on a sawhorse. "Doesn't seem the foal is takin' too much from 'er."

"She's in fine condition. And I can hardly wait for the foal—Noble's foal."

Woodman grinned. "Ought ta be a beaut."

Rebecca ran her hand along Chavive's side, smoothing the chestnut coat. "It'll be a fine one, all right." Her mind carried her back to the death of her mare Miss. Before foaling, Miss had seemed fine, and then so quickly she'd been taken. Fear rolled through Rebecca. "I just pray everything will be all right."

"No reason ta doubt that, mum. Chavive's strong and

healthy. There'll be no troubles with this one." Woodman smiled, his dark eyes offering sympathy.

"I'm sure you're right and I'm worrying over nothing." Grabbing a brush out of a bucket of tools, Rebecca started brushing Chavive. "No use fretting about it."

Woodman picked up the saddle. "I'll put this away, and then I'll be goin' inta town ta pick up Daniel."

"I wish I were going along."

"Ya can if ya like."

"I don't know if I ought to. That ride unsettled my stomach a bit."

"Seems ta me the doc said no riding last time, with Joseph. How's he feel 'bout it now?"

"I'm allowed to ride, just not to overdo. I was good. I only went for a short ride, and it was leisurely."

Rebecca's thoughts went to Daniel. She did want to meet him. She knew he must be nearly done in. The trip from Brisbane to Thornton Creek was exhausting.

"I'll be back with yer husband in no time." Lugging the saddle, Woodman walked toward a lean-to they'd been using for tack.

Rebecca's mind turned to the reason for Daniel's trip to Brisbane. Had he managed to procure a loan? If not, what would they do? Anxiety coursed through her, and she brushed harder. She wasn't sure which would be worse, getting a loan or not getting one. Her arm stopped its rhythmic sweeps, and she leaned on her mare, resting her forehead against Chavive's side. She breathed in the aroma of horse. *Lord, please see to it that whatever happens is what's right for us.*

She straightened and returned to brushing.

"You'll scrub the hide right off her if you're not careful," Daniel said.

Rebecca swung around. "Daniel? Daniel!"

He scooped Rebecca into his arms and held her close.

She hugged him hard. When he settled her on the ground,

she rested her cheek against his chest. The feel of his cotton shirt and the sound of his beating heart comforted her. "Oh, it's so good to have you home! But how? Woodman was just about to leave."

"The stage was ahead of schedule, and I got a ride with Jim. After he hauled some grain over to Cambria's place, he stopped in town. I managed to catch him before he left."

Rebecca rested her hands on Daniel's chest. "So how did your meeting with Mr. Marshal go?" She thought she saw a flicker of hesitation before Daniel smiled.

"Good. Right good. I got the loan. And we'll be able to set things right again."

"And Mr. Marshal, what did you think of him?"

"He has a fine business there in Brisbane. Seems right prosperous—must be doing well."

"What kind of man is he?"

Daniel's eyes slid away from Rebecca's. He removed his hat and combed back blond hair with his hand. "Good business-man, I'd say. He got down to it right off."

"And?"

"And what? What else is there?" Daniel's tone was sharp.

"I just wondered how you felt about him . . . in general."

Daniel replaced his hat. "I'd say he's shrewd. And that he can be tough when he needs to be. I don't see that we'll have any trouble though."

Still feeling a vague sense of unease, Rebecca returned to brushing Chavive. "She picks up a lot of dirt and dust when we're out. The dust settles deep in her coat." She stopped and, without looking at Daniel, asked, "Are you telling me everything?"

"Of course." Daniel's attention went to Chavive. He combed her mane with his fingers. "When have I ever lied to you?"

Her hand gripped the brush, and she moved it along Chavive's back. "I've never known you to lie, but sometimes it's easier to hold back something that needs to be said."

29

Daniel laid a hand on Rebecca's back. "You don't need to worry. Everything will be fine."

She turned to Daniel and searched his face. "I'm sure you're right. You have experience in these kinds of dealings."

He kissed her. "It's good to be home. I ordered supplies so we can finish the work 'round 'ere. I told the man it was urgent, so we can expect deliveries soon." He smiled. "I've got a house to build. I'd better get to it."

Rebecca stepped close to Daniel and wrapped her arms around his waist. "It will be so wonderful to have a house again." She looked up at him. "We've finished the cleanup. What can I do to help with building?"

"You can take good care of yourself. You've a baby to look after."

"Being pregnant is not an ailment. I'm strong and healthy, and I want to help."

"Most of what's to be done is man's work, luv."

Rebecca stood with her hands on her hips. "You know me. I need to keep busy."

"Yes. I do know you." He grinned. "You can be right stubborn. But I like that about you."

"So what shall I do?" Rebecca looked at him wide-eyed. "If you don't give me a job, I'll think of something on my own."

"Perhaps Mum could use more help with the paperwork. She's getting on in years. You should ask her. And Lily and Callie have extra work—living outdoors isn't easy. I'm sure you'll find something." He kissed the tip of Rebecca's nose. "I've got work to do."

"But you've barely gotten home." Rebecca pouted.

"Now that we have the funds, I don't want to wait. There's still plenty of daylight left and a lot a man can do." He smiled. "I'll see you at supper."

"All right." Rebecca folded her arms over her chest and watched him walk away. She did want to help with the house, but what could she do if Daniel wouldn't give her any tasks? She blew out a breath. Sometimes life was just plain exasperating.

𝒟

With Chavive brushed, Rebecca removed the mare's bridle and set her free in the paddock. She moved the gate into place, then watched Lily work at a makeshift table. Perhaps she could use help with dinner preparations. Rebecca rested her hand on her stomach. It still felt upset; food didn't sound appealing.

She strolled toward the servant. The wind whipped up dust and settled it on a cloth draped over rising dough. "Lily, where's Joseph? He was with you." Rebecca felt panic, remembering the day he'd nearly perished in the fire.

"He's sleepin', mum." Lily nodded at a nearby tent. "He plays and plays, and then all of a sudden he drops."

"I wish I had all his energy." Rebecca glanced about. "And Willa? Have you seen her?"

"She's gone up ta 'er tent, mum." Lily frowned. "I'm a bit worried 'bout 'er. She looked done in. I don't think she's feeling well."

"I'll check on her." Rebecca hurried to her mother-in-law's tent. Standing outside the entrance, she said, "Willa. Are you all right?"

"Yes. I'm fine. Come in."

Rebecca pulled back the door flap and walked inside. The space looked surprisingly like a home. Willa had managed to purchase some comfortable furnishings, and the neighbors had been more than generous by providing a bureau and a bed. A vase filled with flowers sat on a small table in the center of the room. Willa lay on the bed, propped up by pillows.

"Lily said you weren't feeling well," Rebecca said.

31

"I'm fine. Just a bit tired. A midday nap will see to me."

"Are you sure?"

"Yes. Absolutely. But I dare say, I'm not as young as I once was. I fear napping is becoming more and more of a necessity. As it should be for you these days."

"I'm fine," Rebecca said, sitting on a straight-backed chair beside the bed. "I was just thinking that you might need some help. What would you like me to do?"

"You do so much already. And with the baby coming, well, I don't want you overworked."

"That's the last thing I am. Actually, I was hoping I could help with the building that will be going on, but Daniel's uneasy about it."

"Is he home?"

"Yes. And he got the loan, so work on the house will begin soon."

Willa looked thoughtful but said nothing.

"There's a lot I could do if I were allowed."

"Daniel's only thinking of your welfare, dear. And the baby's." She smiled. "Perhaps you could crochet some new doilies to replace the ones we lost. And I dare say, the baby will need clothing. You could make a nice layette for her."

"Her? You think it will be a girl?"

"Oh, I don't know really." Willa smiled. "But I feel like it just might be."

"That would be nice." Rebecca sighed. Sewing and needlework were fine, but she wanted to do more. Standing, she said, "I'll let you rest and see if Lily needs help with supper."

𝒟

Lily patted a handful of dough between her palms. "Good ta 'ave Mr. Thornton home, eh?"

"Yes. Life is back in order."

32

A furrow creased the servant's broad forehead. "How did things go for 'im in Brisbane?"

"If you're asking if he got the loan, the answer is yes." Rebecca smiled.

Lily's face looked flushed, and she made a point of not looking at Rebecca.

"Nothing around here stays a secret for long. You don't need to be self-conscious about wanting to know about the future of Douloo."

"Figured it wasn't really me business, mum, but . . . I was curious. And I care 'bout ya."

"I hope taking out a loan from a stranger was the right thing to do."

Lily pushed the lump of dough down on a kneading board. "And why would ya think not?"

"Last Sunday I overheard Mr. O'Brien ask Mr. Oxley about that man Marshal. He said something about there being rumors. I think he said rumors."

"Is that all ya heard?"

"Yes. Just that."

"Wal now, ya don't know just what was bein' said, then, and ya can't listen ta rumors. I figure ya'll soon know 'im well enough." Lily dropped the dough into a bowl.

"I suppose." Rebecca unbuttoned the cuffs on her blouse and rolled up her sleeves. "Can I help you with supper?"

Lily thought. "Wal, there's a recipe I was hopin' ta use, but I can't read it. Maybe ya could read it for me?"

"I thought you didn't use written recipes."

"Roight, but Mrs. Thornton likes this 'specially, and since she's feelin' a bit down, I figured it's a good day ta make it for 'er."

"You don't know how to read at all?"

"Oh no, mum. Blacks don't read. Never did, never will."

"Where's the recipe?"

"Ah, it's roight there." She nodded at the table where a

piece of paper lay. "Was hopin' someone would give me a hand."

Rebecca picked up the paper and glanced down at the ingredients. "Do you ever wish you could read?"

"Yais, for sure. But I don't think I'm smart enough. Figure there'll be no readin' for Lily." She glanced at Rebecca. "That's all roight by me. No need. I got along well so far. Figure I'll do fine yet."

Rebecca nodded, her mind trying to get hold of a scrap of an idea. What if she were to teach the aborigines on the station to read? It would be a good thing. They could become more independent. And she'd have something important to fill her time.

She sat at the table. "Lily, if you could . . . would you like to read?"

"Oh, sure. I sometimes see ya or Mrs. Thornton readin', and I think how lovely it'd be ta disappear inta one of them stories. Course, there's always the storytellers. We got us a couple 'ere on the place. Some nights we all gather 'bout and listen ta the tales of the beginning and 'bout how we come ta be."

Rebecca's mind continued to work. Callie had learned to read without difficulty; why couldn't the others? She could open a school and maybe even teach several subjects. The idea seemed fine until she considered Daniel. He wouldn't like it. He wanted her to do less, not more. And there weren't even any buildings up yet. Adding a school would only complicate things.

"So . . . if you could learn, you'd want to?"

"Wal, sure. But I figure I'm too dumb."

"Of course you're not."

"Maybe, but that's all I heard since I was a gal."

"Well, it's not true." Rebecca stood. As the idea grew, she could feel a pulse of excitement move through her. "Do you know where Callie is?"

"I sent 'er out ta the garden ta pull me some carrots."

Her mind formulating a plan, Rebecca left the recipe on the table. "Would it be all right if I read the recipe to you later?"

"Oh, sure. But not too long, eh?" She smiled, the gap between her front teeth adding to her good-natured appearance.

"I won't be long," Rebecca said.

She hurried toward the garden. It was blackened like the rest of the earth, but the carrots and potatoes had survived. With a canvas bag draped over her shoulder, Callie leaned down and pulled a carrot from the ground. She brushed it off and dropped it into the bag.

Rebecca strode across the field. "Callie," she called.

Callie straightened and watched Rebecca approach. *She's got that look*, she thought. *She's up ta something.*

"What is it, mum? Is everything all roight?"

"Yes. In fact, things are wonderful, actually."

Callie waited for Rebecca to explain.

"I have a grand idea."

"Grand, eh?"

"I was talking to Lily . . ." Rebecca hesitated.

"Mum?"

Rebecca glanced back at the tents and at Lily working over supper. "I doubt you'll like my idea."

"Can't know what it is if ya don't tell me, eh?"

"Right. Of course. Well, Lily needed me to read a recipe to her. She doesn't know how to read. And when I asked if she'd like to learn, she said yes, only she said she didn't think she could." Rebecca barely stopped for a breath. "While she was talking, I started thinking . . . wouldn't it be marvelous if we opened a school right here at Douloo?"

Callie felt instant apprehension, but rather than responding immediately, she allowed the proposal to rest inside her where she could consider it. She dug away the soil around a carrot, grabbed hold of the root, and pulled.

"A school for aborigines . . . here at Douloo," Rebecca said.

Callie brushed dirt from the carrot. She knew Rebecca meant well, but the idea wouldn't work. Finally she asked, "For what purpose, mum?"

"What do you mean?"

"What are blacks goin' ta do with readin'?"

"How can you ask such a thing? *You* know how to read."

Callie added the carrot to those already in her bag. "Yais. But not much, and there's no need for it."

"I thought you liked reading."

"Sometimes, but I don't understand all that's in yer books." She moved down the row to the next singed carrot top.

Rebecca followed. "Eventually you will, and more of the world will be open to you as your reading improves."

Callie pulled the carrot and straightened. *I thought she understood.* "The world is already open ta blacks, mum. Just not yer world."

Rebecca studied Callie. "Books can tell us so much about different people and cultures. Don't you want more knowledge and wisdom?"

"Not really, mum. I know enough. And wisdom will come." She looked to the west, toward Thornton Creek. "If ya open a school, people gonna get mad."

"Some won't like it, but I think most of the people in the district are good, fair-minded citizens." Looking hurt, Rebecca met Callie's eyes. "I thought you'd want your friends to be educated."

"Just don't want no trouble."

"I'm sure everything will be fine." Rebecca scanned the empty fields. "Where do you think we should meet?"

36

Irritation needled Callie. Rebecca wasn't listening. Callie looked about. "Don't know. There's nothin' roight now—no place. Everything's all burned up."

Rebecca's eyes searched. "We could meet outdoors, or we could put up a tent. It will keep the sun off, and if it rains, we'll stay dry."

Callie said nothing more.

Rebecca took her arm and started walking, dragging her friend along with her. "Come on. Let's have a look around. We'll need to find just the right spot."

Remaining silent for a long while, Callie walked along beside Rebecca. Although Rebecca seemed determined, Callie tried again to explain. "Mum, I think yer goin' ta 'ave trouble. And even if we 'ave a school, it'll make no difference for us."

Rebecca stopped. "You can't know that. Don't you think the other servants here deserve an opportunity to learn, the way you did? And I think people in the district will trust educated aborigines more—give them credit for having intelligence."

"I thought ya knew better." Callie shook her head. "The ones that hate us will keep on hatin' no matter what."

"Some perhaps, but people change." She studied the area. "We have to begin somewhere." Rebecca smiled. "Wouldn't it be grand if we were able to have more schools in the district and educate all the black children?"

Callie's eyes opened wide. "It'll never happen, mum."

"You have to believe, Callie. God can do anything."

Callie would have liked to believe, but she knew there was no god powerful enough to do what Rebecca wanted.

4

Rebecca ran her index finger down her watch chain and lifted the watch. Pushing in the clasp, she flipped open the front of the case—eleven forty-five. *Time to finish up.*

With satisfaction, she watched her students. Six of them were bent over their slates, working on sums. Two others, the oldest, had completed their arithmetic and were focused on their early-elementary readers.

They've made such progress, Rebecca thought, feeling the warmth of satisfaction. They'd not only taken the first steps in reading and writing but had gained skills in mathematics and had even grasped some of the cultural studies. *There's no telling what they can accomplish if given the opportunity. Even Lily has learned some basics.*

Rebecca smiled. She didn't want class to end for the day, but she had other responsibilities—her family—and she'd promised the doctor she'd stay off her feet. She glanced over her rounded abdomen. Her ankles looked swollen.

"All right, then. Time to hand in your slates. We'll resume tomorrow morning."

There was a flurry of hurried writing and cleaning of slates, and then quietly the children filed past Rebecca, handing her their slates before hurrying out the tent door.

Alice, one of the older girls who'd managed to move ahead of the other children, held her book against her stomach. "I was wonderin' if ya'd mind me takin' it with me, mum?"

"Not at all. I know you'll take good care of it."

Alice smiled, and her dark eyes shone. "Thank ya, mum." She skipped off toward the doorway.

Rebecca tidied the books on her desk, then moved to the stove and made sure the fire was tamped down. After that she straightened the benches and picked up bits of chalk. She was suddenly famished, and the idea of a cup of tea with biscuits sounded appealing. Giving the room a final glance, she moved to the door and stepped outside.

A cool, brisk wind and the sounds of hammering greeted her. She pulled her shawl more closely about her and studied their nearly completed home. It wasn't as grand as the original house Daniel's grandfather had built, but it was sturdy and comfortable. This time they'd chosen to forgo a second story. Instead, the house was low-slung and sprawling, like many of the homes on the flats. A rambling veranda draped with newly sprouted greenery bordered the home, offering a shaded sanctuary. She started toward the house, and her eyes moved to Willa, who worked in the garden.

When Rebecca reached the front porch, she sat on the bottom step and breathed in the fragrance of fresh-cut timber. The baby kicked vigorously, and she laid a hand on her abdomen. She had only three months to wait for her little one to arrive. Imagining what the baby might look like, she smiled and hoped it would be a girl. Lily had said it would be. She shivered and rubbed her arms, studying the clouds moving in from the south. Perhaps they would bring much-needed rain.

Willa stopped her work and straightened. "How did class go today?"

"Just fine. The children are coming along splendidly."

"And you. How are you feeling?"

"Quite well."

Joseph pushed through the front door and tottered toward the porch steps. He stopped at the top and sat on his bottom. "Mum." After studying the stairway a moment, he got onto his hands and knees and started to climb down frontwards.

"Try it this way," Rebecca said, standing and moving to him. She turned the toddler around so he could climb down backwards.

He caught on to the idea right away and started down.

Willa watched her grandson. "I dare say, he's been full of energy all morning. I've caught him in one adventure after another."

"Since the first day he learned to get around on his own, he's been on an endless journey of discovery," Rebecca said with a grin. She watched the toddler climb back up onto the porch. Tottering slightly, he pushed himself upright and made his way to the railing. He grabbed the top of the balustrade and clambered onto the bottom rail. Rebecca held her breath, watching as his pudgy hands gripped the top railing and he tried to swing one leg onto the top of the banister.

"He could fall," Willa said.

"Yes. I know. But he needs to experience new challenges. I'm trying to give him a bit more freedom." She moved toward the little boy. "All right. That's all for now." Rebecca lifted him and dragged him off the railing and planted him safely on the porch.

Seemingly unruffled, Joseph headed toward a box of toys resting beneath a front window. Before reaching them he spotted his father walking toward the house. "Daddy," he called and toddled toward the front steps. This time he turned and clambered down backwards.

When Joseph reached the bottom step, he stood and held up his arms. "Daddy. Daddy."

Wearing a broad smile, Daniel moved to his son and lifted him. Holding the little boy firmly, he pushed the youngster above his head and smiled up at him. "Looks as if you're having a fine day, lad." He settled Joseph on his shoulders. "There you go, then. Now you've a fine view, eh?"

Perched happily, Joseph planted pudgy hands on his father's hat and gazed about.

Willa dropped a weed into a bucket and pressed her hands against the small of her back as she watched the two. "He always loves it when you carry him about like that. His eyes are bright as the afternoon sun."

Daniel grinned and bounced a couple of times. Joseph chortled.

Willa tugged at the tips of her gardening gloves and pulled them from her hands, then draped them on the edge of the bucket. She retied her wide-brimmed hat and glanced at a blue sky sown with tattered clouds. "It's a grand day."

Daniel eyed approaching heavy clouds. "It's a beaut so far, but things could change." Joseph lifted his father's hat, and Daniel grabbed for it. "Hey now, I need that." He settled Joseph on the ground, and after taking the hat from the youngster's grasp, he returned it to his head. "Good news. We have another well flowing."

"Grand. That makes four, then."

"We'll make it through the drought and be ready for the next one, I'd say." Daniel wore a satisfied smile.

"We can praise the Lord for that." Willa walked to her son. "And I'm sorry to say that we can count on there being more droughts." She smiled. "But this one seems to be easing."

"Things are better. The streams are flowing again."

"Everything is coming back to life." Willa gazed about. "God has restored what the locusts devoured." She turned to her son. "I'm proud of you. You've done well."

Rebecca moved in close to Daniel. "You've done a splendid

job of restoring this place. I don't know anyone who could have done better."

"*Everyone* worked hard." His gaze moved from the partially built barn to the servants' cottages. "Things are better, but we've a ways to go. There are still cabins to be built, the house needs finishing. Plus, I've a mob of cattle to drive south. I need to get to that. Figure we ought to do well with the number of new calves born." He draped an arm over Rebecca's shoulders.

Leaning into her husband, Rebecca asked, "If you think everything is going well, why do you look so worried?"

"I look worried?"

"Yes. You do."

"I'm fine. No worries, luv." He smiled down at Rebecca.

Looking up at her husband, Rebecca yielded to his cheery manner. "All right, then. I won't worry." She looked at her son and then at her rounded abdomen. "It won't be long before we've an addition to the family."

"It will be nice having another baby about," Willa said.

"Joseph's not really a baby anymore," Rebecca said. "He's a year and a half already."

Willa watched the little boy grab a rock and toss it. "I suppose you're right. He's not a baby anymore. I just hate to see the time go by so quickly. He's growing so fast."

"That he is." Rebecca glanced up at Daniel. "I love the house, Daniel. How much longer before it's finished?"

"A couple of months, maybe. We'll have to get the barn up first though, and then we'll finish the house." He gave Rebecca a squeeze.

"There it is again."

"There's what again?"

"That worried look you've been wearing. Something *is* troubling you."

"Nothing's troubling me," Daniel said almost too easily.

He clamped his jaws together and looked toward town as if expecting something.

"I don't believe you."

Daniel smiled. "What have I to worry about with you at my side, eh?"

Joseph tromped through newly turned garden soil, then picked up a hoe. Unbalanced by the length of the tool, he teetered as he pitched the steel end into the earth and tugged. The weight of it knocked him off balance, and he fell on his bottom.

"Oh my. Not quite big enough just yet, I'd say." Willa chuckled and helped him to his feet.

Watching the interaction between grandmother and grandson, Rebecca let go of her worries. Daniel had told her all was well. She needed to have faith in him and in the Lord.

The baby kicked again, only quite hard. "Ah," Rebecca exclaimed.

"You all right?" Daniel asked.

"Yes. It's just the baby. She's a strong one."

"She?" Daniel asked with a grin.

"Yes. She. Lily said it's a girl, and I'd rather like to believe it is." She glanced at her stomach. "Wouldn't it be nice if we had a girl?"

"That would be fine by me."

"I was thinking I'd like to name her after my mother, Audry."

"It's a lovely name," Willa said. "I quite like it."

"All right, then." Daniel patted Rebecca's stomach. "Audry you shall be."

"Aaady," Joseph said. "Aaady." He returned to the hoe and his work.

Lily appeared at the top of the steps. Hands on her hips, she smiled. "He's a hard worker, that one, eh?"

"We can hope," Daniel said.

"I made some tea, and seeing it's a cool day, I was wonderin' if ya'd be wantin' a cuppa?"

"That sounds lovely," Willa said, taking the hoe from Joseph, who was working hard to create a furrow. She rested it against the porch railing and then picked up her grandson. "I think we'd best get you out of the garden." Dusting off dirt from his pants, she carried him up the stairs.

Lily disappeared indoors while Willa dropped into a cane-back chair, settling Joseph on her lap. "A rest is just the thing." Joseph wriggled off his grandmother's lap and ambled toward the toy box. Willa removed her hat and set it on a table at her side, then settled deeper into the chair and rested her head against its webbed backing. "I do love these cool June days. And my flower garden is doing splendidly, all except the roses. They're struggling a bit. They need more sun."

"It's a beautiful garden. And the roses will flourish again," Rebecca said, sitting. "I love the flowers you've added, especially the honeysuckle. We had quite a lot of it in Boston. It's always been one of my favorites."

Memories of riding Chavive across lush pastures at her father's Boston estate traveled through her mind. There had always been honeysuckle growing along the gates and fence lines. Its heavy, sweet fragrance had saturated the air.

She turned to her mother-in-law. "It reminds me of home and of Father."

"And one day it may remind you of Douloo as well."

"I never plan to leave Douloo. Although I wouldn't mind going on holiday." She settled a knowing smile on Daniel.

"Soon, luv. I promise."

Rebecca closed her eyes and took in a long, slow breath. "I was thinking the coast would be just the place for quiet, restful days."

"You'll have few of those after the baby comes." Willa smiled. "Perhaps if you have a little girl, she'll look like you."

"If she does, she'll be a lucky one." Daniel stood behind

Rebecca's chair and caressed her dark hair. "I figure she'll have the same brown eyes and wavy hair as her mother. She and Joseph will be quite a pair—one dark and one fair."

"I must say, I think it's going to be a girl, but I don't suppose it's really proper to act as if we're sure just because Lily envisions a girl," Willa said. "She's a fine person, but she's not a prophet."

Rebecca opened her eyes and looked at Willa. "Of course she's not, but there is something special about the aborigines. They know things we don't."

"That may be, but they can't tell the gender of a baby before it's born." Willa smiled. "However, if it is a girl, I do hope she looks like you. I read somewhere that girls favor their mothers and sons their fathers."

"Really?" Rebecca sighed. "Well, only time will tell." Rebecca gazed at Joseph and then looked at his father. "Joseph is the image of Daniel."

Clasping a ball against his pudgy stomach, the little boy made his way down the stairs and wandered toward a newly constructed paddock. "Joseph. You come back here," Rebecca called.

He stopped and reluctantly turned and faced his mother. Glancing at the ball in his hands, he looked from one parent to the other but remained in place. Rebecca's mind returned to the day fire had consumed Douloo, and her pulse picked up. She'd feared her little boy had been lost to the flames. Now he stood defiantly challenging her. It was difficult to be angry with him.

"Joseph. Mind your mother," Daniel said sternly. He moved to the boy, took his hand, and led him back to the house and up the steps.

Rebecca's thoughts stayed with the fire and the days that had followed. They had months of labor invested in restoring Douloo, and there were many more weeks of work to come.

Rebecca accepted tea from Lily. Using a tiny silver spoon, she dipped sugar from a china bowl and stirred the sweetener into her tea. Setting the spoon on her saucer she took a sip. "Delicious. Thank you, Lily." She turned to Daniel. "So we've another good well, then?"

"Right. Good clear water too. We've been lucky, I'd say."

"I doubt luck had anything to do with it." Willa took a drink of tea and set her cup on its saucer.

"Right." Daniel rested a hip against the banister. He watched Joseph make his way toward the steps again. "Joseph. No."

The lad looked at his father, then walked toward him and held up his arms. Daniel hefted him up, supporting him in one arm.

"We've had a hard time of it, but we've survived," Rebecca said. "In fact, I'd say we've flourished."

Looking at his son, Daniel said, "The fire could have taken everything. Nearly did." He gave Joseph a squeeze.

Rebecca held her cup and saucer in both hands. "From now on I'm convinced all will be well."

"I dare say, we'll have more troubles," Willa said. "It's the way of life."

"Yes. I suppose." Rebecca stared at deep grasses bending beneath a sharp breeze.

When she'd first arrived at Douloo, she'd seen her new home as stifling and intolerable. Over time she'd managed to accept her fate. And then somewhere along the way, she'd learned to love this empty, quiet place. It had become home. Still, there were days that seemed interminably long, and the land could be inhospitable. She was thankful for the school. It had been stimulating, and the students' progress gave Rebecca a feeling of accomplishment. She was contributing something of value to the aborigines.

Rebecca looked for Chavive, who stood placidly in a nearby corral. She'd soon have a foal. Rebecca was certain it would be a fine horse, especially with Noble as the sire. "Daniel, will we be purchasing new horses soon?"

"I hope so. It will depend on money," he said, his jaw taking on a hard line.

"I was just wondering if we might be able to purchase Noble."

"No. I can't imagine his owners letting him go." Daniel's tone was harsh.

"We got Chavive. Remember?"

"Right, but Noble . . . well, they'd want too much for him."

Uneasiness moved through Rebecca. Daniel had that look again, and he'd suddenly become disagreeable. Something was wrong. She thought of asking him again but held her tongue. In due time he'd tell her what was troubling him.

"I'll be needing supplies for the school. We've been going through things so quickly. The students are so hungry to learn." She gazed at the tent where she met with the children several days a week. "Will you be able to build the new school soon?"

"I figured you'd be taking time off from that," Daniel said. "Your confinement date isn't that far away. You ought to be doing more resting. You need to build up your strength."

"I'm plenty strong."

"Right. I guess I would have to agree to that." Daniel grinned.

"After the baby's born, I could close it for a while, or someone else could teach." Rebecca knew Daniel was unconvinced. "I love to teach, Daniel. It doesn't make me a bit tired. I feel as if I've been called to it. Can you understand that?"

"Called in the way a reverend is called to preach?"

"Well, not something so grand as that, but yes, you might say so. I know I'm a help to the children, and to Lily. She comes whenever she can." She glanced at Callie, who was sweeping the front entrance to the house. "Callie has been helping."

"What about the children?" Daniel asked. "Having two is much more difficult than one."

Rebecca looked at Joseph, who was scrambling out of his father's arms, and wondered if it was mothering that God had intended for her. She felt a crushing love for her son. Still, a sense of calling to do more remained.

"I know it won't be easy," she said, "but two children can't be that difficult to manage."

Daniel smiled and nodded. "All right, then. I must admit, I thought you'd do this until the new baby arrived and then mothering would be enough for you. But you must do as you like. You have my blessing."

With a basket of clothing cradled against her side, Callie walked to a clothesline beyond the garden. Rebecca was happy for the distraction. The servant set the basket on the ground, lifted out a pair of blue jeans, and shook them to dislodge the creases. Using wooden pins, she hung them on the line.

"Perhaps Callie could take over for me while I convalesce after having the baby. What do you think?" Before Daniel could answer, the sight of dust billowing just beyond the rise caught Rebecca's attention. "Someone's coming," she said.

A moment later two men rode into the drive. They were young and good-looking. One was tall and lean. He looked at Rebecca, and the coldness in his brown eyes made her want to recoil. The other man removed his hat, revealing shaggy blond hair. He combed it off his face with his hand while staring at Daniel. He didn't look any friendlier than the first man.

"Do you know these men, Daniel?" Rebecca asked, alarm pulsing through her.

Daniel was on his feet. "I . . . I don't know," he hedged. "Maybe." He walked down the porch steps and strode into the yard. "G'day."

The men didn't smile or offer a greeting. Her heart pounding hard, Rebecca stood, clasping her hands. "What do they want?" she asked no one in particular.

"I dare say, they'll take care of their business and then be on their way," Willa said.

"Need ta talk," the tall man said, his voice brusque.

"Right." Daniel looked about, glancing at Rebecca. "Mind if we walk?"

"I'll ride," the blond man said. His companion didn't respond but remained on his horse.

Daniel started walking away from the house.

Rebecca's stomach churned. "Willa, what could men like that want with Daniel? He acts like he knows them."

"They probably just want to speak to Daniel about cattle or some such," Willa said.

✿

"If you're here about that last payment, you needn't have come all the way out 'ere. I always pay my debts. And I'll pay this one. It's just delayed a bit. I've got to take a mob of cattle south for sale before I can pay Mr. Marshal."

Jack moved his horse in close to Daniel. "Don't think ya understood when ya signed those papers. Mr. Marshal frowns on late payments. Money's due when it's due. No later."

"Right, I agree. But a bloke's got to have a bit of room now and again. Money doesn't just fly in on a schedule, not 'round 'ere, anyway."

"We don't care how the money comes in, just so long as it does." Luke gave Daniel a malicious grin.

Daniel knew he was in trouble. "I don't have the money."

"Get it." Jack nudged his hat down slightly in front. "Mr. Marshal will be right annoyed if we come back without it. His words to us: 'Don't care how ya get it. Just get it.'"

"Tell him I'll have some of it in a few weeks. A bloke's buying a couple of horses from me."

"We're 'ere t'day." Ruthless pleasure touched Jack's eyes.

Daniel lifted his hat and ran his fingers into his hair. Where would he get any money? "I have a bit in the bank. But . . ."

"Get it," Jack said.

"Right. I'll do that . . . tomorrow."

"T'day. We'll go along ta see that ya take care of it."

"I don't have enough to cover all the payment. I'm just getting back on my feet."

"We'll take what ya got. And I don't care 'bout yer feet." Jack looked at Luke. "Ya think we ought ta give him a bit of time on the rest?"

"What do people say? Can't get blood out of a turnip? Might like to try." Luke snickered and then turned a hard stare on Daniel. "When will you have it?"

"Two or three weeks."

"What is it, two or three?" Luke asked.

Daniel felt his anger rise. He didn't care who these blokes thought they were. They weren't bullying him. "I'll let you know when I get it," Daniel snapped.

In a flash, Luke lifted his foot and thrust the heel of it square in Daniel's face. Daniel reeled back. Covering his bleeding nose with his hand, he stared at the man who'd kicked him. He wanted to drag him off his horse and teach him a lesson in manners.

"When I ask ya a question, I expect a civil answer." Luke grinned. "Two weeks. We want a payment in two weeks."

5

With a canvas bag draped over one shoulder and balancing an armload of slates, Rebecca ducked beneath the tent flap and walked into the temporary schoolroom. The barn was finished, and Daniel had gone back to work on the house; perhaps a proper school could be next.

A breeze billowed the sides of the tent, and Rebecca shivered. *I best not ask him. He's already fretting over expenditures.* She remembered the men who'd come to Douloo and roughed up Daniel. Did their visit have anything to do with money troubles? She cringed inwardly at the memory of Daniel's poor bruised face and injured nose. He hadn't told her what the men had wanted or why they'd hurt him, but every time she thought of them, she felt afraid.

She looked across the room to one of the station's roustabouts. He was setting up a blackboard on a wooden easel. Thank goodness for the school. It had provided a welcome distraction. *A blackboard will be such a help.*

"That's perfect," Rebecca said. "When Mr. O'Brien offered us the board, I was dumbfounded. He said he wanted to help."

"Is that the bloke who owns the mercantile?"

51

"Yes. He's a fine man."

"Roight nice board," the young black man said.

"It's a blessing. It will make teaching much easier." She glanced down at the new slates she'd purchased. "He may have taken a risk giving us the blackboard. I guess there are some people who would rather we didn't have a school here for the aborigines."

"Could be trouble. But I'm glad yer doin' it." The man smiled, and his face softened, making him look almost handsome.

"I've seen you about the last several days. You're new here, right?"

"Yais. Hired on a coupla weeks ago. Glad ta be 'ere. Heard this is a roight fine place ta work."

"I'm glad that's the word in the district. It's nice to know people hold us in high regard." Rebecca set the slates and the bag containing chalk, pencils, and papers on the desk.

"First school I ever saw in a tent. Looks nice though."

"Thank you. I'll be glad when the permanent schoolroom is built. But for now this will do." She noticed two fuzzy-headed youngsters peering in the doorway. "Good day," she said.

With a giggle, the children dashed out of sight.

"I'm not sure the students' parents are in favor of my teaching their children."

"Don't know the people 'ere well, so I couldn't say, mum." The young man was quiet a moment, then asked, "Will ya let someone like me come ta yer school?"

"Anyone who is interested in learning is welcome. Do you read?"

"No. But I was thinkin' 'bout it."

"You may join us if you like. We start at nine o'clock."

"Thank ya, mum. I'll try ta be 'ere. Got plenty of work ta do, so I don't know that I can come all the time."

"Whenever you can attend will be fine."

"Thank ya."

"Can you tell me your name?"

"Koora, mum." He smiled, and his dark eyes warmed. "Be roight fine ta learn readin'. Can ya teach me how ta write me name?"

"Absolutely."

"Good, then." He turned and walked to the door.

Just as he started out the doorway, Callie walked in, and the two nearly collided. They looked at each other but didn't speak. With a slight nod, Koora continued on his way.

"Who was that?" Callie asked, walking to the chalkboard. "Don't remember seein' 'im 'round the place."

"He's new, but you must have seen him. He's been working for us a couple of weeks now. His name is Koora."

"A drover?"

"No. I don't think so. He said he wanted to come to school, and drovers are out and about too much."

Callie's eyes moved to the doorway.

"He's rather handsome, don't you think?"

The servant's dark face flushed. She shrugged. "Fine, I guess." She rested her hand on the cool surface of the blackboard and then traced a finger across it. "Never seen this before."

"Mr. O'Brien gave it to us."

"Roight nice of him."

The tent flap opened, and Daniel stepped inside. He didn't look happy. "I was told you needed more benches." He surveyed the room. "Looks like you've got plenty."

"I was hoping for a couple more. It seems every day there are new children." Rebecca could still see a bit of bruising along Daniel's cheek and beneath his left eye. She fought the urge to touch his face. Daniel had been very brusque about the whole business and had refused to speak of it.

"The children won't care about having benches. The ground will suit them fine."

Rebecca leveled a reproving look at her husband. "If it

was you, would you prefer sitting on the ground or having a bench to sit on?"

"Right. Well, we have a few benches 'round the place. S'pose I could get some from a couple of the cottages."

"I don't want to take them from the help. Couldn't you make some?"

"Yeah, but not today. I'll just look 'round and borrow some for tomorrow, and then I'll have two made up later in the week." He offered Rebecca a halfhearted smile.

She could feel Daniel's annoyance. "I know this gives you more work, but it's not much, really, and this school is a proper endeavor that will make a difference in the children's lives." Rebecca moved to him and placed a hand on his chest. "Please don't be annoyed with me."

"I'm not." He half grinned. "Well a bit, maybe. There's a lot of work to be done without adding to it." He glanced about the room. "Looks like a proper schoolhouse."

"It does, doesn't it? I'm quite happy with it. It's served me and the children well." She motioned toward the blackboard. "And look what we have now."

Daniel looked at the board but didn't seem impressed.

"It's from Mr. O'Brien. He's been very kind."

"Right. He's a good bloke." He stared at the board. "Never liked school much." He grinned. "Mum said as a lad I was more interested in riding and swimming rather than studying my lessons."

"She's been a wonderful help to me. And Callie has helped some. She's making progress with the parents. If only she can reach more of them."

"And what about that new fella? I saw him leave a few minutes ago."

"Koora?"

"I heard some talk about him wanting to take part in your school?"

"Yes. He said he'd like to attend. Would you mind?"

Daniel looked displeased. "He's got a job to do."

"Of course. But he said he'd only come when he's finished his duties."

"He seems like a fine bloke. Works hard and does a good job. I don't care if he joins your class as long as it doesn't get in the way of his responsibilities." Daniel picked up a reader lying on the desk and thumbed through it. "You know, for generations the blacks have done right well for themselves . . . without books."

"I don't know what you think *right well* is, but it doesn't appear as if they've done well at all."

"They're happy enough." He set the book back on the desk.

"Having an education will be good for them." Rebecca could feel her anger flare.

Daniel crossed his arms over his chest. "S'pose you're right. Well, I better get to those benches." He left without another word.

Feeling deflated, Rebecca watched as he walked toward the barn. "It seemed he'd be just as happy if there were no school."

Callie picked up a broom and started sweeping the dirt floor. "He's got a lot ta think 'bout, mum. Seems the school is more a bother roight now. Shoulda waited, eh?"

"You're probably right. Rebuilding has been an enormous weight on him. But if I'd held off too long, it would mean waiting until after the baby is born. And I was afraid that delaying would mean there'd never actually be a school."

"Yer never one ta let things go, mum. Ya would 'ave seen that it was taken care of." Callie grinned. "I'll see if Mrs. Thornton needs anything more done before we start." She strode outside and toward the house.

Rebecca tidied her desk and then picked up a piece of chalk and moved to the small blackboard, where she proceeded to write the date and the day's assignment. She was careful to make her lettering just so. When she'd finished, she stepped back and looked at her work. The white, perfectly slanted lettering looked nice on the black surface, but as she studied it, she realized how pointless it was to write out instructions. The children couldn't read script yet. She started to erase what she'd written and then thought better of it. *It will be good for them to see the words.*

She set the chalk on the rim of the blackboard and turned and looked at the room. It was organized, spotless, and ready for students. She pulled her shawl more tightly about her. It was cold in spite of the wood stove. She opened the door of the stove and peered inside. A fire flickered but needed more tinder. She picked up two pieces of wood and set them in the flames.

"Rebecca?" Cambria, Rebecca's closest friend, pushed open the door flap and stepped inside. Her eyes inspected the room. "It's quite nice. You've done a lot since I was here last. Now it looks like a real schoolhouse." Her blue eyes were bright.

"It is at that." Rebecca moved to Cambria and embraced her. "How good to see you. I've missed you."

"I've been wanting ta come by, but ya know how things are—there's always work and more work. Never much time for socializing."

"I've heard you find time for Jim." Rebecca smiled.

"Yais. I suppose I do." Her cheeks turned pink. "I want ya ta be the first ta know. Jim and I are engaged ta be married."

"How wonderful! I'm thrilled for you. When is the wedding?"

"Don't know quite yet. He's looking for a piece of land so he can build us a house. Says he's not about ta let a wife of his live in a cabin owned by someone else, even if it is a Thornton cabin."

"I hope he finds something soon. Of course, we'll miss having him here. Will he continue to work for us, or do you plan to run your own stock?"

"He'd like ta have his own, but that's going ta be a tough one ta manage. It takes money. He has some savings, but we don't know if it will be enough."

"Jim's a fine drover and has a good head on his shoulders. He knows the business. Perhaps Daniel would consider selling him a piece of Douloo." The moment the words were out of her mouth, Rebecca knew it was an outlandish idea. She remembered the time she'd suggested selling off a portion of the station. Daniel's response had been immediate and harsh. He'd never let any of Douloo go. "Now that I think on it, I don't believe that's likely."

"Course not. And anyway, Jim and I want our own station."

"I hope you'll be close to us. That way we can continue to ride together and visit often."

"Yais. Wouldn't want it ta be otherwise." She settled an affectionate gaze on Rebecca. "I was hoping ya'd stand up with me . . . when we get married. Yer me closest friend."

"I'd be honored." Rebecca hugged Cambria. "How exciting. I'm so happy for you. Jim's a good man." She grinned. "However, I do recall that our first meeting wasn't exactly friendly. He was quite angry with me for moving here."

"He told me he didn't know ya then, and he thought ya were just another Yank with dreams muddling yer brain. He didn't expect ya ta make a go of it."

"Well, I have." Again Rebecca felt the stir of excitement over her latest project. "And now life is quite thrilling—the school and your getting married." She glanced at her rounded abdomen. "Another baby. There's so much happening."

Cambria scanned the room again. "This is grand, really. Even if it's just a tent. I dare say, you're doing a fine thing by teaching the children." She walked to the blackboard and picked up the piece of chalk Rebecca had left on the bottom rim. She wrote out "Cambria Keller" and then stepped back to look at the name. "I quite like that." She smiled. "It's fine, eh?"

"Yes. It is."

"I'll be happy the day my name becomes Keller. But I may have a long wait yet." She returned the chalk to the board.

"Most likely not." Rebecca draped an arm over Cambria's shoulders and gave her a squeeze. "It's all in God's hands anyway. And his timing is perfect."

"True enough." Cambria moved to the desk and picked up a book of basic grammar. "I'd like ta help if ya need me."

"Thank you. I'm sure I'll be needing assistance, especially after the baby's born."

"Are ya feeling well?"

"Yes. Just getting anxious for her arrival."

"Her?" Cambria smiled. "I hope yer right. Douloo could use more females." She set down the book. "'Round town there's talk 'bout the school."

"I know. I've been told." Rebecca sighed with exasperation. "I'm not going to worry about it. Each time something new comes along, everyone seems to have something to say."

"I figure folks will get used ta the idea."

"I hope I'm up to it all. Sometimes I feel as if I'm doing nothing except filling time." She wiped a smudge off the blackboard. "The children don't always seem happy to be here."

Cambria smiled. "Right. Don't ya remember how it was? There were lots of days I'd rather have been out riding or fishing or doing just 'bout anything other than lessons."

"Yes. I do remember. There were times when I couldn't think about anything but riding."

Two girls Rebecca had never seen before walked into the tent. Their hands clasped, they stood and stared at Cambria and Rebecca. Finally the taller of the two said, "We're 'ere for the school."

"Welcome. It's so good to have you," Rebecca smiled, hop-

ing to set their nerves at ease. "You can sit right over there."
She nodded at a bench in the front.

The children moved quietly to the places indicated and
sat. The smaller of the two was tiny, and her legs dangled
above the floor, so she swung them back and forth.

"Where are you girls from?" Rebecca asked.

"We from the McCleary place, mum," the older girl said.
"Heard 'bout the school and was hopin' ta learn."

"That's fine. I'm very happy to have you."

"Can't stay," Cambria said. "Just wanted ta give ya the
news. Hope ya have a fine day." She moved toward the door.
"See ya later in the week, then."

Callie walked into the schoolroom just as two boys jumped
up on one of the benches. As if competing with each other,
they leaped from one bench to the next, landing between
other students. When the larger lad shoved the smaller one,
they dropped to the floor and fought over who was the stronger of the two.

"Stop! Stop that!" Rebecca hollered, trying unsuccessfully
to step between the two. "Please. Stop this." The boys kept
going after each other.

Callie walked up to them, grabbed each by an ear, and
yanked them apart.

"Ah!" one of them cried.

"That's enough of that! Ya straighten up roight now. This
is no place for mischief. Yer 'ere ta learn." She let them loose.
"Behave yerselves now."

The lads stared at her, then returned to their seats.

"Ya tell Mrs. Thornton yer sorry."

"Sorry, mum," both youngsters mumbled.

"Thank goodness you showed up. I've been having difficulty with those two. They're brothers, and it seems they started their squabbling while on the way here this morning." Rebecca folded her arms over her chest and studied the boys. "They're bright and very good students, but sometimes they have too much vigor." She smiled.

"Seems ya 'ave a good group this morning," Callie said.

"Yes, ten in all. We've two new students. I think there are still some hanging back because their parents don't want them here. Perhaps you could speak to the parents."

Callie didn't say anything right off. She didn't feel comfortable trying to convince anyone that their children ought to attend school. She wasn't even certain how she felt about it herself. It could raise false hopes. Finally she said, "I'll try, mum."

"Thank you. I'm sure if we persevere, more parents will be supportive of an education for their children."

Rebecca sucked in a breath. "However, I must say, this is a challenge, having children dribbling in. Every time there's a new student, I'm forced to take time to teach him the basics. Most have no concept of the written word, or even how to use a slate. The training slows down the rest of the class."

Rebecca glanced at the students. They were already working on their slates, practicing the letters they'd learned the previous week. "I guess time isn't of any real concern. For the most part, the children seem happy enough to linger, and they truly enjoy helping one another."

"It's roight fun," Callie said, picking up one of the small wood-framed boards and a piece of chalk and writing out her name. She admired the word, then said, "I quite like writing."

"Do you think you can help the children with their letters and their sounds?"

"Yais," Callie said, battling against uncertainty about her skills. "It'll be fine if ya don't expect too much. I still 'ave a lot ta learn meself."

"I understand. But we can learn together and from each other."

Callie was a bit taken aback. "How can ya learn from me?"

"I've already learned so much. Don't you know?" Rebecca smiled. "When I first arrived in Queensland, I didn't know a thing about this world."

Someone cleared his throat, drawing Rebecca's and Callie's attention. Koora stood just inside the door. Callie's heart picked up its pace, and she felt flushed.

"Good morning, Koora," Rebecca said. "Welcome."

"G'day mum. I'm done with me work for now and was wonderin' if I could come ta yer school?"

"Of course. Please sit."

Koora glanced at Callie and nodded. Callie refused to acknowledge him. She wasn't about to give him the wrong idea. Wearing a knowing smile, he took a seat on the bench in the back of the classroom.

What is he smilin' 'bout? What does he think he knows? Callie felt furious and embarrassed.

"You'll need one of these," Rebecca said, handing Koora a slate and a piece of chalk. "You can write on it," she said and demonstrated.

Koora smiled broadly. "This is fine. I like it." He settled serious eyes on Rebecca. "I figure if I learn ta write and ta read, I can do more than be a roustabout. Maybe 'ave me own place one day, eh?"

"Big dream for a black man," Callie challenged. "Ya'd be wise ta think more reasonable." She'd known others who had dreams, but no matter how much they believed or worked, their hopes came to nothing.

"Won't get nowhere bein' reasonable," Koora said.

"Humph," was Callie's only response. She walked out of the tent.

"Callie! Wait!" Rebecca went after her, stopping at the doorway just long enough to tell the children she'd return shortly.

61

Callie picked up her pace and didn't look back. She didn't want to talk with Rebecca. She didn't want to speak to anyone.

Rebecca caught up to her. "I thought you were going to help me. Where are you going?"

"I remembered I 'ave some wash ta do." Callie kept walking.

"Please wait," Rebecca said, her tone sharp.

Callie stopped and faced Rebecca. "I said I'd help, but not 'im."

"Why not? He has a right to learn just like everyone else."

"No. It's not good."

"Why?"

Callie hesitated, then said softly, "He's one of those who makes us believe we can 'ave more. And it can't be. We just end up feelin' like fools."

"You can't know it will be like that. Things can change."

"They're not goin' ta change, mum."

Rebecca's demeanor softened. "I kind of like him. Daniel said he's a good worker, and he's obviously ambitious. I thought you might want to get to know him better."

'Ere it comes, Callie thought. *Well, why not.* Her mind returned to a time she'd tried to forget. "I knew a man better once. He was s'posed ta come for me. But he never came. And now no man's goin' ta fancy me. I'm near thirty." She glanced back at the tent. "But I figure I'll be roight fine on me own. Don't need no one."

"Callie, there's nothing wrong with a man and a woman loving each other. And I thought you wanted babies. You told me you did."

An ache rose up inside. Callie had wanted babies. "No. There'll be no bybies for me," she said and walked toward the house.

6

Koora and a young boy each carried an armload of firewood and dumped it into a wood bin alongside a small firebox.

"Thank you," Rebecca said, tucking her shawl snugly between her arms and her body. "It's rather chilly today."

The wood-burning stove held off the cold but made for a crowded schoolroom. Rebecca opened the stove door and picked up a piece of wood.

"I'll do that, mum," Koora said, taking the chunk of acacia from her and shoving it into the fire. He added two more pieces and then closed the door and latched it.

"That should help," Rebecca said, enjoying the odor of burning wood and smoke. The combination of that and the sound of light rainfall on the canvas roof reminded her of Boston.

Koora took his place on a back bench beside Callie. The boy squeezed between two other lads in the second row.

Rebecca studied the children. The girls were dressed in light cotton shifts, and the boys wore pants and cotton shirts. None of them had a coat. Although the children didn't complain Rebecca thought they must be cold. *I wish there was something I could do for them*, she thought.

"Are any of you cold?" she asked.

The children stared at her. A little girl sitting in the front row said, "No, mum. Are ya?"

"Why, yes I am, a bit."

"Me mum says whites got thin skin. That's why ya get cold."

Rebecca smiled. "Hmm. I hadn't thought of that." She glanced at Callie, who offered her a knowing look.

She walked to the front of the classroom and picked up a piece of chalk from the lip of the blackboard. With arithmetic completed, it was time to move on to the writing lesson. Careful to use perfect script, Rebecca wrote out the alphabet, using upper- and lowercase letters.

After writing the letter *T*, she turned and said, "We're going to learn a new letter and a new sound today. But first let's read the preceding letters."

Pointing at each, she and the students recited one at a time.

"Very good. You're making great progress."

She underlined the letter *T*. "Does anyone know what this letter is?"

Silently the students stared at the board.

Finally Koora said, "Is it a *T*?"

Rebecca smiled. "Correct."

Koora grinned. "I been studyin'." He held up his slate to show off the letters of the alphabet he'd written.

"Very good, Koora."

"Yer a fine teacher." He stood. "Wish I could stay, but I got work ta do." He moved toward the classroom door and then stopped. He lingered there a moment, then said, "Mum, I was wondering if I could do some extra work for school, after my chores are done."

"Of course. But you'll need instruction."

Koora looked at Callie. "Maybe Callie could help, eh?"

Callie looked surprised but said nothing.

"Would that be all right with you, Callie?" Rebecca asked.

Callie didn't answer right away, then said, "I could do it."

"Fine, then. Perhaps you two can put together some kind of schedule."

"That would be roight fine with me." Koora placed his hat on his head. "Maybe tonight, eh?"

"Fine." Callie barely glanced at Koora, then looked back at the blackboard.

Koora stepped through the door and disappeared outside. Callie returned to writing on her slate.

"All right, then," Rebecca continued. "Can anyone tell me what sound the letter *T* makes?"

Silence.

With emphasis Rebecca made a *T* sound. The class imitated.

"Can anyone think of a word that starts with *T*?"

A small boy with wild, curly hair raised his hand. "Tr . . . ee, mum."

"Yes. That's correct."

Another hand went up, and Rebecca nodded to the girl.

"What about tooth, eh?" She pointed at her large front teeth.

"Right. Excellent." Rebecca smiled inside.

It had been two months since the students had started their schooling, and already they knew most of the alphabet and its sounds. Plus, they were having great success at writing out the letters. Soon they'd be reading.

This is what had been missing in Rebecca's life. Each morning when she woke, her first thoughts were of the students and the lesson plans for the day. It all seemed so perfect. School took up only a few hours each day, leaving her with plenty of time for her family and for rest. Now all she needed was a proper building.

"Can anyone else think of a word that begins with *T*?" she asked.

Skinny arms shot up.

"How about teacher?" a voice boomed. One of the men who'd accosted Daniel stepped into the classroom. Detached brown eyes settled on Rebecca. "Teacher starts with *T*, roight, mum?" he taunted.

Alarm surged through Rebecca. She managed to nod.

Two other men moved into the room. They looked arrogant and cruel.

The first to step in said, "Let me 'ave another go at it, eh? How 'bout I use it in a sentence?" He looked up at the ceiling in an exaggerated way and drawled, "Wal now, let me see . . . I 'ave it. The *teacher* won't be *teachin'* no more if 'er husband don't do as he's told." He sneered. "What ya think 'bout that, eh?"

Rebecca's stomach churned, and her nerves jumped. She was angry and scared. Unconsciously she rested a hand on her stomach as if protecting her unborn child. Managing what she hoped was a look of nonchalance, she met the man's eyes. "Who are you, and what do you want?"

"Name's Jack. This is Luke. Ya don't want ta mess with 'im." He nodded at the other man. "And this 'ere is Wade." Jack grinned. "Wade's a friendly type. When he wants ta be, anyway."

Jack folded his arms over his chest and scrutinized the room, his eyes stopping at each child. Every youngster met his glare and bore the scrutiny without flinching.

"Roight nice ta 'ave a school for the unfortunate."

"What do you want?" Rebecca repeated.

"Our boss, Mr. Marshal, sent us ta give yer husband a message."

"My husband's not here." Rebecca's skin tingled with apprehension.

"We figured ya could give 'im the message for us." Jack

66

paused, then in a menacing tone continued, "Yer husband knows what's expected. If he doesn't want ta see the people he loves get hurt, he better do as he's told."

Luke moved to Rebecca and laid a hand on her arm. His face looked sculpted and too perfect. His nostrils flared slightly as his fingers lightly touched her skin and his hand trailed up to her neck. "You have a right lovely look to you."

Rebecca swiped his hand away. Her heart hammering, she looked at Jack. "There's nothing I can do for you."

"Not true." Jack walked to the front of the room. He stopped at Rebecca's desk and picked up a book, then rested his hand on a globe before fixing his eyes on the children. "Ya wouldn't want yer teacher hurt, eh?"

Wide-eyed, the children stared at the intruder without responding.

"Figure the youngsters have homes ta go to. Figure there's work ta be done. Perhaps they ought ta get ta it?"

The students turned confused expressions on Rebecca.

"Children, practice your letters. Mr. . . . Jack will be leaving momentarily."

"I'll be staying as long as I see fit." His grin tipping sideways, he took a heavy step toward the children and brought his hands together in a pronounced clap. "Go on now! Get!"

The youngsters flinched. They looked as if they might flee, but they remained seated and looked at their teacher for direction.

Struggling to remain calm, Rebecca said, "Go along. We'll carry on with our lessons tomorrow."

The children hurried out of the room.

Callie moved closer to Rebecca. Rebecca could feel her fury, and she could taste her own.

She remained silent until the last child stepped out of the door, then lashed out at the intruders. "How dare you come into my classroom and behave in such a manner! You have no right to give orders to me or to my students!"

An expression of disbelief touched Luke's chiseled features. "You still don't understand. I, we, can do whatever we want."

Rebecca lifted her chin slightly. "Get off my land."

"Your land, is it?" Luke chuckled and looked at the other men. "She says it's her land." He laughed outright. His smile disappeared, and he turned venomous eyes on Rebecca. "You might want to talk to Mr. Marshal about that."

Fear spiked through Rebecca, but she refused to show it. "If my husband were here . . ."

"If he were here, he'd shut you up."

"I order you to leave! Now! Get off this station!"

"No sheila orders me to do anything." Luke stepped back a pace, lifted his rifle, settled it on his shoulder, and pointed it at Callie. "Be real easy to pick her off. Won't be missed. No better than a dingo anyway."

Rebecca stepped in front of Callie.

Luke left the rifle in place and stared down the barrel at Rebecca. "You're so pally with your black friend there—would you take a bullet for her?" He squeezed the trigger slightly.

Inwardly Rebecca shuddered and tried to convince herself he wouldn't actually shoot her. She stared into his merciless blue eyes and knew he would. He was enjoying this.

She straightened her spine and threw back her shoulders. "I'll give my husband your message."

Ignoring Rebecca, Luke stepped to the left, giving him a clearer shot of Callie. "I seen what happens when blacks get cocky. Think they can do what they want. You're a fool if you think she's loyal to you. She'd never protect you." He settled a hateful gaze on Callie. "Figure she'd kill you if she got a chance."

Rebecca glanced at Callie and a message of allegiance was conveyed between the two. "Go. Please."

"Seems I heard you're a Yank. You know nothing about things here. You're a fool. It'd suit Mr. Marshal fine if you disappeared. We could make that happen." He glanced at Jack and Wade. "Right?"

The two didn't reply, but their posture seemed to affirm the statement.

"Makes me sick at my stomach to think of them mongrels getting high and mighty ideas just because they can read and write," Luke continued. "Course, I figure most of them can't learn anyway." Luke lifted his rifle for emphasis. "Waste of good time."

"Put the gun down. Now!" Willa said, stepping into the classroom. A rifle rested on her shoulder and was pointed at Luke.

With a look of surprise, he glanced at Willa. "You won't shoot me."

"No? I suppose you can keep that rifle right where it is and find out, then." Her expression was unyielding. "Put down your firearm." When Luke didn't move, she added. "Put it down. I'll not have you or anyone else threatening my family."

Luke didn't move.

"We got our message across. Time ta push on," Jack said.

"No! We're staying!" Luke barked. He turned to Willa. "You go back inside that fancy house of yours and have a cuppa. This doesn't concern you."

Willa kept her rifle as it was. "Anything that has to do with my family is my business. I'm telling you as nicely as I know how that you'd be wise to go on your way."

Rebecca felt a swell of pride for Willa.

"I don't take orders from sheilas." Luke stared at Willa, challenging her.

Willa took a step forward. "You go, or you'll taste gun-powder."

"We can come back later," Wade said. "We done what we were asked."

"Put the gun down," Jack told Luke, then settled a brutal

look on Rebecca. "Ya tell yer husband he better do as he's told or we'll be back. Next time someone will get hurt. Might even be that precious little boy of yers."

Rebecca felt a surge of rage and horror. "You touch my son, and I'll—"

"Ya'll what?"

"Come on, let's go," Wade said. He took a step toward the door.

"You'd be wise to listen to your friend," Willa said. "I'm a good shot."

Luke's lips lifted into a sneer. "Right. I'm real scared."

Willa quickly pointed the rifle at his feet and squeezed the trigger. The room exploded with a deafening boom, and the ground just in front of his boots splintered and spit dirt pebbles. She quickly leveled the rifle at the young man's chest, smiling slightly.

Rebecca had never seen Willa like this. She'd always seemed serene and sweet, never tough. Admiration for her mother-in-law grew.

"I'll shoot you if I have to." Willa's tone was implacable.

Jack moved toward the door. "We'll go," he told Rebecca. "But ya tell yer husband what we said."

Reluctantly Luke lowered his rifle. "Do as you're told, or there'll be consequences."

Willa pressed her cheek against the stock of the rifle and sighted it in on Luke. "Your threats mean nothing."

Finally the men backed out of the schoolhouse. Willa followed, keeping the rifle trained on them. Rebecca stepped to the door. Luke moved his horse around behind Jack's, and before Rebecca knew it had happened, he'd lit a torch and tossed it onto the roof of the schoolhouse. The three men quickly rode off.

For a moment Rebecca was rooted in place, then realizing all that was about to be lost, she ran to the tent and ducked inside. Callie had her arms full of slates. Rebecca grabbed books off her desk and piled them in her arms. The torch burned through the roof, and then flames climbed across the ceiling and down the walls.

"Get out! Get out!" Rebecca screamed.

Callie sprinted through the door, gulping in deep breaths of air. Smoke billowed down and around Rebecca. Her eyes burned, and her throat felt scorched. Holding her breath and keeping her head down, she ran for the doorway. As she stepped outside, cool, damp air fell over her like a moist balm. She took in several deep breaths, then turned and watched as the tent blazed.

Willa moved close and laid an arm over Rebecca's shoulders. "There's nothing to be done except be thankful the earth is wet."

"All my work," Rebecca cried.

"You can begin again. Benches can be rebuilt, and another tent can be set up." She rested her hand on Rebecca's back. "Everything will be fine, dear."

"Fire. Shall it always be fire that destroys us?"

"Of course not." Willa smoothed Rebecca's hair as if she were a child. "And we've not been destroyed."

Rebecca wanted to believe that, but she felt something different. The men—what did they want?

Willa pulled her close, but Rebecca felt no comfort as she watched the tent become singed tatters and listened to the popping of wood as the benches and desk burned. When Daniel returned he would tell her what those men were after whether he wanted to or not.

She rested her head on Willa's shoulder and gradually felt better. Finally she straightened and blew out a long breath. "I thank the Lord for you and your rifle." She smiled at Willa. "I had no idea you could be so fierce."

"Fierce? I'm shaking from head to toe. I've never had to do such a thing in all my life. And I dare say, those men will be back. But I don't understand why. What do they want?"

"I don't know exactly. But it has something to do with Mr. Marshal . . . and Daniel."

"So it's the loan, then." Willa's hand shook as she brushed hair off her face. "I pray my son hasn't made some terrible mistake." She watched the puff of dust in the distance marking the men's departure. "Thank the Lord I didn't have to shoot anyone."

"You would have, really?"

"What choice would I have had if they hadn't yielded? I'd never allow anyone to harm you or Callie." Worry lines creased Willa's brow. "I'm not sure what Daniel has gotten himself into, but he'd best make it right, and soon."

7

Joseph leaned his elbows on the table and stared down at his plate.

"Sit up straight and eat your lunch," Rebecca said, her own appetite nonexistent. She picked up her fork, but instead of eating she pushed her meat and vegetables around in her bowl. She stabbed a carrot.

Steps sounded hollow on the veranda, and then Daniel walked through the front door. Rebecca stood. "Thank goodness. You're home. I was beginning to worry."

"No reason to. I'm fine." He kissed Rebecca lightly on the cheek, then moved to the table and sat down. He grabbed a roll and took a bite. Then as Rebecca sat he looked from his wife to his mother. "Is something wrong?"

Joseph spoke up first. "Bad man."

Daniel took a drink of water. "What? What bad man?" He looked at Joseph, then back to Rebecca.

"You didn't notice the school?"

"What about it?"

Rebecca felt her anger and frustration grow.

Willa laid a hand on her arm. "We lost the school today. It burned."

"What? What do you mean it burned?" Daniel pushed away from the table and moved to the window. He stared at the blackened spot beyond the cottages. "What happened?"

Rebecca felt a swell of anger. "You say it so casually, as if we'd lost the broom or something."

Daniel returned to the table. "I don't feel casual about it at all. Was anyone hurt?"

"No. Everyone is fine . . . for now."

"Tell me what happened."

Willa wiped her mouth with her handkerchief. "Some men came by with a message from Mr. Marshal, and before they left they thought it would be fitting to burn down the school."

Daniel squared his jaw. "From Marshal?"

"Yes," Rebecca said, barely able to unclench her jaw. "You know two of them. They were the men who came to see you a few weeks ago—Jack and Luke. You remember—the ones who bashed in your face?" Rebecca knew her tone was snippy, but she had reason to be vexed. "This time there was another man with them called Wade." Rebecca's heartbeat picked up at the thought of the confrontation. "They barged into my classroom and threatened me, the children, and Callie."

Lily stepped out of the kitchen, carrying a large pot. "Yer mum did quite a job of scarin' them off though. Callie was there and said Mrs. Thornton is roight handy with a rifle." Lily grinned and then ladled stew into Daniel's bowl.

Daniel settled a questioning gaze on his mother. "*You* chased them off?"

Willa picked up her fork. "I did at that. And they were wise to go." She smiled slightly and speared a piece of beef. "Your father believed it would be best if I knew how to defend myself. And I'm quite good with a rifle."

"Right, I knew that, but I won't have you chasing off bush-rangers. You might have been hurt."

"We were hurt," Rebecca said. "Those men destroyed the

74

school, Daniel. And they threatened us. They're horrible. They wanted me to give you a warning."

"A warning? About what?"

"They said you were to do as you were told . . . or they'd come back and . . ." Rebecca looked at Joseph, who was too attentive. She leaned close to Daniel and whispered, "They said they would hurt one of us, and they mentioned Joseph."

Daniel's expression turned hard. "They'll not touch anyone in this family."

"Why would they want to?" Rebecca demanded. "What is going on? What do they want?"

"They're just troublemakers. I'll handle them."

"It's more than that. What is it you're supposed to do, Daniel?" Rebecca couldn't keep the accusation out of her tone.

"Nothing. I don't want you to worry."

Willa folded her napkin and set it beside her plate. "Obviously we do have something to worry about. That man, Luke, nearly shot Callie. I think he would have if Rebecca hadn't stood in front of her."

Daniel looked grieved. "You did that?"

"Yes." Rebecca gazed at her husband. "Please. Tell me what's going on."

Daniel scooted away from the table and stood. "I don't want you involved, none of you."

Rebecca pushed to her feet. "But we are involved."

"I think it's best you stay indoors for the next few days. And I want you to close the school, at least for now."

"And what is the reason? Give me a reason." Rebecca folded her arms over her chest.

Daniel didn't answer right away. Finally he leveled a serious look at his wife.

"Those blokes could have done more than burn down a tent. You or one of the children could have been killed."

"I know that. I want to know why. Why are we in danger?" Rebecca settled a hand on her abdomen. "I'm about to have a baby. Do I need to be afraid for her? And what about Joseph?"

Daniel moved to the window. "It might take me a bit of time to straighten this all out, but I will."

"Daniel, it's not fair to leave me out of this. Those men . . . they're evil. They enjoyed frightening us. If they come back—"

"They won't. I'll take care of it," Daniel snapped. He swiped a hand through his hair. "Let me handle things my way. It's better if I can resolve this peaceably." He turned a dark look on Rebecca. "No school. Not until I say."

"But—"

"It will be closed," Daniel snapped. He stared at Rebecca for a moment, then turned and strode out of the room and then outside.

Frustrated and afraid, Rebecca watched through the window as he walked toward the barn. Why wouldn't he tell her what was going on? What was so terrible that he couldn't be honest with her? *Lord, I know something is terribly wrong. Please help us with whatever it is.*

Anxiety still washing over her in waves, Rebecca stepped into her bedroom and closed the door. She moved to the window and stared outside. There were still remnants of the devastating fire that had struck them six months before. Blackened trees stood guard over the yard, where new grasses had sprouted. Burned-out buildings had been replaced by new ones. The barn stood, new and fresh and needing paint. There were newly built cottages and others in varying stages of construction.

Then, her mind returning to the morning's events, she

stared at the blackened ground where the schoolroom had been. What had Daniel gotten them into?

She took a long, deep breath and then blew it out. She needed to remain calm. Being distressed might be harmful to the baby.

She crossed to her bed stand and picked up a book she'd been reading. Sitting on the bed, she lay back on her pillows, opened the book, and tried to read, but her mind wouldn't quiet. In frustration she set the book aside. *Lord, please show me what I'm to do.*

She waited for an answer, but when none came she sat up and put the book on the night table and then crossed to the window. Her eyes wandered to Chavive. Her belly was large and round. It wouldn't be long now until her foal arrived. Unconsciously Rebecca rested a hand on her own stomach.

I wish I could ride, she thought. She looked at her abdomen. It wasn't so large. She could probably ride. And today the weather was cool. Chavive would enjoy an outing. Perhaps a short ride would be all right.

No. That's foolhardy. I'm too close to my confinement. Rebecca wanted to be alone on the open flats, and a chat with Cambria would be grand. *Perhaps I can take the buggy. There's no harm in that.*

Anxious to be on her way, she grabbed a hat from the closet and hurried outdoors. When she stepped into the barn, she nearly collided with Jim. "Oh," she exclaimed, ducking sideways.

"Sorry," Jim said. "Wasn't watching where I was going." He grabbed Rebecca to steady her.

"No trouble. It wasn't your fault. I was in a hurry." She avoided his eyes.

"Where you off to?"

"I was hoping to take out the buggy and maybe stop and see Cambria." She smiled. "I'll tell her hello for you."

Jim eyed her, then said, "You think going out on your own is a good idea?"

"I'll be fine."

Jim didn't speak right away. Finally he said, "Maybe someone should go with you."

"I really need time alone."

"All right, then." He smiled. "Tell Cambria I'll do my best to stop by tonight or tomorrow."

"I'll tell her."

Jim started to move on, then stopped. "Did you tell Daniel or Willa that you're going?"

"No. Daniel's a bit miffed at me. Would you mind telling him?"

"I can tell him, but after what happened this morning, I don't feel good about you traipsing off across the flats. What if those men are out there?"

"They're on their way back to Brisbane by now, or they've found a pub somewhere." She glanced out at the flats. Perhaps Jim was right. It might be unsafe to travel far from the house.

Jim lifted then resettled his hat. "Maybe I ought to go with you. I can talk to Daniel and see if he could do without me for an afternoon."

Rebecca contemplated the idea. She wanted to experience the openness of the flats alone, but Jim was right. She really shouldn't go by herself. "All right, then. You may accompany me."

Jim set off to find Daniel.

While Jim readied the horse and buggy, Rebecca grabbed a handful of grain out of a bucket, and walked to the corral. "Hello, girl," she said to Chavive, trying to keep the tension out of her voice. The horse nickered and immediately moved toward Rebecca. Her soft lips snuffled up the grain. Rebecca caressed the front of Chavive's face, relishing the aroma of horse. She could feel her stress dissipate. "What would I do without you?"

She patted the mare's neck, then moved her hand over the animal's enlarged abdomen. "A nice easy ride would be pleasant, eh? But it will have to wait until our little ones arrive."

Chavive bobbed her head as if understanding the invitation.

Jim drove up in the buggy. "You ready?"

"Yes."

"Couldn't find Daniel. He rode off on business." He climbed down and helped Rebecca up onto the seat. "I brought some water in case you get thirsty."

"Thank you."

Jim gazed at Chavive. "She's looking good."

"She is. It won't be too much longer before she foals."

"The both of you." Jim grinned and climbed onto the seat beside Rebecca.

She looked at the house. More than likely Willa was napping along with Joseph.

"Come on, then. I need to get moving. Can scarcely wait to feel the freedom of the flats. And I need the quiet after all that's happened."

⌥

Jim seemed to understand Rebecca's need for solitude and said very little as they traveled. Rebecca gazed out over the open grasslands. She loved Queensland and now saw the countryside as striking and picturesque. Today, however, the empty plains felt too quiet. The silence was unsettling and pressed down on her. There was no birdsong; even the grasses didn't stir.

By the time they had traveled a mile or so, Rebecca was well aware of her advanced pregnancy. The movement and bouncing of the buggy made her back ache and strained the muscles in her lower abdomen.

"I need to get out and stretch a bit. Would you mind?"

"No. This is a fine place." Jim stopped alongside an acacia, jumped out, and hurried around to help Rebecca down.

"Thank you," she said, moving to the shade of the tree.

Jim offered her a canteen. "Figured you'd be thirsty."

"I am."

She drank and then handed the canteen back to Jim. He gulped down several mouthfuls, then poured some into his palm and offered it to the horse.

Gazing up at the hazy blue sky, Rebecca said, "I truly enjoy the winter days here. Interesting that summer and winter are reversed. I'm still not completely used to it."

A tromping sound interrupted the quiet. Rebecca looked in the direction of the noise and saw a bull, enveloped in a dust cloud, charging toward the buggy.

Fear spiked through her. *A scrub!*

"Not good," Jim said. "Wild bulls can be dangerous. And this one looks like he's up to no good."

The horse whinnied and yanked away from Jim.

"Come on, Rebecca, get in the buggy." Jim kept his hand on the horse's bridle, trying to keep him calm. "I'll give you a hand up."

Rebecca was starting toward the buggy, when the horse yanked free of Jim and trotted away, dragging the buggy with him. Jim chased after him.

The bull was getting close and had turned his attention on Rebecca.

"Jim," she called, trying to keep her voice calm.

The bull was so close, Rebecca could hear its huffing. There was no time to wait for the buggy, and she couldn't get to it quickly enough. Clumsily she ran for the tree. Grabbing hold of a low-hanging branch, she hefted herself up the narrow trunk of the acacia. The weight of the baby and her added girth slowed her down and made it difficult to climb.

Still not out of reach of the angry bull's horns, she moved higher. Leaves scratched her face, and small limbs caught at her clothing. She looked down at the ground. She wasn't high enough! *Lord, help me,* she prayed. Pushing with her feet, she moved up toward the top branches and clung to the fragile refuge.

The horse was still skittish, but Jim managed to get hold of its bridle. He looked at Rebecca. "Hang on!"

The bull continued his charge. At the last moment, he veered away, skirting the tree. Blasting air from his nostrils, he battered the lower limbs and trunk with his broad horns. The tree quaked as Rebecca clung to her unsteady perch. Finally the scrub trotted around the tree, huffing and pawing at the dry ground.

Still clinging tightly to the scrawny limbs, Rebecca settled her bottom on a crook between two branches and stared down at her foe.

"Just stay put. He'll lose interest and move on," Jim called.

The bull turned its attention on Jim and the buggy. Jim climbed into the buggy and slapped the reins across the horse's back. He trotted away.

The bull lowered his head, settled an angry gaze on the horse and buggy, then snorted and dug at the ground. He charged. Jim again slapped the horse's back with the reins and moved away as fast as was safe. The scrub charged after him, coming so close he nearly gored the horse as he cut away at the last moment.

Jim kept moving, and the bull stood and watched, huffing. Finally, seeming to think he'd had his way, the animal trotted off. Keeping an eye on the departing bull, Rebecca climbed down from her perch.

"That was a close one," Jim said with a grin as he drove the buggy to Rebecca.

"How can you smile about it? You and I were nearly killed."

"Yes, but we weren't. And I must say, you were quite a sight perched up there on your limb."

Rebecca struggled to quell a smile. "I guess I was a sight at that." She moved toward the buggy. "We best be on our way."

"You sure you don't want to go back to the house?"

"We've come this far. We might as well go the rest of the way."

⁂

When Jim and Rebecca approached the Taylor home, Cambria sat in a chair on the front porch with her bare feet propped on a post. She rocked forward and stood. "Jim? Rebecca? What are ya doing 'ere?"

"I was needing your company, and Jim offered to escort me," Rebecca said. With a sideways glance at Jim, she added, "I expect he may have had ulterior motives, however."

"Is it good for ya ta be so far from home so close ta yer confinement?"

"It's perfectly all right."

Cambria smiled brightly. "Well, then I'm glad for the company." She gave Rebecca a hand down from the carriage. "What's happened ta ya?"

"What do you mean?"

"Yer face is all scratched up."

"Oh, a scrub."

"What?"

"Let me get settled, and I'll tell you."

"I'll put the horse up," Jim said.

"When ya get back, I'll have something sweet for ya and something cold ta drink too." Cambria smiled demurely, then turned her attention to Rebecca. The two women walked to the porch. "Seems that baby's getting bigger every day," Cambria said.

"She is. I've only got about seven weeks until my confinement date."

"Oh. Ya shouldn't be out and about like this."

"There's nothing wrong with a little drive. And Jim was with me." She grinned. "Of course, as I said, I met up with an ornery bull."

"What happened?"

"We stopped to rest, and he came after us. It could have been bad. He nearly got me, really gave me a fright. I'm a bit slow these days. I had to climb a tree to get away from him."

Cambria laughed. "What a sight that must have been."

Rebecca smiled. "It sounds funny now, but at the time it wasn't funny at all. I feared for my life and the baby's." Rebecca chuckled. "And I'm sure I looked quite ridiculous sitting up in that tree." She smoothed back her hair, then looked at her hand. "I'm still shaking."

"Ya poor thing. I'm sorry for laughing."

"Well, then the beast went after Jim. He had to move fast to stay out of the animal's way."

"No. Really?" Cambria sat and nodded toward a chair beside hers. "Now, what's on yer mind? Ya don't generally ride all this way for nothing. I can see something's troublin' ya."

Before sitting, Rebecca dipped water out of a barrel and took a drink. "Mmm. That tastes good." She set the dipper back on its hook and sat. "When I left home, the day felt cool, but it's heating up."

"Right. Generally, July's cool. But 'round 'ere ya never know."

Silence enfolded the two women. "It's awfully quiet," Rebecca said. "Is your family gone?"

"Yais, it's just me. Everyone's off ta town. They'll be back shortly though, I expect." Cambria folded her hands in her lap and rested her feet on the railing. "Now, what is it ya come ta talk 'bout?"

"You know me so well." Rebecca hesitated, then said, "Daniel's in some kind of trouble."

"Why do ya think that?"

"Some men came to the station a few weeks ago. I knew immediately that they were up to no good. One of the men kicked Daniel in the face."

"So that's what happened ta him."

"Daniel wouldn't say then who the men were or why they'd come. And they came back this morning—threatened Callie and me. And they torched the school."

"Oh, my Lord! No! What did they want?"

"They just said to tell Daniel he'd better do as he was told."

"And what's that?"

"I think it has to do with a loan he got from Mr. Marshal. Daniel won't tell me what's going on, but I know he owes money, and I don't know how he could be paying on it right now."

Rebecca remembered how her mother-in-law had faced off with the intruders. "I was scared to death, but you should have seen Willa. She pointed a rifle right at those men and ordered the three of them off the station. She was marvelous!"

Cambria laughed. "I knew there was fire in her."

"I was proud of her. But those men are truly wicked. I can't imagine why Daniel's dealing with people like them."

"What are ya going ta do?"

Rebecca shrugged. "If there was a constabulary in Thornton Creek, I'd report all of this, but there isn't anyone to enforce the law. And I know Daniel doesn't want anyone to know what's going on. So what can I do? He refuses to confide in me. He's shut me out."

"Try not to worry. You can trust Daniel."

"I've always believed that." Rebecca blew out a shallow breath. "But I'm sure he's in trouble. I want to help, but he won't let me. Men. They can be so pigheaded."

"Not my Jim," Cambria said with a smile.

"He's a man just like the rest of them."

"Maybe so, but he's a fine bloke." She dropped her feet to the porch floor and rocked forward, planting the front legs of her chair on the wood planks. "I must say, I'm surprised at Daniel. I've never known him ta be secretive. Guess all ya can do is wait and trust him ta see ya through, eh?"

8

Rebecca stepped onto the veranda, which smelled of fresh paint. Joseph pushed through the front door and toddled past his mother, then clumsily galloped across the broad porch.

Rebecca moved to a chair and dropped heavily into it. She was exhausted, and the baby felt heavy in her abdomen. She rested her head against the back of the chair and stuck her legs out straight in front of her.

"My, now, don't you look ladylike," Willa teased, moving up the front steps.

"I'm shameless, I know, but I feel like a bloated cow and don't care much about good manners."

Willa sat beside Rebecca. "I recall the feeling," she said with a smile. "But it won't be long now. You've only a month more to wait, and one never knows if a baby might arrive a bit early."

"It seems that just a few weeks ago, I felt fairly lithe. I'm certain this child has doubled its size since then."

"The last month is always the most difficult." Willa patted Rebecca's leg.

The sound of a galloping horse carried from beyond the rise. With all that had happened in recent months, Rebecca couldn't keep from immediately being on alert. She sought out Joseph, who was moving toward the steps. Instinctively, Rebecca pushed out of her chair and picked him up.

Woodman appeared a moment later. He was riding hard and didn't slow up until he'd reached the porch steps. "I need ta talk ta Daniel."

"I think he's in the barn," Willa said. "What's wrong? You look upset."

"Those men took Dusty. They dragged 'im off."

"What men?" Willa asked.

"The ones from Brisbane that come ta talk ta Daniel."

Holding Joseph more tightly, Rebecca walked to the balustrade. "What do you mean they took him?"

"Me and Dusty were workin' on a hayrack, and they just rode up, lassoed 'im, and dragged 'im off."

"Oh, my Lord," Rebecca said. "Daniel!" she called, starting down the porch steps.

Woodman turned his horse toward the barn.

Daniel emerged from the dark interior and strode into the yard. "Rebecca, did you call me?" His eyes landed on Woodman. "Something wrong?"

"It's Dusty. Those men took 'im."

Rebecca was still lugging Joseph when she reached Daniel. Willa stayed close by her side.

Woodman snatched his hat from his head. In spite of the coolness of the day, sweat mixed with road dust lay in droplets on his forehead. Rivulets tracked into his heavy brows. Using the back of his hand, Woodman swiped away the grime. "One of 'em said they were gonna hang 'im."

"Where did they take him?"

"Headed toward town."

Daniel ran to the corral where his horse was tied and already saddled. "We'll need more help. Where's Jim?"

"He's workin' the east border along with the rest of the crew."

A frown creased Daniel's brow. "Guess it's just you and me, then," he said, leading his horse out of the corral.

Rebecca walked alongside Daniel. "Please, Daniel, must you go? Those men are truly evil. I know they'll do something awful."

Daniel stopped and looked at Rebecca. "And what about Dusty? I can't just leave him."

Rebecca nodded. "Of course." While hanging on to Joseph, she hugged Daniel with one arm. "I love you. Please be careful."

With a quick kiss for Rebecca and Joseph and a nod to his mother, Daniel climbed onto the stallion's back and joined Woodman.

Callie approached. "Heard what ya said. Dusty's a fine bloke, Mr. Thornton. He's got a family." She looked squarely at Daniel. "Wouldn't want ta give bad news ta Nan."

"I know, Callie. I'll do all I can."

"We gotta go," Woodman said.

"Right." Daniel kicked his horse, and the two men rode away.

Rebecca moved closer to Willa and clasped her hand. "I'm frightened."

Willa didn't answer but squeezed her daughter-in-law's hand.

D

Daniel's heart hammered against his rib cage, pulsing in rhythm with the beat of his stallion's hooves. He rode alongside Woodman. The two traveled as fast as they dared over the uneven ground.

What if we don't get there in time? Daniel thought, then forced the unimaginable from his mind. *Lord, where are they?* His eyes scanned the open land. Patches of grass and dry ground passed beneath his horse's belly. *Faster. Faster*, his mind chanted. Leaning forward, he permitted his body to flow with the horse's strides.

His mind moved to Dusty. He didn't know him well. Dusty mostly kept to himself, but he seemed a good sort, a hard worker. Woodman knew a lot of people but called only a few friend. Dusty was one of those few, which told Daniel he must be first-rate.

He glanced at Woodman, whose dark eyes were hard with resolve. The aborigine leaned forward, holding the reins loosely and urging his horse to an even faster pace. They had to find Dusty—soon.

Without speaking a word, Daniel and Woodman kept moving. The huffing of horses, the beating of hooves, and the whisk of lathered thighs harmonized with Daniel's inner voice of distress.

And then Daniel saw Dusty. His hands were tied behind his back, and a rope held him to one of the bushrangers' horses. He knelt on the ground. Blood trickled from a gash above one eye, and his face was swollen and bruised.

Daniel and Woodman slowed but moved closer. Wind sighed, picking up bits of dirt and leaves. The sound of creaking leather and the heavy breathing of horses seemed loud. Daniel's stallion shook his head, and his silver bridle jangled.

Luke stood beneath an acacia tree. He tugged on a rope hanging from a heavy branch. It had a noose at the end of it. When he spotted Daniel and Woodman, he sprinted for a gun leaning against the tree. Jack was still on his horse, rifle in his hands. He raised it and pointed it at Daniel. Wade grabbed his out of a holster on his saddle.

Daniel and Woodman kept moving forward.

"Stay back," Jack called. "We've got business ta take care of 'ere. And we don't need the likes of ya."

"Let him go," Daniel said, stopping his horse.

"Why would I do that?" Jack glanced at Dusty, then leveled

a malevolent gaze on Daniel. "This is yer fault, ya know. It's time ya saw how Mr. Marshal deals with blokes who don't pay their debts."

"I said I'd pay, but I need more time. I told Mr. Marshal. I know he doesn't want this." Daniel glanced at Dusty, who staggered to his feet.

Jack grinned, exposing perfectly straight, white teeth—they seemed too perfect. "I only do what Mr. Marshal tells me ta do."

Daniel was taken aback. Up until this moment, he hadn't truly believed Robert Marshal had ordered the despicable tactics employed by the three bushrangers. He knew him to be crafty, even shady, but not a murderer. He glanced at Woodman. How could they save Dusty's life?

"I'll pay," he said, unsure just where he'd get the money. "But I've got to go into town."

"Yer out of time."

"Let's be reasonable . . ."

"The reasonable thing to do was to pay your debt," Luke shouted. "But you were so high and mighty, too grand to be bothered. So now this here blackfella will pay for your arrogance."

Dusty looked from Daniel to Woodman; his eyes were lit with fear.

"Can't just hang 'im," Woodman said.

"You shut up!" shouted Wade, the quietest of the three.

Daniel's mind frantically searched for a solution. "No one has to die. I'll see to the debt." Daniel prodded his horse forward, hoping Luke would give way.

Rifle in hand, Luke stepped toward Daniel. "Not another step." He aimed the gun directly at Daniel.

"Hang him," Jack said.

"Right," Luke said. "You watch them two." He moved toward Dusty.

Keeping an eye on Daniel and Woodman, Luke grabbed

hold of the rope binding the black man. He pulled a hunting knife from a sheath attached to his belt and cut Dusty free of the horse but left his hands tied. Holding the young man with one hand and grabbing the horse's bridle with the other, he dragged Dusty toward the tree, then positioned the horse beneath the limb where the rope hung.

Daniel dismounted and walked toward Jack. He knew Jack was the one he'd have to convince. "There's another way. I could get the money and give it to you. You could keep it. Or I could give you extra. Mr. Marshal never has to know."

The men seemed to be thinking. Wade spoke first. "I could use a bit of cash. Been a long time since I felt the touch of a woman."

Jack seemed uncertain.

"I could get it now, right out of the bank," Daniel said.

Jack studied him. "Thought ya didn't have no money."

"I do," Daniel lied. "Just had other things to pay with it, but that doesn't matter now. I'll get it for you."

"He's lying," Luke said. "He's got no money or he would have paid us. He'd do anything for his wife and kid."

Jack straightened. "We do what Mr. Marshal tells us." He turned to Luke. "Hang him."

Luke grabbed Dusty, and with a grunt, hefted the small man onto the horse's back.

Keeping his gun and his eyes leveled on Daniel and Woodman, Jack moved his horse close to Dusty and settled the noose over the man's head, yanking it tight about his neck.

Luke laid a hand on the horse's rump.

"You do this, and you'll be sorry," Daniel said. "The law will hunt you down. And you'll be facing the same fate as Dusty. You've no reason to follow Mr. Marshal's orders. Just walk away. I won't say anything about this."

"No one cares 'bout a blackfella," Jack said. "We follow Mr. Marshal's orders. If not, he'll know. And once yer in his sights, there's no stepping out of 'em."

"So Marshal runs your life? You have no say in what you do?" Daniel let a smile touch his lips. "Sounds to me like you're as much slaves to him as any black man might be."

Jack's eyes turned cold, and his mouth tightened into a grim line. "I do as I like." Without warning, he swung around and fired at Woodman, grazing his left arm. Woodman lifted his rifle in response. "Don't move," Jack said, keeping his gun aimed at Woodman. "It'll be the middle of yer face next time." He spit. "We'll be doin' our job now."

Woodman lowered his gun, ignoring his wound.

Jack nodded at Luke, and Luke lifted his hand off the horse's rump. "Maybe next time ya'll think before ya let Mr. Marshal wait on his money."

Daniel took a step closer.

"Told ya ta stay put," Jack said, raising his rifle to his shoulder.

"What did this man do to deserve hanging?" Daniel asked.

"He works for ya." Jack smiled. "I'll be doin' ya a favor. He's probably been robbing ya blind."

"He's a good man." Daniel looked at Dusty and offered him what he hoped was a look of encouragement. "He's got a wife and three children."

"Means nothin' ta me."

Woodman remained silent, his jaw set. Daniel could see rage boiling beneath his composed exterior.

"I never robbed Mr. Thornton," Dusty said. "I been a good worker and do as I'm told. No reason ta 'ang me. What'll me kids do, eh?" His eyes wide, he looked at Jack.

"That's none of my business."

Daniel's fury grew along with a sense of helplessness. "If you do this, it's plain murder—nothing less. I'll see to it that you hang."

Jack grinned. "Ya try. Ya'll get nowhere."

Daniel knew Jack spoke the truth. And he knew that the time for reasoning had ended. He and Woodman would have to kill the men. He glanced at his black friend. There was no sign of fear or pain on his face. His stance was relaxed and he had his rifle lowered, but Daniel knew that didn't mean Woodman wasn't ready.

"I can't let you hang him," Daniel said. "Cut him down."

The three men grinned. Luke chuckled.

Daniel raised his rifle. "I'll kill you if I have to."

Almost immediately a shot rang out, and Daniel felt a searing pain in his thigh.

He went down but fired at Jack, who clapped a hand over his shoulder where Daniel had hit him.

Woodman fired at Jack but missed.

Wade sprinted to Daniel and pressed his rifle against Daniel's head. "Drop your guns. Both of you."

There was nothing to be done. Daniel loosened his grip on the rifle and let it drop.

"You too," Wade shouted at Woodman.

Woodman's brown eyes went from Daniel to Dusty. Finally he released his hold, and the rifle clattered to the ground. Luke snatched up both rifles.

"Now we'll do what we came to do," Jack said, glancing at his shoulder where blood oozed through his shirt.

"Civilized people don't hang men for nothing," Daniel said, gritting his teeth against the pain in his leg.

"Who said we were civilized?" Jack chuckled.

Dusty sat with his back straight and his eyes staring at the ground in front of the horse.

"I'll not forget this day," Daniel said. "And God will give you your just rewards."

Wade pressed the barrel of his rifle harder against Daniel's head. "Figure the Almighty would just as soon clean these beggars off the face of the earth than not, eh?"

Nausea swept through Daniel. Dusty was going to die. He looked at the young man. The rope was tight about his neck. Fear showed in his dark eyes, but he sat steady and sure. He made no sound of protest nor fought the men. He'd accepted his fate.

Dusty's eyes settled on Woodman. He nodded at his friend.

"All is well, mate," Woodman said. "Our mother the earth is waitin' for ya."

"Anything you want to say?" Luke asked Dusty. He looked as if he were enjoying himself.

"Did nothin' wrong. That's it."

"Right, then."

Luke swatted the horse, and the animal reared and then ran, dropping Dusty with a hard jerk. There was a sickening thud, and then he hung limp, unmoving. A sharp breeze picked up dust and swirled it around the tree.

Woodman stood silently staring. Daniel pressed his cheek against the dry ground. It was the only thing that felt solid or real.

"We'll tell Mr. Marshal you got his message," Luke said as he swung up onto his horse.

Without another word the three men rode away.

9

Pulling his knife from its sheath, Daniel hobbled toward Dusty. He didn't want to look at the young man. Only minutes before he'd had a life. Now . . . now he had nothing.

Woodman hurried to Dusty. "Shouldn't 'ave happened," he said.

Daniel could think of no appropriate response. Fighting down nausea, he held Dusty's body against his and sawed at the rope.

Woodman kept an unreadable expression as he stood in front of Dusty and held him steady. The rope gave way, and he winced slightly as the body dropped against his chest. Stoically he hefted the man onto his shoulder and then turned and eased him to the ground, where he leaned his friend against the tree. Blood from Woodman's wound stained the front of Dusty's shirt.

He stepped back and gazed at his friend. "Sorry, mate. Not roight they done that."

Daniel moved to Woodman and rested a hand on his shoulder. "I'm sorry."

"Nothin' ya have ta be sorry 'bout. Ya couldn't 'ave done more."

"You all right?" Daniel asked.

Woodman glanced at his arm. "Yeah. It's the bleedin' ya can't see that hurts a man."

Daniel understood. Dusty's death was one more injustice done to a black man, a scar Woodman would carry, like so many others. He stared at Dusty and then glanced at the place he'd last seen Marshal's men.

They think they've won, but they've lost. They'll pay. I'll see to it. Bitterness felt like a salve.

Feeling as if a poker were impaling his thigh, Daniel limped to his horse and grabbed the canteen from the saddle. He took a swig, then poured water into his hand and splashed his face, rubbing it hard against his skin. No amount of scrubbing could clear away what had happened. The image of Dusty's death lingered. Daniel knew it would remain always. He screwed the canteen lid on, draped the container over the saddle horn, and then dusted off his hat.

"Ya all roight?"

"Yeah. I'll be fine."

Settling the hat on his head, his eyes returned to Dusty. Daniel had never been able to fully grasp the reality of death. Minutes ago the young man had breathed the same air Daniel breathed. His heart had beaten, and blood had coursed through his body. And then . . . he'd gone, calmly accepting mortality.

Daniel's chest tightened, and anger heated his belly. *No man deserves to die like that—innocent.*

"He's fine now. Gone ta our mother."

Daniel barely heard. His mind reeled with what had taken place. Could he have done more? He looked at the rope still hanging from the tree, suspended like a serpent. He moved to the tree, stopping directly in front of the rope. With ferocity he grabbed hold of it, yanked it down, and pitched it away. Dirt puffed into the air, and the rope lay still. Daniel watched it a moment as if it might move and writhe away.

96

"The world's a mess, eh?"

"Yer roight there."

⌗

Daniel looked out over the land. Except for an occasional clump of scrub and a small, twisted gum tree, the flats were empty. Often he'd sought out the land's stillness, receiving its offered tranquillity. Today it left him bereft, its silence pervading the plains with sorrow. A breeze sighed and bent dry grasses. The ground beneath the heavy steps of the horses seemed bleak.

Daniel's thoughts looped back to Dusty and the ugly way he'd died. He considered the man's family, and a knot formed in his gut. He'd see to the care of Nan and the children. They could stay on at Douloo as long as they liked. He'd provide whatever they needed. Still, as he considered their future, he realized it offered little. Nan could hire herself out as a house-maid or a field worker. Daniel's malaise grew. She had no good options. Perhaps if her children had an education . . . For the first time Daniel grasped the importance of Rebecca's school. An education offered the aborigines their only hope.

His thoughts returned to Dusty. He'd been stoic. The vision of the man's courage made Daniel feel small. How had he let those men get the better of him? All of this was his fault. All of it.

And what of Dusty? Had he gone to some mythical place where his earth mother cradled him in her arms? Like a drying leather strap, guilt tightened around Daniel's chest. *I should have told him about Jesus*. His mind took him back to missed opportunities and then to the man Dusty had been. He'd believed in the ancient cultures. He'd never have listened to Daniel.

The agony of guilt and shame crashed down on Daniel. *I am to blame, aren't I? All of this is because of me and my foolishness.*

He gazed at the distant horizon. Already pink touched the sky and the tufts of clouds hanging in its vastness. He forced himself to look at Woodman. "I'm sorry. I . . . I'm sorry."

ᴅ

As Daniel approached the house, he tried to quiet his inner tension, but no matter how many times he wiped his palms on his pants, the reins remained damp in his hands. He was so besieged by the weight of his blunder and his guilt that he barely felt the throbbing in his leg. Rebecca pushed out of a chair on the porch and walked toward the steps. He had to tell her, but how? How could he explain that Dusty had been killed because of the deal he'd made with Marshal?

Her hand resting on her rounded abdomen, Rebecca moved slowly down the front steps. Daniel couldn't look at her. He turned the horse toward the cottage where Dusty had lived with his family. Nan stood in the porch shadows, remaining there even when Daniel and Woodman stopped in front of the little house.

Daniel dismounted and walked up onto the porch. Woodman stayed with the horses.

"I'm sorry, Nan," Daniel said. "We tried to save him."

The aborigine woman's eyes held Daniel's for only a moment, but he could see her distrust.

"Me Dusty's gone. Done in by them mongrels." Nan compressed her lips, and her black eyes glittered with loathing, but there were no tears. She waved away a harassing fly. "He's in a better place now though, eh? This world's no good." She gazed at three youngsters huddling just inside the door. "Me bybies 'ave no father now."

"I'm sorry," Daniel said again. "We tried to stop them, Woodman and I."

Nan managed a stiff nod, then looked at Woodman. "I'll need help with 'im."

"Roight," Woodman said. "Daniel and me can carry 'im inside."

Nan looked at the ground and then nodded toward Daniel and said, "Not 'im."

Woodman glanced at Daniel. His broad face had lost its comfortable quality. He looked worn out. Deep lines cut across his forehead and angled down his cheekbones. His graying, bushy eyebrows rested heavily on his eyelids. With a wince of pain, he took a handkerchief out of his back pocket and wiped dust and sweat from his face. He replaced the handkerchief, then looked back at Daniel. "I can get 'im, then."

Koora stepped up to the horse. "Yer bleedin'. I'll help ya." With a grunt, he hefted Dusty onto his shoulders. Bent beneath the man's weight, he followed Nan and Woodman inside the cottage.

Daniel turned and watched his mother and Rebecca walk toward him.

"What happened?" Willa asked.

"They hanged him."

Willa's golden complexion paled. "Why would those men hang Dusty? What has he done to them?"

"Nothin'," Woodman said, stepping onto the small porch. "He got hanged 'cause of bad judgment."

Guilt building, Daniel glanced at Woodman. This was his fault. If he'd been wiser, Dusty would still be alive.

"We'll talk about that later," Willa said matter-of-factly. "You're hurt, and so is Daniel. We need to get the doctor out here."

Feeling contemptible, Daniel watched Woodman step back inside the cottage. He felt a hand on his arm and looked into Rebecca's dark, compassionate eyes.

"Come into the house." She settled his left arm over her shoulders and braced him as they moved toward the porch.

"I tried, but we couldn't stop them. They . . ."

"I know you did all you could."

Willa walked alongside Daniel. "We'll settle all the rest later, but right now I'm thankful you're alive. You best get out of the sun." Willa moved up the steps.

Rebecca took Daniel's hand, and he grasped the railing and slowly made his way up the stairway. He stopped and looked back at Dusty's cottage. "Where do you think he is now?"

"Oh," Rebecca said, the word escaping as if someone had thumped her chest. "I don't know." She thought a moment. "Do you think anyone told him about Jesus?"

"Probably not. He was a blackfella."

"But . . . maybe someone did," Rebecca said weakly.

"Maybe."

⬥

Dr. Walker bandaged Daniel's leg. "You're a lucky one. It was a clean entrance and exit. Didn't hit the bone. And the damage to the muscle is slight." He straightened and smiled. "That ought to see you for a while."

"Thank you, Doctor," Willa said.

Daniel sat back on the sofa. "You better have a look at Woodman. He got hit in the arm."

"Right. I had a quick look at him when I first got 'ere. Doesn't look too bad."

"Thank you for all your help, Doctor," Willa said.

"And for getting here so quickly," Rebecca added.

"That's what I get paid for." The doctor smiled and closed his bag, then placed his hat on his head and ambled toward the door. "Told Woodman to wait for me on the porch. I'll see to him there."

While Willa accompanied the doctor to the front door, Rebecca sat on the sofa beside Daniel. She took his hand in hers. "Now, are you going to tell me what this is all about? Seems we ought to know—people are getting killed." Rebecca's voice sounded tight and grew higher with each word. "It's bad, isn't it?"

Daniel took a deep breath. He didn't want to tell Rebecca about his dealings with Marshal, but there was no way to avoid it. Now she'd know how foolish he'd been. "I made a deal with Marshal. He loaned me what we needed so we could get back on our feet. I explained that it would take me a bit of time to come up with the cash to repay the loan. I thought he was all right with that. Seems he's not."

Daniel stopped as the rustle of skirts announced Willa's return. She stood in the doorway. "Go ahead, son. It's time we heard the truth. All of it."

Callie stepped to the doorway. "I have tea, mum. Would ya like it in 'ere?"

"Yes. Thank you. Just set it on the table."

Callie moved silently into the room and set the tea tray on the parlor table in front of the sofa. She straightened and walked to the doorway but remained in the room.

Daniel glanced at her.

"Can I stay? Dusty was a friend."

"You might as well. What I have to say will affect you too." He looked at his mother and could have wilted under her reproving gaze. He cleared his throat. "Well, as I was saying, I thought I'd have time to raise the money, but he insists on being paid the balance immediately."

"Is that why those horrible men came here before?"

"Yes. I went to the bank that day and paid them some of what I owed, but . . ." Daniel glanced at Callie. "It wasn't enough."

"I'm sure if you speak to Mr. Marshal, he'll—"

"No. He's the one who ordered those blokes to hang Dusty.

Course, he didn't know who Dusty was. I figure they were just supposed to pick someone."

Willa moved to the window. With her hand resting against the hollow of her neck, she gazed outside. "So what shall we do?" She turned to Daniel. "Is there anything we can sell in order to pay Mr. Marshal?"

"No. Nothing we have is worth enough. And he's not going to wait until I can get the cattle south to sell."

Rebecca faced her husband. "Daniel, how could you have gotten involved with a man like that?"

"I didn't think I had a choice. It was get the money or lose Douloo. Now . . . well now, it's clear I should have found another way."

"You didn't see that he was evil?"

"Sometimes it's not so easy to spot it in a man." Daniel started to lean forward, but the pain in his leg stopped him. "I knew better." He glanced at his mother. "Paul said it, eh? In the book of Romans. 'For the good that I would I do not: but the evil which I would not, that I do.'" He felt the apostle's shame and frustration. His eyes moved to Rebecca. "I'm sorry, luv. I'm vile. I wish I could undo it, but I can't."

Rebecca rested a hand on his arm. "I know you would. And I know that when you decided to borrow from Mr. Marshal, you were doing what you thought was best."

Daniel took Rebecca's hand and kissed it, then pressed it to his cheek. "I don't deserve you." He glanced at Callie and then looked at his mother. "All this is my fault."

"It's not," Rebecca said. "How could you have known? How does anyone explain people who are so vicious?"

"Men been killin' blacks long as I can remember." Callie's voice was hard.

The weight of his guilt building, Daniel looked at Callie. There was nothing he could say. She was right.

Callie rocked from one foot to the other. "It's easy ta kill a black man. No one cares when a blackfella's murdered.

Figure there are some who won't be content 'til there's no blacks left."

"Most folks don't feel that way." Daniel offered what he hoped was an encouraging smile. "You're family to us. You know that, don't you?"

Callie didn't answer right away.

"You can't think we're like those men," Rebecca said.

"No. I don't think yer like that, but . . ." Her dark eyes settled on Daniel. "Dusty would be 'ere if ya'd done roight."

"That's not fair, Callie." Rebecca's voice was plaintive. "Daniel couldn't have known the consequences."

"Maybe so, but it's always us blacks that pay for whites' mistakes. Ya don't see us as bein' the same, so ya don't give it no thought."

"We've treated you fairly." Rebecca stepped close to Callie. "Don't you remember the day I first came? Right off I asked you to join me for breakfast and a visit."

Callie pushed frizzy hair away from her face. "No, mum, ya asked me ta sit and listen while ya had yer breakfast. Ya didn't ask me ta join ya."

An expression of surprise crossed Rebecca's face. She pressed her hand against her mouth. "Oh. I did do that. I'm sorry."

"No need."

"Sometimes we don't see things as clearly as we should," Daniel said.

Callie nodded. "I'll see ta Woodman. The doctor might need some help, eh?" With that, she left the room.

The parlor turned quiet.

Rebecca sat on the sofa beside Daniel.

"What about Joseph? Is he in danger?" Willa asked.

Daniel stared at the floor. "Yeah."

103

10

Rebecca slowly pushed away from the kitchen table. "I'm feeling the weight of this child today." She picked up her half-eaten bowl of oatmeal.

"'Ere, let me have that." Daniel took the bowl and limped to the sink, where he set it on the counter. "Not hungry this morning?"

"I've no room for food," Rebecca said with a crooked smile, glancing at her rounded stomach.

"Won't be long now, mum," Lily said with a wide grin. "We'll 'ave us a bybie 'ere soon, eh?" She scraped the leftover cereal into a slop bucket.

"I hope you're right," Rebecca said, returning to her chair. "I'd say it's time this child met the family."

Joseph banged his spoon against his cereal bowl, and Willa gently placed a hand over his to quiet him. "I dare say, I can scarcely wait to hold the little one in my arms."

Daniel grabbed his hat off a hook alongside the back door. "I better get to town. I'll speak to Charles Oxley like we talked about." Just the thought of meeting with the banker made him feel like he had grit between his teeth. "Doubt it'll do any good though."

"I realize it's a difficult undertaking, but you must make the effort," Willa said.

"Right."

"You're still limping," Willa said. "Dr. Walker told you to stay put for a couple of weeks."

"My leg's better. A week of rest did the trick." He settled his hat on his head.

The day of Dusty's death, Daniel had agreed to speak to Mr. Oxley; again it seemed the only reasonable thing to do. Now, given time to think on it, he wished he hadn't promised to give the banker another try. He could already feel the humiliation that would come with the meeting.

"You know he'll make me squirm," Daniel said.

"He may at that," Willa said. "But there's no way around it."

"He's the one who recommended Marshal in the first place." Anger building, Daniel leaned on the counter and gazed out the kitchen window.

Then he remembered how Mr. Oxley had thrown the name in the trash. *I'm the one who dug it out.* The hurt and betrayal he saw in Nan's eyes haunted him. Every time she looked at him, she silently accused him, and he deserved it. He studied the open land, half expecting to see the three men who'd hanged Dusty riding across the flats.

"He didn't recommend him. Oxley told me about Marshal, then threw his address in the trash bin. I dug it out." Still staring outdoors, he said, "Stay close to the house. And keep Joseph inside."

"We can't hide indoors forever," Willa said. "If we do, then those men will have won."

"And if they grab one of you?"

Willa rested a hand protectively on Joseph's back. "We've got the good Lord to watch over us. We can't forget that."

"Maybe Daniel's right." Rebecca looked at Joseph. "I couldn't bear it if something happened . . ." Her eyes teared, but she straightened her spine and cleared her throat and said, "Some of the children have been asking about school. I suppose we could teach them in the house for the time being."

Daniel straightened and looked at Rebecca. "That might work."

"I think it's a splendid idea," Willa said.

"All right, then. School will resume, but indoors." Daniel eyed Rebecca. "And only as long as you're up to it."

Rebecca rested a hand on her stomach. "We do need a few supplies. The children have been such enthusiastic students that they've nearly gone through the chalk and ink." She let out a sigh. "And I'll need two more slates," she said apologetically. "One was broken, and we've a new student."

"You'll have to make do," Daniel said. "I don't mean to be unsympathetic, but we've bigger problems just now."

"Of course. You're right. I'll have the children share."

He smiled kindly. "I do wish you'd postpone school altogether until after the baby is born. I don't want you doing too much." He limped across the room and dropped a kiss on her forehead. "But of course, it's up to you, luv."

"I'm fine, and I don't want to disappoint the children or Lily. She's doing splendidly. And Koora always looks forward to school. He's one of my finest students. Did you know he plans to have his own place one day?"

"He'll have a difficult time of it."

"He knows that. That's why he works so hard." She smiled. "I really do long to go back to teaching. In truth, I think the school occupies my thoughts. With all that's been happening, I feel better when I'm busy. And I must admit to being distracted by my coming confinement. I've been a bit anxious about it all, especially after what happened after Joseph's birth."

Daniel rested a hand on Rebecca's shoulder. "You'll be fine, luv. No worries." He forced a smile, but at the idea of the birth, he felt a tightness in his chest. He hadn't forgotten how sick Rebecca had been after Joseph was born. "Have you talked with Dr. Walker?"

"Yes. He's assured me he'll be close by. And he says I have nothing to worry about." Rebecca glanced at Lily. "Actually, I think what helped me last time was Lily's medicine."

"Roight good remedy, that eucalyptus tea," Lily said.

Rebecca leaned her elbows on the table. "I'm simply not going to worry about it. I'd say we've enough to think about. And we can't forget Chavive. She's due to foal any day. She's seemed a bit out of sorts the last few days. And she's been off her feed."

"Wouldn't it be grand if the two of you had your babies the same day," Willa said with a smile.

"No. It would be dreadful. I want to be with her. And if I'm laboring, I'll be seeing nothing of Chavive."

"We'll have to trust God with it," Daniel said more cheerfully than he felt. He planted his hat on his head. "Well, I'm off." He moved slowly toward the back door, careful not to put too much weight on his injured leg.

"Are you sure you're well enough to ride into town?" Willa asked.

"I'm fine, just a bit sore."

Rebecca pushed out of her chair and crossed to Daniel. She kissed him. "Please be careful."

"I will be. And you be praying that I have a proper go at Mr. Oxley."

"We'll be praying," Willa said, offering a warm smile.

 ⁊

Anxiety set Daniel's nerves to popping as he walked toward the bank. He glanced at the overcast sky, then tried to relax tight muscles as he stepped onto the sidewalk. He wouldn't grovel. He'd already decided that. But he figured Mr. Oxley would demand it.

He placed his hand on the doorknob and, with a heavy breath, turned it decisively. Pushing open the door, he stepped inside. The room was empty except for Mr. Oxley, who sat at an oak desk, bent over paperwork. Daniel strode across the room, purposely setting his boots down hard against the wooden floor.

"Be right with you," the banker said without looking up.

Daniel stopped at the clerk's window, keeping his back straight and his shoulders back. He tried to relax his jaw. Just the sight of Mr. Oxley made him angry. *If he'd just given me a loan in the first place, everything would have been fine.*

"Right, then," Mr. Oxley said, turning in his chair. When his eyes landed on Daniel, a question touched them and then annoyance. "What can I do for you?" he asked, moving to the window.

Daniel put on a smile. "G'day. Trust you've been well."

"Right fine." Mr. Oxley waited.

"Glad to hear that." Daniel swallowed hard and tried to force his request from his throat. "I'm in need of a loan, sir," he finally managed.

"We've already been down that road, Daniel."

"Right, but—"

"Things the same at your place?"

"No. We've got the house mostly finished, the barn's up, and some of the cottages are rebuilt. And I'll be on my way south to sell off some cattle soon."

Mr. Oxley studied Daniel. "I thought you secured a loan from Robert Marshal?"

"I did. But he's an unsavory type. Unreasonable."

"But you got a loan?"

"Yes. But I need to pay him off right away. That's why I'm 'ere. There's been a misunderstanding between him and me . . . about the payment—when it's due. He's being a bit irrational about it."

"Irrational, eh? Seems to me when a man loans money to a stranger, he ought to be able to count on punctual payments."

"Right. But as I said, there was a misunderstanding."

"Straighten it out, then."

"Well, that's the problem. I can't seem to do that." Daniel hadn't wanted to tell Mr. Oxley about what had been going on, but there was no way around it. "Marshal sent some of his men to my place, demanding the money."

"Yes. I seem to recall a visit from you several weeks back. You made a sizable withdrawal."

"Right. But that wasn't enough for him. He sent his men back again and threatened my wife."

The banker lifted his eyebrows. "Not what I would call good business practice, must agree."

"And then last week they grabbed one of my roustabouts and hanged him."

"Hanged him?" Mr. Oxley's voice sounded startled. "Who was it?"

"Dusty."

"Right, a young blackfella. I've seen him around." Mr. Oxley grasped his bow tie and nudged it up slightly. "Well, don't figure a black is worth too much fuss, eh?"

Daniel's anger surged, but he kept his teeth clamped shut and forced the rage down. Finally he said, "He was a fine man. And his wife and children are left with no one to care for them."

"I'm sure you'll see to them."

"Can't do that if I lose Douloo." Daniel glanced at a piece of lint on Mr. Oxley's suit. "I need a loan, sir. My family's in danger. You knew what kind of man Marshal was when you told me about him. I figure you owe me another chance."

"I owe you nothing," Mr. Oxley said, smoothing his perfectly clipped mustache. "You knew the type when you went to him. Everyone 'round 'ere knows about Mr. Marshal."

"What do you mean everyone?"

"There're quite a few blokes who've done business with him over the years. Some turned out fine, some didn't."

"Who?" Daniel pressed.

"Let me see, now. There's the Burstows, and Patrick Crotty had a run-in with him couple years back, and . . ."

"How many people had to borrow from Marshal because they couldn't get it from you?" Daniel couldn't keep the accusation out of his voice.

Mr. Oxley leaned back slightly, looking annoyed. Evenly he said, "Can't say for sure. Several."

"Write down the names for me."

The banker gave him a suspicious look. "Why? What do you want with them?"

"I need to talk with the blokes, find out more about this Mr. Marshal." Daniel slowly shook his head back and forth. "Figured a neighbor like you, a man I've done business with for years, would know better than to suggest I do business with the likes of Marshal."

Mr. Oxley smoothed the front of his suit jacket, finding the lint and removing it. "I simply told you he made loans from time to time."

Daniel wanted to throttle the man. If not for the counter being in his way, he might not have been able to restrain himself. "You're no better than the dingoes that slink 'round this town." He leaned on the counter and pushed his face close to Mr. Oxley's. "Write down the names."

Mr. Oxley walked to his desk and took a piece of paper from a drawer and an ink pen from the top of the desk. Bending over the note, he wrote down several names, then carefully folded the paper in half. He walked back to Daniel.

"Hope I didn't smudge the ink," he said, sliding the folded halves across each other.

Daniel snatched the list from him.

"What are you going to do with them, anyway?"

110

"Don't know just yet. I'll figure it out."

Mr. Oxley's lips turned up in a satisfied smile.

"I'll be back the end of the week to close my account," Daniel said.

The banker's smile disappeared. "What do you plan to do without a bank?"

"I'll do just fine." Feeling like he might explode at any moment, Daniel turned and strode out of the bank, doing the best he could not to hobble.

He was glad he'd ridden his stallion. He needed a good ride. He yanked the reins free of the hitching post and slung himself up onto the horse, gritting his teeth against the pain from his wound. He pulled hard on the reins and turned the animal into the street. With a tap from the heels of his boots, he leaned forward and galloped out of town.

By the time Daniel reached the home of Stephen Burstow, the first name on the list, his anger had quieted. His horse was in a lather, but he felt better. His mind felt more focused, and he was set on finding out what kind of business dealings Stephen had had with Marshal.

Stephen pounded a nail into a corral fence as Daniel approached. He straightened and smiled. The creases at the corners of his eyes deepened. "G'day to you."

"G'day." Daniel carefully dismounted; the pain in his leg had become a throb. He led the stallion to a trough, where the horse slurped up water.

"Right good to see you, Daniel. It's been too long." Stephen lifted his hat and smoothed back graying hair.

"I wish it was pleasure that brought me 'ere. I've been having trouble with a bloke from Brisbane. Heard you've done business with him."

"Maybe."

"I need you to tell me what you know about Robert Marshal."

Stephen's eyes narrowed, and his expression turned grim. "Right. Marshal. About all I know is he's no good. And that you shouldn't have anything to do with the likes of him."

"Too late. I'm already indebted to the wog."

"Sorry to hear that." Stephen studied the brim of his hat, turning it in his hands. "The drought and the fire push you too hard?"

"Right. I needed money to get on my feet, and he was the only one who would give me a loan."

"Oxley wouldn't give it to you, eh?"

"Nope."

Stephen thought a moment, then said, "Marshal's a snake. Nearly did me and my family in." He glanced at the house. "I managed to get him paid, but only because of a generous brother-in-law." He settled his hat on his head. "You needing help?"

"Maybe. Right now I need information and money. Marshal's gotten hostile. If I don't pay him . . ." Daniel let the sentence trail off, unwilling to give voice to the possibilities.

"Wish I had the money to give, but the drought's been hard on me." He pulled off his gloves. "Anything else I can do, I will. The stink of that man's stayed with me. I paid more than twice what I borrowed."

Daniel rubbed his neck. "That's the way of it. You have any advice?"

"Get out from under. Marshal won't give up. He's got no qualms 'bout hurting folks. He's a bad one."

"He killed one of my roustabouts."

Stephen thought a moment. "Ol' Patrick Crotty had a run-in with him a while back, and John Oliver too. I know they'd help. None of us would object to turning the tables on that viper." He grinned. "Wouldn't mind having a go at him myself."

"Be fine if we could get a leg up on him. Might if we stick together, eh?" Daniel smiled, but inside he felt dismal. "I'll let you know if there's a need. Be on my way, then."

He shook Stephen's hand, a plan formulating in his mind. If he made a stand against Marshal, there might be enough blokes in the district to trounce the man and his thugs.

11

Rebecca stood at Chavive's stall, resting her arms on the top of the gate. The mare shifted her back feet, then lay down. A few moments later, she stood up again.

"She's been doing that all morning," Rebecca said. "She'll foal soon."

Daniel laid an arm over Rebecca's shoulders. "It'll be a fine one too. Noble was a grand stallion."

"If she has a colt, it will be like having him back again," Rebecca said wistfully. "He was splendid, wasn't he?"

"He was at that. I hated selling him."

"You did what was necessary." Rebecca felt the ache return to her lower back. It intensified and moved to her abdomen. She managed to smile, ignoring the pain but knowing she'd soon be forced to give way to it. The contraction continued to build, and she closed her eyes against it.

"You all right, luv?"

Rebecca nodded. The pain eased. "I'm fine." She blew out a breath. "But I might be having our baby today." She smiled up at him.

"Rebecca. Why didn't you tell me?"

"I haven't known long. And I don't want your mother to force me to bed."

"I thought you'd been acting a bit peculiar. You're moving slower than usual, and you've been awfully quiet."

Rebecca looked at her rounded abdomen and rested a hand on it. "Of course I'm moving slowly. How would you be getting around if you were carrying this bundle?" She grinned. "You don't expect me to be leaping about, do you?"

"No. Course not." Daniel gave her a gentle hug. "But maybe you ought to go to bed."

"No. I want to be here for Chavive."

Rebecca turned her attention back to the mare, who was now lying on a fresh bed of straw. "I'm a bit worried. This is her first foal. One never knows just what kind of trouble a mare might have."

The death of Miss had been nagging at Rebecca. The mare had seemed fine, the foal healthy and strong. There'd been no hint that something was so wrong.

Just like when Joseph was born. Rebecca felt herself tense. Taking a deep breath and releasing it slowly, she told herself, *Everything will be fine.*

"No need to worry," Daniel said. "Chavive's in fine health. She's got a strong spirit that will see her through. Like you."

"Sometimes a strong spirit isn't enough." Rebecca thought of the men who had been threatening them. "Daniel, what if those men return? What are we going to do?"

"I'm working on a plan. There are some other blokes who might be able to help us."

She opened the gate and walked into the stall. "What do you mean—a fight?"

"Maybe if we have to."

Chavive lifted her head and looked at her as Rebecca approached. In spite of her advanced pregnancy, Rebecca managed to squat beside the mare. She stroked Chavive's neck. "You're a fine one," she said, running her hand over the horse's chestnut coat. She looked up at Daniel. "Do you think it will come to that?"

"Maybe."

"I pray not."

Chavive blew air from her nostrils and pushed to her feet with a grunt. In a resolute way, she stared at the stall's wall. Rebecca straightened and rested a hand on the mare's abdomen. She could feel the muscles tighten. "She's contracting. This is a strong one." She looked at Daniel. "It shouldn't be long now."

Without warning, a sharp pain hit Rebecca, and she let out a gasp, clutching her abdomen.

"Rebecca? Are you all right?" Daniel moved to her side.

Through gritted teeth, Rebecca said, "I don't know who's going to have her baby first, me or Chavive."

"Mum said she hoped you and that horse of yours would have your babies on the same day."

"It appears she'll get her wish." Rebecca gripped Daniel's hand as the pain intensified.

"It's time you went to your bed. I'll send for the doctor."

"I want to stay here with Chavive. But yes, send for the doctor." The contraction ebbed, and Rebecca loosened her grip. "The pains aren't lasting long. I'm sure I have lots of time yet."

"I won't risk your health. We'll let the doctor decide if it's safe for you to stay with your horse."

"All right, then."

Daniel studied her. "I won't have a child of mine born on the barn floor."

"I won't let that happen. I promise."

"You shouldn't be on your feet so much," Daniel said, hurrying out of the stall and reappearing a few moments later with a wooden chair. He set it beside Rebecca. "Sit. I'll have one of the roustabouts go for the doctor, and I'll make sure Woodman is here to help with the foal."

Gratefully Rebecca sank onto the chair, resting a hand on her stomach. "That's much better."

"I'll tell Mum and Lily. They'll see to you."

"Please don't. They'll force me to bed."

"You? I doubt they can force you to do anything you don't want to do." Daniel grinned.

"All right, then. Tell them. But I'm staying put as long as I can."

"Right," Daniel said, heading for the barn door. "I'll be right back."

$\mathcal{D}$

Chavive's labor continued, as did Rebecca's. Woodman oversaw Chavive while Dr. Walker watched over Rebecca.

"It seems she should have produced a foal by now," Rebecca said, trying to breathe through a contraction. She rested her forehead against Chavive's side. When the pain relented, she straightened and looked at Woodman. "I think she ought to be checked. Something's not right."

"Ah, she's probably fine, but I'll check 'er if ya like." Woodman removed his shirt and stepped next to the mare. He ran a hand along her side and felt as she contracted. "Good strong pains. This is her first one; it takes time with a first foal, mum." He carefully reached inside the horse, his arm disappearing up to his shoulder.

As he felt for the foal, Rebecca held her breath. What if it wasn't presenting right? What if Chavive was damaged the way Miss had been? "Is she all right?"

Woodman removed his arm and wiped it clean on a rag. Wearing a smile, he said, "Roight fine. We'll 'ave a foal 'ere before long."

Rebecca felt herself relax. "Oh, thank the Lord." She sat on

117

the chair and wondered if she'd make it to Chavive's birth; her own contractions were becoming nearly unbearable.

Finally, with a little help from Daniel and Woodman and a strong, protracted grunt, Chavive pushed her foal from her body.

Daniel stepped in and removed the remaining bag of waters and cleared the foal's nose. "It's a colt!"

"He's a beauty!" Rebecca said, momentarily forgetting her own circumstances.

Chavive turned and sniffed her new baby, then started licking him clean.

"He looks fine," Daniel said. "The image of Noble."

"He's wonderful." A contraction gripped Rebecca, and she was forced to pant through it.

Dr. Walker, who'd been standing by and observing Rebecca, stepped into the stall. "It's time you tended to your own child," he said.

"I believe you're right." Rebecca reached for Daniel's hand.

He helped her stand, and he and the doctor assisted her to the house. The contractions were coming so often that Rebecca was forced to stop twice before making it indoors.

As she moved toward her bedroom, Willa, Lily, and Callie hovered. Another contraction stopped her at the door to her room, and water gushed from between her legs. "Oh dear. I'm sorry," Rebecca said, overtaken by a powerful contraction. She leaned against Daniel, unable to speak.

"No trouble, mum," Callie said. "I'll take care of it." She hurried toward the kitchen.

The pain built, and Rebecca forced down a scream. Finally, after an agonizing minute and a half, she took a deep breath. "I think my time is near, Doctor."

"Well, let's get you to bed, then, and see what we have." He smiled kindly.

Lying on the bed did nothing to lessen Rebecca's misery.

The pains came one on top of the other. With each Rebecca felt a gripping need to push. "I have to push."

"Go ahead, then," Dr. Walker said.

Lily appeared at the doorway with a bowl of water. Towels were draped over her shoulder. "I thought ya'd need these, eh?"

"Right. Just set them there next to the bed." Dr. Walker rolled up his sleeves. "Let's have a look."

"Time for you to leave," Willa told Daniel, ushering him out of the room.

"Wait a moment." Daniel returned to Rebecca. He leaned over her, taking her hand. "I'll be right outside, luv."

Rebecca nodded.

Daniel pressed his lips to her forehead.

Rebecca wished he could stay. She needed him. Then another contraction swept over her, and all she knew was that she had to push.

☙

Dr. Walker placed his stethoscope in his medical bag. "You're just fine, Rebecca." He snapped the bag shut.

"You don't expect any trouble like last time?" Daniel asked.

"No. But be watchful. One never knows." He leveled serious eyes on Rebecca. "I want you to stay in bed."

"I'll be happy to," she said, feeling so worn out she craved sleep. She looked at the infant in her arms, and the weariness dissipated a bit. An ache of love squeezed her chest as the little girl scrunched up her face in an effort to look at her mother.

Willa leaned over Rebecca and gazed at the infant. "She's beautiful. Looks just like you."

"She does at that," Daniel said, sitting on the bed beside Rebecca.

The doctor moved toward the doorway. "I'll see you in a couple of days."

"Thanks, Doc," Daniel said, shaking the man's hand. "You did right well."

"I'd say it was Rebecca who did right well." Dr. Walker smiled and opened the door.

"I'll see you out," Willa said, accompanying him into the hallway.

Rebecca turned her attention back to her daughter. The infant blinked and then studied her mother's face through dark eyes. She pursed her lips.

"So it turned out just as you wanted," Daniel said. "Chavive delivered a fine colt and you a daughter."

Rebecca smiled and took a contented breath. "Yes. It's a fine day."

"I'd say." Daniel touched the baby's hand. She instinctively grasped his finger. "Ah, she's a strong one."

Rebecca lifted the little girl and kissed her cheek, delighting in the velvety softness and the perfume of new life. "Audry. That is your name."

"It's a grand name."

"Father would be pleased, especially since she looks like my mother." Rebecca felt the sting of tears. If only her father and mother could have been here to meet their granddaughter.

Willa stepped into the room with Joseph resting on her hip.

"You really think she looks like me?" Rebecca asked.

"She does, absolutely." Willa shifted Joseph around in front of her. "There's someone here who wants to meet his sister." She set the little boy on the floor beside the bed.

Rebecca held the baby in such a way that Joseph could see her. "This is your little sister, Audry."

Joseph laid his pudgy hand on the baby's cheek. "Au . . . dy." He touched her dark curls. "Soft."

Joy swelled within Rebecca. "You're such a big boy. You'll have to look out for her, take good care of her."

"Right," Joseph said. "I'm big." He grinned, his blue eyes lit with delight.

"Come on up 'ere, lad," Daniel said, scooping up the little boy and setting him on the bed beside him. "Would you like to hold her?"

Joseph reached for the baby.

"You have to be gentle with her," Rebecca said, carefully placing the infant in Joseph's arms while keeping a protective hold on her.

Joseph cradled the baby, smiling at the little girl. "Sister, Au . . . dy."

Fear unexpectedly jolted Rebecca as an image of the men who worked for Marshal penetrated her bubble of joy. They'd be back. Daniel still hadn't paid what was owed. She caressed Joseph's soft blond hair and kissed him, then gently took back the baby. "I think I need to rest."

"Of course," Willa said. "We'll leave you alone."

Rebecca didn't want to be alone. She looked at Daniel. "Could you stay for a while?"

"Right." Daniel smoothed back Rebecca's dark hair. "You all right, luv?"

"I'm fine. Just tired." She leaned against her pillows and closed her eyes. The baby burrowed close to her mother.

"Time for Mummy to rest," Willa said, lifting Joseph off the bed. "Come along. Maybe Lily will let us help her with the baking."

"Can we make cake?" Joseph asked, his words only partially distinguishable.

"I think that would be a fine idea." Willa looked at Rebecca. "Can I get you anything, dear?"

Forcing her eyes open, Rebecca smiled at her mother-in-law. "No thank you. Nothing right now."

"Right, then. We'll be off." Willa grasped Joseph's hand and led him out of the room.

"Would you like me to put the baby in the cradle?" Daniel asked.

Rebecca looked at her daughter and then offered her to Daniel. "That's probably a good idea. I'm suddenly exhausted."

Daniel settled Audry in her cradle, then sat in the chair beside the bed. "You sure you want me here? I don't want to be a bother."

Rebecca reached for Daniel's hand. "No. Never. I need you. I'm . . . I'm frightened."

"What is it? Are you unwell?"

"No. It's not that." She glanced at the window curtain suddenly set to dancing by a breeze. "It's those men. What are we going to do if they return?"

"We'll stand up to them, that's what. But they may leave us alone. I sold off some bullocks and paid some of what I owe. I figure it'll hold Marshal off for a while."

"Daniel, I'm frightened. What if they were to take one of the children?"

"It'll work out. Right now you need to take care of you and the baby. That's all you need to think about." He offered a tender smile.

"Yes, but she and Joseph . . ." Rebecca couldn't even bring herself to say the words.

"They'll be fine. Marshal won't touch them. He wouldn't dare."

Rebecca closed her eyes and forced herself to take slow, deep breaths. Still, her mind wouldn't rest as images of the three despicable and heartless men who'd shown up in her classroom pressed down on her. "What if he does dare, Daniel?"

12

Rebecca watched Daniel ride off and then turned to Willa. "I need to go into town. Could you teach the class for me this morning?"

"Of course. But do you think you're up to a trip into town?"

"It's been nearly three weeks since Audry was born. And I'm feeling quite robust."

"What is it you intend to do?"

"The school needs supplies."

"Daniel could have done that for you."

"Yes, I know, but I hate to ask him, and I'd like to get out for a bit."

"Do you think it's safe for you to travel about on your own?"

Rebecca felt a spike of the old fear but refused to accept it. "It's been weeks since the trouble. Perhaps Daniel's partial payment has satisfied Mr. Marshal for now. And as you said yourself, we can't hide indoors forever."

"Perhaps you ought to have Woodman go for you."

"No. I'd like to go. I've been inactive too long." Rebecca offered what she hoped was a confident smile. "Callie said she'd accompany me. I'm sure we'll be fine." Rebecca's eyes went to Lily, who was patting out a batch of bread dough. "I'll need someone to watch Audry and Joseph though. I really don't want to take them with me. Lily, would you watch the children?"

Lily rested her hands on the plump dough. "Be happy ta."

"Thank you. I just fed Audry, so she should be fine until I get home. She's sleeping right now."

Joseph dropped his spoon in the middle of his mush. "I want to go."

Rebecca moved to her son and planted a kiss on the only clean spot on his face. "Not today. You stay with Lily."

Joseph pouted, but only for a moment. "Bye," he said and returned to eating his cereal.

Rebecca glanced out the window at the new schoolroom. "The children are already arriving for school."

"Oh dear. I better hurry, then," Willa said. "Tell them I'll be right there."

"Thank you." Rebecca hurriedly left the house. Lifting her skirts out of the dirt, she walked toward the temporary schoolhouse. The idea of getting out on the flats again and enjoying the unrestricted feeling of freedom offered by the grasslands was exhilarating.

She stopped at the corral where Chavive and her new foal were confined. The colt dashed across the enclosure, kicking and bucking. Rebecca chuckled. "So you're already letting the world know you intend to challenge it."

Chavive stretched her neck over the fence, and Rebecca rested a hand on the mare's forehead and caressed the front of her face. "You did well. I'm proud of you." With a final pat to Chavive's neck, Rebecca hurried on toward the school.

Callie stood just inside the doorway. Koora stood beside her. The two of them looked a bit uncomfortable.

"Good morning," Rebecca said.

"G'day." Koora flashed a smile.

"G'day, mum," Callie said. "We goin' inta town?"

"Yes. Willa will be out shortly to see to the children."

"Roight." Callie glanced at Koora. "Maybe ya can help Mrs. Thornton, eh?"

"I'd like that fine. She's a nice lydie." His gaze lingered on Callie, who in spite of her serene exterior, was unable to conceal a flush. She was obviously fond of the young man.

Rebecca liked Koora. He was eager to learn and never missed an opportunity to be at school, which might explain his quick grasp of the basics in reading and math.

"I got ta go now," Callie said, shyly leaning toward Koora.

He put his hand on her arm. "See ya later, then?"

"Roight." Callie looked at Rebecca. "Will we be gone long?"

"No. I just need a few things from the mercantile." Rebecca studied the couple. *They love each other*, she thought, warming at the idea.

She remembered the days when she and Daniel had fallen in love. It hadn't happened before they married nor soon after; not until months later did she recognize her devotion. Those days had been a mix of confusion and fear as well as joy.

Rebecca stepped inside the tent and faced the students who were already seated on the benches. "Children, the senior Mrs. Thornton will be your teacher today. She'll be here in a few minutes. You mind Koora until she arrives."

The children bobbed their heads in assent.

With a smile, Rebecca moved outside and hurried toward the carriage house. Callie walked beside her. "Can't afford to dawdle," Rebecca said. "We must return before Audry gets hungry."

"Roight, mum."

Rebecca stepped inside the carriage house, and Woodman looked up from a piece of harness he was working on. "G'day."

"Good day," Rebecca said. "We'll need the surrey. We've errands to run in town."

Woodman knit his brows. "Daniel know?"

"No. But I'm sure he wouldn't mind."

"Just wondered, with the—"

"Yes. I know. But if we're to continue educating the children, we must replenish supplies."

Woodman clamped his mouth shut.

"The Lord will see to us," Rebecca said. "He always has."

Woodman set down the harness. "Figured he might take care of Dusty too, eh?"

Rebecca felt as if she'd had the wind knocked out of her. She said nothing more. She had no answer to Woodman's challenge. Why had God allowed such an atrocity?

✺

Standing in front of a row of shelves containing school supplies, Rebecca thought over what she needed. She glanced at Patrick O'Brien, who leaned on the mercantile counter studying a ledger.

Mr. O'Brien looked up and smiled from beneath a perfectly trimmed mustache. Brushing aside a thatch of red hair from his forehead, he asked, "Anything I can do for you, Mrs. Thornton?"

"I just need a few supplies . . . for the school."

"That's coming along all right, then?"

"Yes. Splendidly in fact."

He nodded. "How's that new baby of yours?"

"She's quite well."

"Good. Tell your husband I heard 'bout his predicament. I'll be happy to help out, if he needs me."

"Help out?"

126

"Right. Word is he's thinking of taking a stand against Marshal."

Rebecca's stomach did a queer flip. "Oh yes. Of course. I'll tell him."

Trembling inside, she picked up pencils and chalk. Rebecca didn't want Daniel to stand up to Marshal. She was afraid for him.

"I just need a few items," she said, selecting two more pieces of chalk along with some drawing paper. "These ought to do nicely." She set the items in a basket she carried on her arm.

Trying to act nonchalant, Rebecca asked, "Just what would you like to do to help Daniel?" She moved on to pens and ink.

"Well, whatever he needs. I'm a pretty good shot." He straightened his short frame and set back his broad shoulders.

"Oh, I pray it won't come to that." She selected three pens and two bottles of ink.

"Never know with a man like Marshal. There's a number of blokes in the district who've had a difference of opinion with that man. Might feel good to get off a round or two." He grinned.

Rebecca felt sick inside. She added a slate to her basket. Approaching the front of the store, she stopped momentarily to admire a bolt of yellow linen. "This is lovely."

"Would you like me to take some down to Elle's?"

"No. Not today. Although I would like an excuse to visit her. It's so nice having her back in town."

"Right you are. And she's been keepin' busy I hear tell."

With a sigh, Rebecca set the yellow linen down. There would be no new dresses while they were in debt to Marshal. She set the supplies on the counter in front of Mr. O'Brien. She smiled at the man and couldn't imagine him shooting anyone.

"That be all, then?"

"Yes." Rebecca wanted to get home. "Do you really think it will come down to a gunfight?"

"Might." Mr. O'Brien sorted the items in the basket and priced them. "That's not what a bloke wants, but you do what you must, eh?"

"I suppose." Rebecca reached into a small change purse and deposited several coins on the counter. "Is that enough?"

Mr. O'Brien counted out the money. "Just right." He dropped the coins into a money box. "You just missed Cambria. I think she said something about dropping by your place though. Told me she couldn't wait to see that baby again."

Rebecca smiled. "She's wonderful with Audry. One day she'll make a fine mother."

"I figured. When do you suppose her and Jim are going to get married?"

"Just as soon as he gets their place set up." Resting the handle of the basket over her arm, Rebecca said, "Thank you. Good day, now."

"Have a fine day, eh?"

"I certainly will."

When the door closed behind her, Rebecca drew in a deep breath, gathered her skirts, and then swiftly moved to the surrey. She'd be glad to be on her way. She needed to talk to Daniel. She couldn't allow him to do something as foolish as start a conflict between himself and Marshal.

Callie sat on the front seat of the surrey. "Ya look troubled, mum."

"I am." Rebecca set the basket on the floor in the back between the seats. "Mr. O'Brien said Daniel and some of the men from the district are planning to take a stand against Mr. Marshal, even if it means a gun battle."

"Sometimes that's what's roight."

"It can't be right. Too many men could be hurt. And he dare not anger Mr. Marshal further."

"I'd say Mr. Marshal's angry enough. Have ya forgotten Dusty?"

Rebecca let out a long breath. "No. Of course not. And I suppose you're right. How could Mr. Marshal be more angry than he already is?" She climbed onto the driver's seat, lifted the reins, and slapped them over the hind end of the horses. Immediately the team trotted into the road. "I just wish there was another way."

Rebecca suddenly realized how little she trusted Daniel in this, or God for that matter. "We need to be praying more," she said.

As the idea of God's sovereign hand being laid over her life penetrated her thoughts, Rebecca quieted inside. He'd always been faithful. Her mind flashed to the day of the fire and how Callie and Joseph had miraculously survived the flames.

"Wal, ya can pray ta yer God, but I don't see that it'll make a difference."

"Oh, Callie," Rebecca said with exasperation. "If only you could understand what it's like to have a God who loves you and watches over you."

Callie pursed her lips and stared at the horses' rumps. "I don't know 'bout yer God, but I know ya, and I wanted ta tell ya I'm sorry 'bout what I said the other day."

"What did you say?"

"Ya know, 'bout yer not invitin' me ta eat breakfast with ya when ya first come ta Douloo."

"Why, that was weeks ago. Have you been thinking about it all this time?"

"I been thinkin', and I meant what I said except that I know ya and Mrs. Thornton and Daniel aren't like the others." She looked Rebecca in the eye. "Ya respect me . . . and Woodman. Ya been fair and kind."

"Thank you." Rebecca rested a hand on Callie's. "But you were right. I can be careless."

Callie nodded assent.

Rebecca turned quiet. She wanted to speak with Callie about God and about her salvation, but she didn't know just what to say. "I know you've read the Bible."

"And I thank ya for teachin' me ta read, but—"

"Have you considered Christianity?"

"I know me own way, mum. No reason ta go another."

"Would you join me at church this Sunday?" Before Callie could refuse, Rebecca hurried on. "I know it's not something you've done and that you may feel a bit out of place, but at least you could experience church. And Rev. Cobb is a fine man who delivers exceptional sermons."

"I'd never be allowed in a Christian church, mum."

"I'm sure it would be all right. Please, just try it once. If you do, I promise never to bring it up again."

Callie gazed ahead, saying nothing. Finally she said, "All roight, then. If ya promise not ta ask me again, I'll go."

"Wonderful!" Rebecca exclaimed, barely able to believe she'd managed to convince Callie.

"I won't be forced inta goin' back. Ya promise not ta ask."

"Yes. I promise."

✵

Callie stood on her tiny front porch and watched as Rebecca stepped onto the veranda. Her insides churned. *What 'ave I done? I don't belong in no church. They'll not want me.* She held her Bible close, pressing it against her chest.

Rebecca hurried down the front steps. She waved at Callie. "Good morning."

Callie nodded but remained where she was. *I'm not goin'. My bein' there will only stir up a bee's nest.*

Daniel stood in the yard, holding Audry, while Joseph galloped back and forth between the porch steps and the surrey. Willa was already seated in the carriage.

Rebecca approached Callie. "You look very nice."

Callie glanced down at her pink floral shift and snatched a frayed blue hat off her head. "I don't 'ave nice clothes, mum."

"You're fine. And you've got your Bible."

"This isn't a good idea. I should stay home, eh?"

"No. Of course you shouldn't." Rebecca's voice was too cheery. She circled an arm about Callie's waist and steered her toward the surrey. "You can sit with me."

"If ya don't mind, mum, I think I'd rather sit up front with Woodman."

"Of course," Rebecca said. "Sit wherever you feel most comfortable."

"Are you ready, then?" Daniel asked.

"Yep," Joseph said, scrambling in and sitting beside his grandmother.

"We're ready," Rebecca said.

Callie stood beside the surrey, wishing there were some way to get out of her promise to Rebecca. She looked up at Woodman. "Don't think this is a good idea."

Woodman smiled. "Ya said ya'd go. Now ya goin' ta back out, eh?"

"I didn't say that." Without another word Callie climbed up and sat beside Woodman.

When the Thorntons arrived at church, Callie remained planted on the seat while the family stepped out of the surrey. Her stomach ached. She glanced at the church, her eyes lingering on the steeple that housed a large, polished bell.

"It's not ringin', mum," she said.

"No. They wait until just before ten o'clock, when the service begins."

"Oh." Callie remained seated, hands in her lap, back straight.

"Come on, Callie," Joseph said. He stared up at the servant, his blue eyes wide and innocent.

Taking a deep breath, Callie glanced at Woodman, who offered her a slight smile and a shrug. Finally she climbed down.

Daniel had ridden alongside the surrey. He dismounted and tied his horse to the back of the carriage, then took Audry from Rebecca and gave his wife a hand down. With Audry in one arm, he held his other out to Rebecca, and then the two of them headed toward the church. Willa walked alongside them.

Joseph held out his hand to Callie. "Come on."

"Roight, then," Callie said, grasping the youngster's hand. She looked about, but when she noticed people staring at her, she set her gaze straight ahead.

When they reached the steps at the front of the church, Callie stopped.

"Don't be scared," Joseph said. "God's here. He's nice."

Parishioners moved past the Thornton cluster. Many gazed at Callie, and some whispered to one another.

"It will be fine, Callie," Willa said, taking her arm and leading her up the steps.

Rev. Cobb stood at the door. He was unable to hide his surprise but quickly recovered and smiled at Callie. "It's good that you could join us. Don't believe I've ever seen you in church before."

"No, sir. Never been."

Joseph tugged on her hand, and dragged her inside the small sanctuary. Talk ceased, and glances were cast at Callie and the Thorntons.

Callie wished she had the power to disappear.

"Come along, then," Willa said with a warm smile, resting a hand momentarily on Callie's arm and moving farther inside the sanctuary.

"We'll sit right 'ere," Daniel said, stopping at the first empty pew near the back of the church.

The bell let out a loud peal, and Callie flinched. It rang again and again. It was too late to leave now.

Parishioners stared and then tried not to. Mothers hushed their children's questions, and then finally, thankfully, the minister stepped to the podium.

"G'day to you all. Welcome." His warm eyes rested momentarily on Callie before traveling over the congregation.

The first chords of the organ played, and everyone stood. Staring at the back of the person in front of her, Callie stood along with the others. Voices merged hesitantly at first and then more vigorously as the song progressed.

Callie wanted to leave and even glanced at the back of the church to measure how many steps it would take to reach the door. Freedom called.

When the song ended, the people sat and Rev. Cobb returned to the podium. "This morning I have something quite significant I need to address, a topic God spent a good deal of time on—our mistaken beliefs about good works." He paused, allowing the congregation a chance to grasp the topic. "If not for his mercy and forgiveness, we would never know heaven.

"While it's true that, to achieve heaven, all that's required of us is to believe in Christ as Savior, the Lord asks more and offers more. Good works are not required if we're to be accepted into his family; however, his desire is that we live a life filled with good works. A bit confusing, eh?" He smiled.

Callie tried to listen to the reverend and to comprehend what he was saying, but her mind was more focused on her surroundings and the fact that every person in the room seemed aware of her presence. Callie strained to understand.

"Now, then, let us go to the Word. In Ephesians chapter two, verses eight and nine, it states clearly that salvation is a gift, freely given." The reverend waited a few moments while parishioners turned to the book of Ephesians.

Callie didn't know where it was located and kept her Bible closed on her lap.

"Now, then, it says, 'For by grace are ye saved through faith; and that not of yourselves: it is the gift of God: Not of works, lest any man should boast.'"

The reverend smiled. "There is nothing we can do to earn a place in heaven. It is God's gift to us, a gift of salvation to all mankind. Salvation is not something we can produce by our works, but rather by our faith."

Had the reverend said that the place called heaven was for anyone who believed in Christ—even blacks?

He leaned on the podium. "Don't misunderstand; God wants us to do good works, but it is not the work we do that saves us. However, we should never forget that good deeds please God. Read the next verse with me."

Cambria sat three rows up. She looked over her shoulder and caught Callie's eye, offering a reassuring smile. Callie felt slightly better as she glanced at the closed Bible lying in her lap.

Pulling himself to his full height, the reverend continued. "So what is God talking about when he speaks of good works?" He glanced down at the Scriptures in front of him. "There are many things we can do that please God. We can give to the poor. We can love the unlovable as Christ did with the lepers. We can help our neighbor." He said the last sentence with emphasis. "But we need to be judicious in how we help one another." He glanced at Daniel. "May we never sin in the effort."

Callie knew he was talking about Daniel's plan to challenge Marshal. Was it a sin to protect yourself and your family? *I'll 'ave ta ask Rebecca 'bout that.*

The reverend continued talking about other ways to do good works, but Callie was too nervous to hear much of what he said. She was thankful when he finally stepped down from the podium. After the closing hymn, parishioners stood and filed out of the church. Callie started down the aisle toward freedom.

"G'day," Cambria said, striding up to her. She clasped Callie's hands. "I'm so thrilled ya came this morning. I hope ya'll come back."

"Maybe," Callie said in a hushed tone while she continued toward the door.

Cambria fell into step beside Rebecca, who seemed to be making every effort to keep up with Callie. "Maybe we can have a cuppa this week, eh? Or go for a ride?"

"That would be lovely."

Callie was nearly running by the time she reached the bottom step in front of the church. She headed straight for the surrey.

Rebecca followed. "Callie? Callie. Please wait."

Callie didn't stop until she reached the carriage. "Yais, mum?"

"You were in such a hurry," Rebecca said, "I couldn't keep up."

"I come 'ere just as I said, mum. But I don't belong."

"Did someone say something to you?"

"No. No one has ta say nothin'."

"Be patient. People need time to adjust, including you."

"They won't. I won't." Callie pursed her lips and folded her arms over her chest, tucking her Bible under one arm.

Rebecca looked at the parishioners filing out of the church and at the reverend greeting each one. "Rev. Cobb is a fine man." She turned a smile on Callie. "What did you think of the sermon?"

Callie thought a moment. "It was good. But it seems ta me, Christians only talk 'bout what they believe; they don't do what they believe."

"That's not true, not exactly. We try. Christians aren't perfect. I never said we were. We make mistakes, do dreadful things, even cruel things sometimes. Everyone does. But most of the time we love and take care of each other."

"I guess that's true enough." Callie climbed onto the surrey seat. "Koora wouldn't like it if he knew I went ta church." She glanced at the families gathering for lunch. "Don't tell him, mum."

"You like him a lot, don't you?"

"Yais. I do."

"He's fond of you too."

"Ya think, eh?"

"Yes. I can see it in his eyes."

Callie smiled. "I did like church, mum. But I won't be comin' back."

13

Dusk fell over the plains, and the Thornton house settled into quiet rest. Glad to have the day done, Rebecca sat in an overstuffed chair with her legs tucked up under her and a comforter across her lap. She turned a page of her book, *A Tale of Two Cities*. She'd read Dickens's historical novel before, but she never tired of the drama nor the battle between good and evil. The characters were vivid and real, their struggle genuine.

Hearing the pop of a floorboard, she looked up. Callie stood just inside the doorway. "Why, hello, Callie. Is everything all right?" When Callie didn't reply, Rebecca asked, "Can I do something for you?"

Still the aborigine said nothing. She studied Rebecca, then tentatively asked, "I was wonderin' if ya'd like ta see somethin' special."

Intrigued, Rebecca let the book rest in her lap. "What is it you want to show me?"

Callie glanced about as if afraid someone might overhear. "Can't say roight yet. But would ya come with me?"

Her interest growing, Rebecca closed her book and set it on the table beside her. "What is it?"

"Somethin' good . . . 'bout me people."

Rebecca pushed to her feet. "All right, then." She folded the comforter in half and laid it over the back of the chair. "I'll tell Willa. She's helping Lily in the kitchen."

"No need ta say nothin', mum." Callie glanced at the stairway. "And Mr. Thornton, mum, where is he?"

"He was exhausted and went to bed."

"The bybies?"

"They've gone to bed as well." Rebecca studied Callie. "Is something wrong? You're acting strangely. What is it you want to show me?"

"Ya'll see." Callie smiled as if she was enjoying her secret. "Come on, then." Silently she moved toward the front door.

Rebecca followed, holding her breath and doing her best to move quietly like Callie.

The sky held on to the last trace of fading light as they moved away from the house. Callie walked rapidly, leading Rebecca out onto the flats. Darkness draped itself over the land and swallowed up the two women as they left the lights of the house behind them.

Rebecca stumbled and nearly fell over a clump of grass. "Slow down," she called in a loud whisper. She stood still and sought out Callie in the darkness. She couldn't see her. Pulling her sweater close, she called, "Callie. Where are you?"

"Roight 'ere," Callie said with a chuckle. It didn't sound like she was more than a few feet away.

"I can't see a thing," Rebecca said. "I don't know that this is a good idea."

"It's all roight. The moon will be up soon, eh?"

Feeling uneasy, Rebecca asked, "Where are we going? What are we doing out here?"

"Ya'll see."

Rebecca threw back her shoulders. She'd have to put a

stop to this silliness. "I won't go a step farther until you tell me where we're going."

Callie moved closer to Rebecca, her silhouette appearing out of the darkness. "I want ta share somethin' sacred with ya. Most whites never seen it."

"If you're talking about rock paintings, we can see those in the daylight. I want to go back."

"No. It's not paintings." Callie turned silent, then continued, her voice soft and expressive. "This is kind of like yer church, mum. I went ta see yer ways. Now I want ya ta see mine."

"You'd like to share a religious ceremony with me?"

"Yais . . . but not exactly. It's a ceremony, but also a secret life. It's taboo for women."

"Taboo?"

"Yais. It's not for women, but I seen it before. Me mum took me once. Sometimes women are allowed to go to ceremonies. But this one . . . well, this one 'as special power."

Rebecca wasn't sure she wanted to see an aborigine rite, especially one with special power. The thought sent shivers through her. She glanced toward the house, but it had disappeared behind the rise. "Do you think it wise to wander so far from home in the pitch black?"

"It's not so dark." Callie smiled and Rebecca could see the white of her teeth reflect the light of a rising moon. "Ya afraid, mum?"

"Should I be?" Rebecca peered at Callie, wishing she could see her better. "It seems that something done in the darkness is meant to be hidden. Perhaps we shouldn't pry into the men's customs."

"It's all roight, mum. No need ta worry."

"Is it far?"

"No. Not far." Callie placed Rebecca's hand on her shoulder and moved on, silently passing through the night.

Even with help from Callie, Rebecca wasn't as sure-footed as her friend and had difficulty keeping up. More than once she tripped over something hidden in the darkness. She worried about scorpions and snakes and kept glancing at the uneven ground, but it was too dark to spot anything.

Just when Rebecca had decided to put an end to the evening's excursion, she heard a distant throaty sound of a didgeridoo. She stopped. "What's that? Is that where we're going?"

"Yais. The corroboree has begun."

Clicking sounds and chants joined the mystical resonance of the didgeridoo. Rebecca's stomach tightened, and her anxiety grew. "Callie, are you sure this is all right?"

"Yais. I want ya ta see. It'll hurt no one if we watch. The blokes won't even know we're 'ere."

"What do you mean?"

"We'll hide." Callie's answer made Rebecca more apprehensive. "If we've nothing to fear, why must we hide? What is it that we're going to see?"

"It's a celebration of our mother the earth and an initiation." Callie slowed her steps. "Lydies not s'posed ta see, but I seen. Like I said, when I was a young gal. I was scared, but me mum explained everything." She smiled. "Come on." She dropped to her hands and knees and crawled toward a strange light penetrating the tall grasses.

Rebecca remained where she was. *I ought to return to the house. This can't be good.*

Curiosity won out. Rebecca knelt and on hands and knees followed Callie. Her long skirt made crawling difficult. It kept bunching up and seemed to catch on every branch or bush.

Dropping to her stomach, Callie moved through the dry grass and stopped at the edge of a large open space.

Heart pounding hard beneath her ribs, Rebecca did just as Callie had. She pressed against the earth. *I can't believe I'm doing this. I don't care what she says; we could be in real danger.* When she stopped, Rebecca peered into the clearing lit by

140

a large bonfire. Men danced around the blaze. They were naked, dressed only in paint.

Rebecca knew she shouldn't be gazing at the men, but she couldn't take her eyes off of them. She'd never seen anything like it. They'd painted designs on their bodies. Some had stripes running up or across their legs, others had painted squiggling lines on their chests, and there were a variety of other designs that looked like leaves or waving grasses or circles.

"We shouldn't be watching," Rebecca whispered, closing her eyes.

"Ya never seen a man?" Callie teased.

"Of course I have. I'm married. But Daniel's my husband," Rebecca whispered.

Callie grinned. "Yer funny, mum. Ya look like ya seen a ghost."

"Well, it's not proper." Rebecca turned her gaze back to the men. "You didn't tell me they were going to be unclothed."

"It's not their naked bodies what matter, mum, but the rest."

"Of course," Rebecca said, making an effort to convince herself this part of Callie's culture was innocent. And if she wanted to understand aborigines, she supposed this was a good place to begin.

Four men sat side by side just outside the ring of the dancers. Two puffed into didgeridoos, and two beat sticks in rhythm. Rebecca studied the dancers' feet as they moved to the song's pulse. Sometimes they kicked up dirt and then shuffled backwards. They chanted and stomped the ground.

The scene felt supernatural, and Rebecca knew she was witnessing something the Christian world considered wicked. And yet she couldn't look away. Something about the movement and the rhythm of the music held her, tantalized her. Shadows of impassioned dancers played on the grasses beyond the fire, and Rebecca felt a chill of fear as well as wonderment.

"They celebrate the earth that gives so much," Callie whispered. "They sing of life; of the rivers, sky, and moon; and of the earth that gave them up and will one day take them back again."

"It's fascinating," Rebecca said, beginning to comprehend that this was a celebration and realizing she had nothing to fear.

When one of the elder men removed a primitive knife from a sheath worn around his waist, the muscles in Rebecca's stomach tightened. She held her breath and then glanced over her shoulder into the darkness, suddenly afraid they were being watched.

The man lifted the knife above his head and held it as if offering it to the sky. Her dread building, Rebecca stared. Suddenly he brought down the knife and sliced into his arm. She could feel a scream rise up but pressed a hand over her mouth to smother it.

Blood trickled down the aborigine's arm and onto his leg. Rather than acting disturbed, the man became more animated. Another one of the older dancers brought out his knife and sliced into his arm . . . and then another man cut himself . . . and another.

The fervor of the music increased, and the dancing became frenetic. The men's song grew louder and more pronounced. They cut themselves again and smeared the blood over their bodies and then on one another. Some drew designs with the blood. The younger men moved close to the ones who had taken part in the bloodletting. They danced in such a way that the blood dripped onto their bodies.

Rebecca was sickened. "Why are they doing that?"

"The young blokes get power from the blood of the older ones, and they are bound to each other always. It's somethin', eh?"

Rebecca was horrified but said nothing. Obviously this was of great importance to Callie. She watched, afraid of what might come next.

A white-haired man moved into the darkness and returned with a boy. Several other lads followed but remained behind when the first was led into the circle.

"What are they going to do?" Rebecca asked, unable to keep her voice from trembling.

"It is initiation."

The boy seemed animated, but Rebecca could also see fear in his eyes. He danced with the men and then was taken aside. The old man took his knife from its sheath, held it up to the dark sky, and then turned to the boy. Rebecca closed her eyes. She couldn't bear it, no matter what it was. She heard a groan and a muffled cry, and then she opened her eyes. There was blood, lots of it, on the youngster's thighs and on the ground in front of him. And yet he joined the men in the dance.

"I can't stay," Rebecca whispered, backing away and then turning and crawling toward the safety of darkness.

She didn't stop until she was certain she'd put ample distance between herself and the aborigine men and their ritual. The music was quieter, the sounds muffled, and the blazing fire was out of sight, but Rebecca couldn't rid herself of the frightening images.

She sat, pulling bent knees in close to her chest. Why would Callie share something so ghastly with her? She rested her forehead against her knees.

Callie joined her. "Mum, ya all roight?"

"Yes," Rebecca said, blowing out a quick breath. "But it was awful. Why did you bring me here? I've never seen anything like that. What is it?"

"I told ya, it's a corroboree. A time for the men to join each other and celebrate life and the wonder of the earth."

"And the boys?"

"It is their passage from bein' a lad ta bein' a man. It's a good thing."

"Circumcision. Is that what it was?"

Callie shrugged. "I don't know what ya call it."

"And how can you say it's a good thing? It was horrid. They were cutting themselves, and then they cut that boy."

Callie sat back. "Why is it horrid?"

"It's so bloody and . . . outlandish."

"Ya 'ave yer rituals, mum."

"Yes, but not like these. Why would you show me such a thing?"

"Ya take me ta yer church so I can see yer ways. And I go. This is me people's way."

Rebecca could see the comparison, but church was quiet and reverent. "This is very different, Callie. What does it all mean?"

"The men grow more powerful. They become stronger, wiser. The songs tell of growing up and becoming wise, of finding water and trees for shade. They talk 'bout the beauty in the stars and the moon. The men sing 'bout growin', lovin', and how the spirits of bybies come inta their women. They ask for help from the earth ta feed their families. And then they speak of the day they return ta the land they come from."

Rebecca started to grasp the importance. "But the blood, why did they do that?"

"The blood of a man has power, mum. I thought ya'd understand. I been readin' the Bible ya gave me. It talks 'bout blood and that it saves men, roight?"

"Yes, but . . . it wasn't like this, with so many men cutting themselves and bleeding on each other." She shuddered at the memory.

"So you say it's better that a man has no choice and is hanged from a cross?" Callie's tone challenged.

"He wasn't just a man. He was the Messiah, the Son of God. And he *chose* to die."

144

Callie smiled. "And they choose to share their spirit with each other—to build up courage and strength. That is wrong?"

"No. Of course not. It's just that . . ."

Callie stood and started toward the house. "Sorry I brought ya, mum. Thought ya would understand."

Annoyed with herself and her inability to remain composed under the circumstances, Rebecca pushed up from the ground and hurried to catch Callie. "Please don't misunderstand. I'm glad I came. I just wasn't prepared. I've never seen anything like it before."

Callie kept walking.

"Can you tell me more about the . . . corroboree. Is that how you say it?"

"Yais. This corroboree is a special one. Women are not allowed." Callie slowed her pace. "Sometimes we sing with the men, but we must turn away from the magic. And sometimes the women dance and sing *after* the corroboree, and then we share the power."

"It's very interesting," Rebecca said, still struggling to grasp the implications of it all.

To Callie this was church. She'd always seemed composed and tranquil. Rebecca wondered how it was possible that pagan beliefs could contribute to her serenity and strength. *I suppose if one believes strongly enough, it would offer a measure of peace.*

"Sometimes the women 'ave secret rituals. I remember when I was a gal, me mum and me danced, and we sang special songs. It was a good time." Callie closed her eyes and held her arms out at her sides. She moved over the landscape, looking very much like a ballerina, her movements fluid and delicate.

"How lovely," Rebecca said.

"I can still 'ear the music, feel it in the earth 'round me." She looked up at the sky. "'Ere is beauty; it's all 'round, touch-

145

ing us, holding us." Her voice low and melodic, Callie sang a song in her own language.

Rebecca felt the presence of God, of his creation. She wished she understood the words. "What are you saying, Callie?"

Callie looked at Rebecca. The newly risen moon glowed against her dark skin. "That I am now part of the dreamtime. That the land beneath me feet brings power, and the dark of night quiets me, and the light of the stars and moon soothe me."

"That's beautiful," Rebecca said, her comprehension growing. "You believe you're part of the earth?"

"Yais, mum. We're bound ta each other. That's why I can't believe in yer God. Ya don't know how it is ta love the earth, ta know it, ta understand it, and ta be part of it."

Rebecca felt sorrow seep inside of her. She'd never given much thought to the importance of God's creation. She'd always admired it but had never seen it as a gift. God had given so much, and she'd barely given it a good look.

"From now on I'll try harder to think about what's around me," she said, hoping to convince Callie of her good intentions, but more so to give credence to her newfound convictions.

"Good," Callie said and hurried her steps toward home.

When the lights of the house appeared, Rebecca felt disappointment. This horrible, powerful, amazing evening was over, and she was no longer afraid. Instead, she was captivated and energized by all she'd learned and all she'd yet to discover.

The two women stopped in front of Callie's cottage. Rebecca rested a hand on her friend's arm. "Thank you for showing me. I understand better now."

Callie nodded and then walked up the steps of the cottage.

After Callie disappeared inside, Rebecca remained for a few minutes more. She gazed at the dark sky with its muted stars gazing down. *God placed them there*, she thought. Her eyes moved to the moon. Bright and bold, it rested comfortably in the heavens as if watching over creation.

The aborigines may have some perplexing and disquieting practices, she thought. *But they know the earth, which is God's creation.*

⁂

When Rebecca climbed into bed beside Daniel, wonderment still held her. She tried not to wake him. Pulling the sheets up under her chin, she stared at the dark ceiling.

"Where've you been?" Daniel asked, his voice cutting into Rebecca's tranquillity. He sounded angry.

"Oh, you startled me."

"I searched for you, and you weren't in the house. I was set to find you, but when I discovered Callie was gone too, I figured you were together. And then Lily said she saw you leave."

Rebecca wasn't ready to share her experience. "Callie took me to see something," she said, trying to sound nonchalant.

"You should have told someone. What if the baby needed you?"

"Oh, well, it was all a bit sudden. I didn't think I'd be gone long."

"Where were you? It's been dark a long while."

Rebecca knew Daniel should know. *But Callie doesn't want me to tell.* She looked at her husband in the dim light. "I can't say."

"You can't say? I'm your husband."

"It's just that, well, I'm certain Callie wants it kept a secret."

"She wouldn't mind my knowing."

"All right, then." Rebecca blew out a breath as if preparing for a race. There was so much to tell. "We went to . . . a celebration. She called it a corroboree."

Daniel sat up. "She took you to a corroboree?"

"Yes, but it was all right. No one saw us." She pushed up on one elbow.

"Why would you do that? They're not for whites."

"Callie wanted me to see it. So I could understand her better." Rebecca sat up. "It was quite enlightening. Callie explained a lot of it to me. And in some ways it's like our own faith. We draw close to God in prayer and song, seeking comfort and power. We praise him for all he's done for us. That's really what they were doing. I understand that the god or mother of the earth or whatever it is that they worship isn't the God of the Bible, but they're worshipping in their own way."

Now feeling animated about sharing, Rebecca brushed her hair back off her shoulder and continued, "I don't understand it all, and I'm sure I never will, but it was important to Callie that I appreciate and respect her beliefs."

"I thought you were praying for her salvation? What good will it do if she thinks you accept her pagan way of thinking?"

"I'm sure she doesn't believe that. She knows how important my faith is to me. And I *am* praying for her."

In the light from the moon, Rebecca could see that Daniel's jaw was set. He was angry.

"I don't want you to ever do anything like that again. It's dangerous. Your curiosity about their religion or your loyalty to Callie is not a good enough reason to take off in the middle of the night."

"She's my friend. I'm sure I was in no danger."

Daniel lay down, pulled the blankets up over his shoulders, and rolled onto his side, his back to Rebecca. "I need you to obey me in this, Rebecca." His voice was stern.

Rebecca stared at his back. He didn't understand. "Why are you so upset?"

He turned over and faced her. "The aborigine ceremonies aren't for us. And they'd be the first to say so." His brows creased. "And definitely not for a woman."

"I must admit, it was a bit frightening at first, but after Callie explained everything, it wasn't so shocking."

"We have to remember that the aborigines are still wild, and we don't always know what to expect. At the very least, it's not safe to go wandering 'round at night." The irritation had gone out of his voice.

"You're right about that," Rebecca said, rolling onto her back and staring through the half light at the ceiling. "But I'm still glad I went."

Daniel sat up and dropped his legs over the side of the bed. He moved to the window and gazed out. "I know you care about Callie, but you have to be careful, Rebecca." He turned to look at her. "I don't know what I'd do without you. And what about the children?" Daniel glanced out the window. "We don't know what Marshal's up to. We have to stay on our guard."

"It's been a long while since we've heard anything."

Daniel turned and looked out on the moonlit yard. "Right, but I still owe him money. We can't trust him."

Heavy silence swamped the room.

"I've been thinking that you ought to go on holiday to Boston, spend some time with your aunt."

"No. I'm not leaving. You need me." Rebecca climbed from beneath the blankets and moved to Daniel. Pressing herself against his back, she draped her arms around him and rested her cheek against his skin. "I can't leave you, not with things the way they are."

"What about the children?"

Rebecca felt fear grab hold of her. "I am frightened for them, but I'm staying." She moved around to face him. With a smile she looked up at him, admiring his handsome, boyish looks. "But I do like the idea of a holiday. Perhaps we could go together."

Daniel pulled her close. "Where?"

Rebecca shrugged. "I loved Brisbane."

Daniel was quiet for a moment. "A friend of mine, Jack Patterson, owns a cottage just north of there. It's on a small bay. He and his family lived there when he was a boy. When they moved to the flats, they kept it so they'd have a place to go on holiday."

"Can we go?"

"I'll work out the details." Daniel rested the bottom of his chin on Rebecca's head. "While we're there I could speak to Marshal. Perhaps I'll be able to reason with him."

14

A knock sounded at the door, and Daniel pushed against the mattress and rolled onto his side. "Who is it?"

"Just Callie. I brought ya some tea."

"Come in." Daniel pulled the covers up over him.

Callie stepped into the room, carrying a tray with tea. "Yer wife thought ya might like something ta start yer day with." She glanced at Daniel but seemed afraid to look at him squarely.

"Right. Just set it on the desk there." Daniel nodded at the desk near the window. With a groan, he pushed up on one elbow.

"Ya hurtin', sir?"

"No. Just a bit stiff. Could be I'm getting old, eh?" He grinned.

"Not you, sir," Callie said with a teasing lilt to her voice.

"Sometimes I wonder." Daniel sat up, folding his legs in front of him.

Callie moved toward the door. "Breakfast will be ready soon. Lily made scones."

"Good."

She grabbed the doorknob when Daniel said, "Callie, I

151

want to speak to you. Could you meet me in the study in half an hour?"

"Roight," Callie said, uncertainty showing in her eyes.

Daniel knew Rebecca wouldn't want him to bring up the previous evening's outing, but it needed to be addressed. "I'll be there shortly."

With a bob of her head, Callie stepped out of the room.

Callie stood outside the study door when Daniel arrived. He opened the door and waited for her to enter. "Please, have a seat," he said, moving around his desk and dropping onto a chair.

Callie moved to a straight-backed chair and sat.

Daniel rested his hands on the desktop. "It's about last night. I'm sure you meant well, but I don't think it was wise to take Rebecca to a corroboree. You placed her and yourself in danger."

Callie's eyes held a question, but she remained silent.

"You can do whatever you like with your ceremonies, but they're not meant for whites. And with all that's happened, it's not safe to wander about, especially at night. We can't forget what happened to Dusty." Releasing a loud breath, he closed his eyes for a moment. "Poor Dusty. I don't want to be responsible for another death."

Callie's dark complexion faded slightly. "Yer roight. I didn't think 'bout that."

"And you may be right fine with aboriginal rituals, but Rebecca's not accustomed to them."

"Did it upset her?"

Daniel wasn't sure how to answer. "Not extremely, but she did say some of it was a bit shocking."

"I just wanted her ta see—"

"Right. I know. She told me, but from now on it would be better if you kept such things to yourself."

Callie looked like she'd clamped her jaws tight. "Roight," she said and stood. "Is that all?"

"Yes."

Callie hurried to the door, and before Daniel could say anything more, she disappeared into the hallway, pulling the door shut behind her.

Daniel stared at the door, his mind still with Dusty. He couldn't rid himself of the vision of his hanging. And although Nan had taken her children and gone to work for another man, he thought of her every day.

Daniel leaned back in the chair and closed his eyes. He was tired. Last night's discussion with Rebecca, thoughts of Dusty, and the threat of what Marshal might do next plagued him. He'd muffed everything. How could he get out from under Marshal's thumb? What could he say or do that would end the fear and the endless watching and waiting? What would it take to save Douloo?

Daniel thought about the holiday he and Rebecca were planning at the coast. Being in Brisbane presented a perfect opportunity to speak with Marshal, as distasteful as the prospect was. He took a sip of cooled tea and then set the cup back on the tray. Could he convince Marshal to accept smaller payments until the station was on its feet again? Daniel doubted it. He stared out the window, looking eastward. His mind searched for a means of convincing the corrupt businessman to ease his conditions. No matter how hard he thought, he couldn't lay hold of a reasonable argument, not one Marshal would accept, anyway. Daniel felt as if he were watching the demise of a loved one—the ruin of Douloo.

He picked up his Bible and riffled through the pages until they fell open to Psalm 1. He looked down at verse 1. "Blessed is the man that walketh not in the counsel of the ungodly, nor standeth in the way of sinners, nor sitteth in the seat of the scornful." He stopped. *I did that. I went to a wicked man for help, and I allowed him to have charge over my life.*

Daniel shook his head in disbelief. He'd been a fool. Closing his eyes, he prayed, *Lord, help me to straighten this out. I know what I did was wrong, but now what do I do? Show me how to set it right.*

Daniel remained there a long while, praying and seeking God's strength and peace. Finally the grumbling in his stomach reminded him of breakfast. And there was work to be done. He couldn't sit all day and worry.

Closing the Bible and pushing to his feet, he meandered toward the kitchen, where he refilled his empty cup and sat at the breakfast table. He drank his tea quietly, watching Lily prepare breakfast.

"Ya look a bit down in the mouth t'day," she said.

"I do?" He took another drink. "I'm fine. No worries."

"Good." She cracked an egg into a frying pan. "Figure everybody gets mad sometimes, eh?"

"Right. Do I look mad?"

"Yais, I'd say."

"I'm not," Daniel said, but he was. He was mad at Marshal and his thugs, and he was mad at himself. "I've made a mess of things," he confessed.

"Nothin' that can't be put roight though, eh?"

"I pray so."

She flipped an egg, and it sizzled in bacon grease. "Ya'll figure it out. I'm sure of it."

Daniel wished he were so certain. "I fear you've too much faith in me, Lily."

"I been 'round 'ere a long while. I know ya. And ya've done roight well since yer father passed on. Ya've grown up." She turned the eggs onto a plate and set a scone beside them. "Some things can't be changed. Ya 'ave ta do the hard thing by facing troubles." She set the plate in front of Daniel.

154

"You've heard the talk." Daniel rested his arms on either side of the plate.

"I 'ave." Lily faced him squarely. "Yer up ta the test."

Carrying Audry against her shoulder, Rebecca walked into the kitchen. "Good morning." She smiled at Daniel. "You slept late. Are you all right?"

"Sleepless night is all."

Joseph followed his mother into the room, hopping instead of walking. "G'day," he said climbing onto his chair. "I'm hungry." He smiled, and his pink cheeks plumped.

"Good, then. I made ya a fine breakfast." Lily set a plate with a scone and an egg in front of the youngster. Joseph took a bite of his scone and then climbed down and galloped around the kitchen.

"Joseph, sit down and eat your breakfast," Rebecca said, sitting at the table. She looked at Audry, who contentedly sucked on her fist.

Joseph stopped for a moment and then galloped back around the table and clambered onto his chair. He took another bite of scone.

"I'm absolutely famished," Rebecca said.

Willa walked into the kitchen. "Good morning. It's lovely, isn't it? Cool and sunny. My favorite sort of day."

Daniel nodded and took a bite of egg. "Cool for October, I'd say."

"Ya like some breakfast, mum?" Lily asked Willa.

"Just a scone, please. No eggs." Willa took a sip of tea. "Did I hear you say you didn't sleep well, Daniel?"

"Couldn't turn off my thoughts." He sampled his scone.

"I must say, the house felt a bit unsettled last night."

Rebecca's and Daniel's eyes met. Her look told him not to say anything about her evening's experience.

"I could hear the didgeridoo in the distance late. Must have been some sort of special night for the blacks."

"Right. I heard it too. That might explain the sense of activity." Daniel ate the last of his eggs and took another bite of his scone, then pushed his plate away. "I've got work to do." He stood and leaned toward Rebecca, dropping a kiss on her cheek. "Have a good day, luv."

"Should I look into the possibility of taking a holiday?" she asked.

"No. I can do that. I'll be in town."

"You going on holiday?" Willa asked.

"Right. We thought it a fine idea," Daniel said. "And the perfect spot would be the Pattersons' cottage north of Brisbane."

"Oh yes. It's a lovely place. It's been so long since we've been there. The last time was before Bertram . . ." She hesitated. "Before Bertram left us. Actually, it was before Rebecca came to Douloo." She smiled gently. "You'll like it, dear."

"I'm sure I will." Rebecca looked at Daniel. "Can we go soon?"

"If you think the baby is up to it."

"She seems sturdy," Rebecca said, glancing at the infant. "I could take Callie with me. She'd be a help."

"That's a fine idea." Daniel moved toward the back door, his mind on Marshal. The idea of disrupting his holiday to meet with the man made Daniel almost wish he weren't going. But there was no way to avoid it. It had to be done.

🍵

After an exciting two-day stay in Brisbane, Daniel, Rebecca, Callie, and the baby prepared to travel north to the cottage on the coast. There'd been no mention of Marshal. Daniel and Rebecca both knew it would be necessary to meet with him, but neither was willing to allow the obligation to ruin their holiday.

Daniel handed Callie and then Rebecca up into a surrey. Rebecca held Audry against her chest. Daniel took the front seat. "I've had a grand time of it. Now we're off to the coast."

"It's been lovely," Rebecca said, moving Audry to her shoulder. "Brisbane is a charming city. And last night's concert was as good as any I've attended, even those in Boston."

"We'll come back, eh?"

"Yes. Soon." Rebecca was silent a moment, then she asked, "Do you intend to see Mr. Marshal?"

"Yes. But not until after we've had a few days at the beach." Daniel lifted the reins and whisked them across the horses' backsides. The animals set off at a brisk pace, and Brisbane soon fell away.

"It's beautiful here," Rebecca said, her eyes wandering over the lush forest pressing in around them. "But I can't help but think we ought to speak with Mr. Marshal as soon as possible and not wait."

"I want a couple of days to give what I'm going to say some thought. To clear my mind a bit."

"I suppose that's wise," Rebecca said, then turned quiet.

Several silent minutes passed, and then Callie said, "It's roight nice, 'ere, but I like ta see all 'round. Can't see for nothin'."

"I rather fancy the coast," Daniel said, the tranquillity of his surroundings soothing his worries.

Broad-leafed plants hugged the trunks of cedar and eucalyptus trees, whose limbs served as perches for countless birds. The variety of colors and voices offered an untamed symphony to passersby. The foliage parted, and an aqua sea with white sand beaches spread out below. Sunlight glinted off a quiet bay.

Rebecca sucked in a breath. "Oh, it's beautiful! I don't think I've ever seen anything so picturesque. Even my favorite spot overlooking the Massachusetts Bay wasn't this lovely." She leaned forward and rested her hand on Daniel's arm. "Thank you for bringing me."

"Wait until you see the cottage and the shoreline where we'll be staying. It's grand."

The cottage huddled among trees at the edge of the sand. Windows across the front provided a spectacular view of a quiet bay. It was ideal. There were no other homes nearby, so they would have absolute privacy.

"It's charming," Rebecca said, inspecting the cottage and then stepping out onto a small veranda, where she gazed at the sea. "I've never spent time in a place quite like this."

Callie gazed out for a moment. "Roight pretty." She turned to Rebecca. "Would ya like me ta see ta the bybie?"

"Yes. She was fed just before we left Brisbane. She ought to sleep for a bit."

Taking the infant, Callie said, "I'll see that she has a nap."

"Thank you." Rebecca watched Callie disappear into the back of the cottage.

Daniel stood behind Rebecca and circled his arms about her. "So you like it?"

"I love it." Rebecca leaned against him.

"Nothing is too good for you, luv." He kissed the top of her head.

Rebecca turned and faced him, studying his features.

Daniel couldn't remember Rebecca ever looking more beautiful. Dark tendrils of hair had come loose of their pins and framed her suntanned skin. Her dark eyes sought his. Passion swept through Daniel. He gently pressed his lips to Rebecca's, then kissed her ardently. For that moment the world with its troubles ceased. Daniel pulled her closer.

"I love you," Rebecca whispered. She rested her cheek against his shirt and burrowed in close.

Daniel gazed over her at the azure sea. "I thank God for

you." He kissed her again. "I don't know what I would do without you."

They stood like that for several moments, and then a large, brightly colored bird flew onto the veranda and lighted on the railing. Rustling its deep blue feathers, the bird gazed at them, seemingly unafraid.

"Oh my. I've never . . . ," Rebecca said.

Startled at Rebecca's voice, the visitor took to the air and swept back up into the woodland.

Keeping hold of Daniel's hands, Rebecca asked, "Shall we go for a swim?"

Daniel studied Rebecca's face, then pressed his lips to hers and murmured, "Not just yet, luv."

✿

Time had passed too quickly. Rebecca didn't want to leave the cottage. It meant facing the world and Marshal. If only she could remain in this place, where she felt embraced by the wilds and her husband's love.

The time here had been like a dream. She'd not allowed the brutality of the world to spoil the delicate bubble of delight that had surrounded her and Daniel. They'd roamed the beaches, played in the surf, picnicked, and made love. However, in the background trouble had huddled. And now it was time to face that trouble and Marshal. Rebecca had decided she'd speak to him. Daniel had tried to reason with him, but to no avail. Perhaps a woman's touch could make the difference.

She considered what she ought to tell Daniel. He'd be against her becoming involved. She poured his tea, then filled her own cup and sat across the table from him.

Daniel captured her hand. "What did you have in mind for the rest of the day?"

"I thought a picnic might be nice." Rebecca glanced at the white beach framed by heavy greenery on one side and the sea on the other. Waves curled toward shore, breaking and then washing onto the sand. "Perhaps we could collect shells."

"Sounds fine. Joseph will like them."

Rebecca felt a pang of sadness. It would most likely be a long while before she and Daniel spent another beautiful week like the one they'd just enjoyed. "I hope we don't wait too long before returning."

"I've decided we ought to come back before the year is out." He kissed her hand. "We'll bring Joseph next time."

"He'd have a grand time." Rebecca took an apple from a bowl of fruit sitting on the table and turned it over and over in her hands, studying its sheen. She needed to talk to Daniel about Marshal, but she didn't want to break the spell.

"Let's go for a walk," Daniel said. "Audry's sleeping, and last time I checked, Callie was reading a book."

"That sounds grand." Rebecca returned the apple to the bowl and grabbed Daniel's hand. "Callie, we're going to the beach," she called. "Be back soon."

She led Daniel toward the shoreline. Then, still holding hands, they ran, tough grasses whipping their legs and the sand giving way beneath their feet. Out of breath, Rebecca stopped, and clasping both of Daniel's hands, she leaned away from him and walked in a broad circle. Water swirled about her feet and ankles. Tilting her head back, she said, "I love it here."

Daniel laughed and swung her around. Together they tripped and fell into the shallow surf. Daniel reached down and swept up a handful of water, spraying Rebecca.

"Oh! You!" she cried, scooping up handfuls of saltwater and splashing him.

Daniel grabbed her and pulled her close. "We'll come back soon, eh?"

"Yes," Rebecca said, leaning against him. The sound of

breaking waves and the aroma of sea and forest applied a tranquil balm. The birds quieted, and the breeze turned soft.

Rebecca felt quiet inside as she watched the waves wash into the small bay. A curl of water swirled up around her feet and then withdrew, the receding water sucking the sand out from beneath her feet. Her thoughts turned dark. Rebecca considered Marshal's men and how they were like the waves, pulling the life of Douloo out from under the Thorntons.

"We have to stop them," she said.

"Them?"

"Mr. Marshal and his men. They'll destroy Douloo if we don't." She looked up at Daniel. "When do you plan to talk to him again?"

"Tomorrow. Afterward we'll spend the night at a hotel and then take the train the next morning."

Rebecca nodded. "I'd like to speak to him. Would you mind?"

"I'd rather you didn't. He's an unsavory bloke. It's not fitting for you to be involved."

"I know, but you've already talked with him and managed to get nowhere. I thought that maybe a woman . . . well, a woman might be able to appeal to him."

"I doubt anything will budge him." The blue in Daniel's eyes cooled. "I don't want you having anything to do with a man like him."

"Please. Let me try. You'll be there. I won't be alone."

Daniel kicked at a rippling wave. "All right. You can speak to him." He looked grief stricken.

"Daniel, don't torment yourself." Rebecca moved close to him. "Everyone makes mistakes." She circled her arms about his waist. A breeze ruffled his blond hair, and she smoothed it back. "You can't do everything right. No one does."

"Yeah, but why this mistake?"

Rebecca caressed the worry lines out of his forehead. "We must trust the Lord."

"Wish I'd done that from the beginning."

✻

Staying close to Daniel, Rebecca stared at the broad shoulders of the surly man who'd met them at the front desk of Marshal's office. His gait was fast and determined. Following him into the darkness of the building made Rebecca uneasy. Were they doing the right thing? Or were they merely giving Marshal the opportunity to carry out another of his despicable deeds?

The man didn't stop at the office door. He turned the knob and walked inside. "Someone ta see ya."

"Ah, Mr. Thornton. Come in." Marshal's small mouth turned up in a deceptive smile. His cold gaze landed on Rebecca. "This must be Mrs. Thornton?"

"Yes." Daniel kept his face a mask of determination. "We've business to discuss."

"With your wife present?"

"My wife's my partner, and I welcome her involvement."

Rebecca felt a surge of love and pride for Daniel. She'd never find a finer man.

"Have a seat," Marshal said, dropping into a plush chair. Draping one leg over the other, he lit a cigar. He puffed, and the acrid smoke swirled about him.

Daniel and Rebecca remained standing. "Are you aware of the damage your men have done?" Rebecca asked.

Marshal's eyes went to Daniel. "You allow her to speak for you?"

"She can have her say."

Rebecca continued, "Your men frightened our entire household, and they hanged one of our roustabouts."

162

"Oh yes. I heard about that. He was just a blackfella, right?"

"He was a man with a wife and children," Rebecca said.

Marshal leveled a detached look at her. "I can understand your being upset, but that was the point, wasn't it?" He studied his cigar, then put it to his lips and puffed. "I figure you're here to pay your loan."

"I can't pay you right away," Daniel said. "I'll need two more months. As I said before, it takes time to get a station back on its feet after a drought. And we had the fire as well."

"I thought I made it clear." Marshal pushed his cigar into an ornate glass ashtray. "There will be no more delays." He stood. "I was quite specific when we started this venture. I can't have blokes thinking they can pay me whenever they feel like it—whenever it suits them. Then where would I be?"

"And I thought you understood that I wasn't sure when I'd be able to pay you but that it would be soon. I'm good to my word. You'll have your money."

"Soon is not soon enough." Marshal leaned on the table, resting his weight on bent knuckles.

"Mr. Marshal, what my husband is trying to say is that we have every intention of paying you. We always pay our loans. However, if you insist on using heavy-handed tactics, we'll be forced to have you arrested."

"Arrested?" Marshal chuckled. "Go right ahead, little lady. You try." He narrowed his eyes and looked at Daniel. "I believe your husband and I already discussed the topic of the police. There's no one in Brisbane who'll touch me."

If it was possible, Marshal's expression became harder. "You'll pay me and you'll pay me now, or you'll hand over your precious station." Sweat beaded up on his face, and his nostrils flared.

"That's impossible," Rebecca said, straightening her spine

and hoping her fear and disgust weren't evident. "We'll need more time, but . . . will you consider something as a down payment in the meantime?"

"Something? Such as?"

"I've a superb mare and her colt. They're the finest in the district, possibly in all of Queensland. She's worth a fair amount. I'd be willing to hand her over to you until we're able to make our next payment."

"There will be no 'payments.' You've gone beyond that. All I'll accept is payment in full." He sneered. "A mare and a colt? You expect me to take you seriously when you make offers like that?"

Rebecca didn't know what else she could propose. "Please, Mr. Marshal, you'll be far better off—"

"Rebecca," Daniel said, his voice hard. "We've given him an offer, a fair one. He can take it or leave it."

Marshal moved from behind the desk and stood directly in front of Daniel. "Your payment in full or the station. If not, anything more happening out your way will be your doing. And from what I've heard, you have a real nice little family out there on the flats. I'm sure you'd hate to see anything happen to them."

"Don't threaten me or my family." Daniel glared at Marshal, then took Rebecca's arm. "Come on. We're leaving."

He strode toward the door. The man who'd seen them in stood and blocked their way.

"Let 'em go," Marshal said.

"I don't give way easily," Daniel said.

Marshal sneered. "But give way you will."

15

Exhausted and discouraged, Rebecca sat in the surrey beside Willa. Although the morning air was cool, she didn't feel refreshed. The journey home from the coast had not been pleasant. She and Daniel had argued. He wanted her and the children to return to Boston where they would be safe, and she'd refused. She couldn't leave him, not while he was in the midst of this terrible strife. Her place was at his side.

Today's gathering at the Taylors' was meant to be a break from the day-to-day strain of living, but Rebecca could summon little enthusiasm for the social gathering and sheep shearing, although she did look forward to a good chat with Cambria. Perhaps her friend could offer guidance.

She watched Daniel, who rode alongside Jim. The two moved just ahead of the surrey. Daniel sat his horse well, holding the reins lightly, but Rebecca could see the tension in his shoulders. She knew his mind was on Marshal. He watched the landscape closely, looking for anything out of the ordinary.

Joseph leaned over from the front seat and planted a kiss on his mother's cheek.

"Love you." He smiled.

Rebecca tousled his blond hair. "I love you too. Now, you sit down. It's not safe to be up and about while we're driving."

He sat down hard and folded his arms over his chest. "Does shearing hurt?"

"No. I don't believe so."

Joseph was quiet a moment, then asked, "Can I shear?"

"No. You're too little."

He stood and leaned over the seat again. "I'm big. I can ride a horse."

"Yes, you can," Rebecca said softly. "But shearing is different. The clippers are too sharp for a little boy."

Pouting, Joseph turned around and dropped back down on the seat.

Willa looked at Rebecca. "Are you all right, dear?"

"Yes. Why do you ask?"

"Since returning from the coast, you seem preoccupied and a bit sad."

"I'm just tired. I haven't had time to rest from the trip." Rebecca wanted to talk with Willa about all the events and questions that had plagued her since Marshal's men first appeared at Douloo, but she didn't want to worry her. And what good would it do to talk with her about it anyway?

"You know, the Lord admonishes us to share one another's burdens."

Rebecca smiled. "Yes. I know." She let out a sigh. "All right, then. I am worried, about Mr. Marshal and what he'll do next."

"Even great challenges aren't too big a problem for God."

"I agree, but I can't seem to stop fretting. And Daniel wants me and the children to go to Boston—just for a while. I don't want to leave."

"Perhaps you should."

"What about the power of God you just declared?"

Maintaining her calm, Willa said, "He asks us to be prudent. And if you were to go, Daniel wouldn't be so worried about you and the children." She looked at her hands folded in her lap, then at Rebecca. "I must say, if Bertram were facing similar circumstances, I'd stay."

Audry started to cry. Rebecca was thankful for the distraction. "You can't be hungry already, little lady." She bounced her gently, and she quieted. "What about now?" she asked Willa. "Will you stay?"

"I have to." She smiled slightly. "Not everyone can leave. I'll be needed."

Once more Joseph climbed halfway over the front seat and draped his upper torso between his mother and grandmother.

"There, now. There'll be none of that," Willa said sharply.

Immediately Joseph retreated to his place beside Woodman, his pout in place once more. It was well understood that when Willa used that tone, she meant business and one would be wise to obey.

"That's better," Willa said. "We haven't far to go."

"If you stay, I can't leave you."

Willa patted Rebecca's hand. "I'll be fine. The real concern is the children. Perhaps sending you off to Boston is what the Lord wants, and Mildred would be so pleased to have you there. She's not seen Audry yet."

Rebecca didn't answer. She watched Daniel, and her heart ached at the thought of leaving him.

Without looking at Rebecca, Willa asked, "How was your holiday? You've barely said a word."

"It was quite nice. The cottage was charming, and I don't think I've ever seen a prettier place. The beach was an unbelievable color, nearly white. And the aqua seas made the sandy beaches look even more spectacular. In some places the water is so clear you can see right to the ocean floor. And of course, there are lush forests. They were a delicious change." She glanced at the flat grasslands, which stretched away in all directions.

"I've always enjoyed the coast," Willa said.

"Did you and Bertram visit Brisbane often?"

"Yes, years ago. The boys always loved it." Willa's expression turned wistful.

"I wish it weren't so far to travel."

Willa remained quiet a few moments then said, "You told me about the scenery at the coast, but you didn't say anything about you and Daniel. Did you enjoy yourselves?"

"Yes. We had a wonderful time while at the coast." Rebecca didn't want to even think about her encounter with Marshal, but before she could stop the words, she was telling Willa about it. "I met that horrible Mr. Marshal."

"Oh. Really?"

"Yes. Foolishly I thought he might listen to me and make some sort of reasonable compromise. But he's just dreadful. He didn't hear a word I said. He doesn't care about anything or anyone. And he'd like to get his hands on Douloo. We were told to either pay him on the spot or he'd come and take the station."

"Oh dear. Why didn't you say something about this?"

"What good would it have done?"

"I would have known how best to pray. And I could have been a better support to you and Daniel."

"I didn't want to worry you. I'm sorry."

"I understand, dear, but we must be honest with each other and uphold one another." Willa clasped gloved hands in her lap. "We'll pray. And then wait to see what God does."

Rebecca nodded. "I'm scared. I don't know what's going to happen."

"God knows. And we can trust him."

"Daniel feels responsible."

"The responsibility does rest on him. All of it, including Dusty's death." Willa was quiet a moment. "I love my son and admire him, but he did make a terrible mistake."

Rebecca knew that Willa spoke the truth. She'd thought it

more than once. But she couldn't bear to think on it for the pain it caused. "Daniel would never have signed a contract with Mr. Marshal if he'd known what was going to come of it."

"Of course not, but we can't rely on our hindsight. He should have paid heed to God's Word. He knew what the Bible said about seeking earthly solutions to our problems." Willa's eyes teared. "It is a harsh lesson, for us all."

Rebecca looked at her husband, her heart aching. "He's suffering, and there's nothing I can do."

"God is compassionate and knows Daniel's heart. My son may have a rough go of it, but the Lord will see to him and to us."

Rebecca glanced at Joseph. He looked up at the sky and quickly opened and closed his eyes several times. She chuckled. "To be young again and discovering the world for the first time."

Rebecca smoothed Audry's dark hair. The little girl rested against her mother's chest. "I've heard that some of the men want to make a stand against Mr. Marshal. How do you feel about that?"

"I've heard the rumors. And I can't say, really. There's a part of me that wants to fight, but Daniel did borrow the money. He owes it to Mr. Marshal. He must make good on the loan."

"But Mr. Marshal's an evil man, and his terms are making it impossible for us to pay. He wants every penny we owe. Right now."

"Then I believe God will provide in the way he sees best."

"We can't live our lives honorably if we yield to bullies," Rebecca said, feeling her anger and hurt well up.

"I agree. But there are grave consequences to be considered." Willa reached across and patted Rebecca's arm. "We aren't going to solve this today. I think we ought to enjoy ourselves. It's time we had a bit of fun." A breeze caught

Willa's hair and whipped it into her eyes. She brushed it back off her face. "Put your worries aside, at least for today."

🦢

Wagons crowded the Taylor yard, and a paddock was congested with horses. Women set out food on long tables beneath a patch of trees, while children climbed wooden fences, chased one another around wagons, and clambered over a pile of hay. The men had gathered inside the woolshed. Two large corrals were crammed with bleating sheep waiting to be sheared.

Rebecca hadn't expected such a turnout. "I had no idea," she said, clutching Audry while she stepped out of the surrey.

Joseph squeezed past her and charged toward the woolshed.

"Joseph," she called.

He stopped and turned to look at his mother.

"You're not to go in there."

Daniel strode up to the youngster. "I'll keep an eye on him," he hollered so his voice would carry over the din of complaining sheep and laughing children. "You've a shoe untied, lad." He quickly tied the lace and then lifted the boy onto his shoulders.

"All right," Rebecca said. "Have fun."

Cambria set a pot on the table and straightened. "G'day," she called.

"Hello," Rebecca said loudly so she could be heard.

Willa looped an arm through Rebeccca's and guided her to a table. "It's a good thing the weather has been dry and the sheep won't need to be washed."

"Good ta see ya," Cambria said. Her eyes moved to Audry. "She's growing like a weed. I can hardly believe how big she is already."

170

"I can feel it too. My arms are tired from carrying her."

"Oh, let me have the bybie," Elle said, joining them. "What a precious lamb," she said, lifting Audry and smiling into her face. "She's a beaut, just like her mum." Audry smiled. "And bright too, eh?" She planted a kiss on the baby's cheek. "I wish I'd had bybies of me own. Although I must admit to never having missed the company of a man." With a sigh, she added, "Now days I'm too old for me own bybies, but I love 'em just the same." She grinned.

"She's taken with you," Rebecca said.

"Mind if I take her with me while I have a bite ta eat?"

"No. Go right ahead. She's content with you."

Elle winked at Rebecca before turning and walking back to a group of women sitting at a table. Her attention on her granddaughter, Willa followed Elle. Rebecca smiled as she watched the ladies fuss over her daughter.

"Hey there," Jim said to Cambria, striding across the yard and joining the two women.

"G'day ta ya." Cambria smiled. "It's grand ta have ya 'ere. Maybe ya can give one of them sheep a tussle, eh?"

"Nope. Cattle's all I know. Don't like sheep much."

"Thought I'd seen enough of 'em ta last me a lifetime, but I'm going ta miss 'em after we're married."

"We'll keep one or two around for company, then," Jim said, resting an arm on Cambria's shoulders and giving her a squeeze.

Cambria laid her head against his shoulder for just a moment. "It won't be the same, but I s'pose I can get used ta cattle." She smiled, her blue eyes bright with mischief and affection. "Course, I still don't know when me wedding day is going ta be."

"Just as soon as I find a piece of land for us and build a house. I'm doing my best." Jim grinned. "I better get over to the shed. Always like to watch the shearing. Those fellas are pretty amazing—single-minded and fast."

"There'll be wagers made, I can assure ya," Cambria said. "I figure ya've got more on yer mind than just watching."

"Wagers? On what?" Rebecca asked.

"They'll lay down bets ta see which of 'em can shear a sheep the fastest."

"They're a spirited bunch," Jim said.

"I'd say the blokes are more like strutting roosters . . . so proud of themselves."

"Yeah, they're that, all right." Jim glanced at Mrs. Taylor, who was busy chatting with a neighbor. He planted a quick kiss on Cambria's cheek. "See you later." He strolled toward the woolshed.

Her face flushed, Cambria said, "Right. I'll see ya on the boards, then."

Jim stopped and called back to her, "Heard you can shear with the best of them."

"That I can. And I'll show ya too."

"Can't wait." Jim lifted his hat, bowed slightly, and then resettled the hat on his head and continued on.

Cambria took Rebecca's hand. "Come on, let's have a look at what we've got ta eat. I'm starving. Been up since before dawn. And the shearers were working soon as it turned light."

"Do you mind if I have a look at the shearing first?"

"Ya can't wait?"

"I'd rather not."

"Come along, then." Cambria smiled and headed for the barn.

Inside the odors of sweat, wool, and animal were overpowering. Rebecca covered her nose with her hand. "It smells awful."

Cambria grinned. "Too right."

The shed was a chaotic mix of men and sheep. Men hauled outraged sheep up from pens and handed them off to shearers, who laid the animals over one leg and clipped them free of their wool. Rebecca watched, amazed at the skill and speed with which the sheep were separated from their coats. While the animals complained, the shearers managed to get the wool off in one piece. When the shaving was finished, the wool was quickly scooped up and laid out on sorting tables while the seemingly traumatized creatures were passed off to another man, who shuffled them into a chute. The defrocked animals scrambled out of the shed, blinking in the bright sunlight.

"How do they do that?" Rebecca asked, watching a large man in a ragged shirt snip a sheep clean of its wool.

"It's not so hard as it looks. Just takes time ta learn is all. Holding them sheep'll break yer back though. Ya want ta have a go at it?"

"Oh no. I think not." Rebecca stepped back and watched the work.

Jim and Daniel stood side by side, hands in their pockets, clearly enthralled over the process even though they must have seen it done many times before. Joseph remained on his father's shoulders, obviously spellbound by what he was seeing. Mr. Taylor stood beside them, chewing tobacco and occasionally spitting brown juice on the floor.

"Me dad said it's a good year," Cambria said. "The sheep are healthy and there's no mud, so the work is easier. The drought took a lot of sheep, but things are better and the grass has been good, so we've had healthy sheep and mostly trouble-free lambing. Course, it's a bit late in the season. Had trouble finding shearers. Too many blokes needing 'em. But we're doing all right."

The two friends stood and watched for a while, and then Rebecca said, "I'm hungry. Let's get something to eat."

"Good. I'm starving." Cambria walked toward Jim.

Rebecca followed.

"I'm going for some lunch," Cambria said. "Ya ready?"

"Yeah." Jim smiled down at her, his brown eyes alight with admiration. "I could use a bite. How about you, Daniel?"

Daniel glanced at Rebecca. "Could do with some lunch." He patted Joseph's leg. "You hungry, lad?"

"Right hungry."

"Come along, then," Cambria said. "There's good food. Me mum's been cooking for days. We better get ta it before the shearers break ta eat. If they get ta the meal before us, we'll be picking at their leftovers."

Jim walked alongside Cambria. Daniel set Joseph on the ground and watched the youngster gallop off ahead of the adults.

Walking beside Rebecca, Daniel took her hand. "Jim said some of the blokes want ta help us out."

"They're going to give you a loan?" Rebecca asked, knowing that wasn't what he'd meant.

"No. Not exactly. There's a bunch of them who said they'd take a stand with me at Douloo. If Mr. Marshal comes to take possession, we'll stop him."

"Oh, Daniel, that sounds awfully dangerous. There must be another way."

"Can't think of one," Daniel said with determination. "But you and the children will have to be on your way. And, I hope, Mum too."

⯎

After Daniel and Jim had finished eating and returned to the woolshed, Rebecca and Cambria lingered at the table over a piece of lemon cake.

"Right good, eh?" Cambria said, chewing with satisfaction.

"Yes. Very." Rebecca took another bite. She watched as sheep disappeared into the barn and minutes later reappeared bald. She chuckled. "They look so peculiar and bewildered after their ordeal."

"Yais, they do at that. But I imagine it must feel good ta

have that load off." Cambria took another bite of cake. "Heard ya went on holiday ta the coast."

"Yes. It's beautiful there."

"That it is. Did ya have a nice time?"

"Yes, quite a fine time."

Cambria eyed her warily. "So what happened? Heard ya met with Mr. Marshal. Is he going to be reasonable?"

Rebecca set her fork on her plate. "No. He said he'll take Douloo."

"Can't say I'm surprised. Heard 'bout him before."

"Daniel is thinking of staying and fighting for it. He said some of the men in the district already promised to help."

"Right thing ta do."

"The idea frightens me."

"From what I can see, ya've no other choice. It's either that or walk away."

Rebecca hated the stark reality. "Maybe walking away would be better than risking lives."

"Maybe." Cambria picked up a crumb of cake and stuck it in her mouth. "Daniel couldn't do that though. Neither could I. And I'd say it was time Marshal was put in his place." She took a drink of water.

"Daniel wants me and the children to go to Boston until things are settled."

"Hate ta see ya go." Cambria was quiet a moment.

"I don't want to leave. Maybe you could talk to him."

"I couldn't do that. What if Joseph or Audry got hurt?"

Her appetite gone, Rebecca set down her plate. She watched Elle make over Audry. She knew it was wise to take the children to a safer place.

"So ya gonna go?"

"I haven't decided. Maybe."

Cambria swept away a fly that landed on her arm and watched as it lit on a partially eaten piece of bread. "I keep

175

thinking about Dusty and what those monsters did to him. Those men would kill anyone who gets in their way."

Rebecca nodded.

"I don't want ya ta go. Yer me best friend. But I couldn't stand it if something happened ta ya or the little ones." Cambria picked up her plate and glass. "I promised me mum I'd give her a hand with the dishes. I gotta go. Take care, eh?"

"I will. I better find Audry. She's probably getting hungry."

Rebecca looked for Elle, who had the little girl on her lap. Sorrow washed over her. She knew what she had to do. There was no other choice.

16

Rebecca stood beside the kitchen sink with a bowl of scraps pressed against her waist. "Joseph and I will feed the chickens."

"I'll feed the chooks," Callie said.

"No. We'd like to." Rebecca took Joseph's hand and led him out the back door. "Here, you take the feed," she said, dipping a small bowl into a barrel of ground corn and handing it to Joseph.

He held it against his body the same way his mother held her bowl. "Chickens hungry?"

"Yes. They're always hungry," Rebecca said, guiding the little boy down the porch steps. The morning air felt hot. Rebecca didn't relish what was certain to be a scorching day.

She moved toward the chicken yard, keeping an eye on Joseph, who very nearly tipped the feed out with every step. When she reached the pen door, she lifted the latch and stepped inside. Chickens flocked to her, strutting and clucking in expectation of breakfast.

Joseph stepped in behind his mother. Immediately he grabbed a handful of scratch from his bowl and threw it into the yard. Squawking and flapping their wings, the chickens mobbed the scattered feed and set to consuming it as quickly as they could.

Rebecca moved farther inside the enclosure and dumped the bowl of leftover vegetable greens and bread. Chickens swarmed the scraps. "You'd think they were starving the way they act."

Joseph tossed more scratch, and the chickens went after it. He giggled. "Hungry, eh?"

"They are. That's because they're working so hard to lay their eggs."

"Good eggs," Joseph said and dumped the last of the feed.

The sound of pounding hooves reached Rebecca, and apprehension swept through her. Pulling Joseph against her skirts, she gazed at the place she knew riders could first be seen when approaching the house. The three men who worked for Marshal rode into the yard, and Rebecca sucked in a breath and picked up Joseph. She hurried to the chicken house and pressed against the wall, hiding in the shadows. What did they want this time?

Daniel stepped out of the barn. He held a rifle in his hands.

Lord, save us, Rebecca prayed. She'd never known Daniel to keep a rifle with him. He'd been prepared for the men's return.

The riders stopped just steps in front of Daniel.

"Go on your way," he said, brandishing the rifle.

"What do ya think yer going ta do with that?" Jack asked. "Ya can't shoot all of us, not before we get ya."

Daniel ignored the question. "What do you want?"

"Ya've got some horses Mr. Marshal wants. We're here to get 'em for 'im." Jack rested his hands on his saddle horn.

Luke, the man Rebecca thought the most vicious of the three, picked up a whip and, before Daniel could respond, swept it over his head and allowed it to snake out and grab the rifle out of Daniel's hands. The gun fell to the ground in front of Luke's horse.

Then Luke flashed the whip again, only this time he aimed for Daniel, laying the lash across his cheek and leaving a cut. Blood dribbled from the wound.

Daniel pressed his hand to the gash. "What do you want?"

"Where's the mare and colt you promised Mr. Marshal?" Luke demanded.

"Chavive," Rebecca said in a frantic whisper. Carrying Joseph, she ran out of the chicken yard and handed the little boy to Willa, who stood at the bottom of the porch steps. "Keep him for me," she said, and holding her skirts out of the dirt, she hurried to Daniel.

"We never promised him any horses," Daniel said. "Marshal didn't agree to the deal." He wiped blood from his face.

Rebecca joined her husband.

"Well, he changed 'is mind." Jack's lip lifted on one side. "And we'll take 'em."

Rebecca's eyes turned to the paddock where Chavive and her colt stood. "It's understood that when the loan is paid they'll be returned," she said.

"Mr. Marshal will do as he likes." Jack's eyes were hard. "I'm supposed ta get the horses. That's all I know." He looked at Chavive and the colt, then nodded at Luke and Wade.

The two men dismounted and walked toward the paddock.

"They're fine animals and are used to being well cared for," Rebecca said, walking toward the corral. "You must look after them properly."

"Or you'll what?" Luke asked as he moved into the corral.

Rebecca knew giving instructions was foolish, but she hadn't been able to stop herself. She could feel tears pressing against the back of her eyes, but she willed them away. These men wouldn't see her cry.

Daniel joined her, resting a hand on her arm. "Rebecca," he whispered. "Don't."

"We'll take care of 'em." Jack's dark eyes found Daniel. "Ya pay the loan, or we'll be back."

Luke hooked a lead on Chavive, and Wade took the colt. They climbed back on their horses.

Rebecca moved toward Chavive.

"Stay back!" Luke yelled. Chavive whinnied and shied away from the man.

Rebecca stopped.

Wade stood aside with the colt. "What'll it hurt if she gives the horse a pat, eh?"

Luke looked at Jack.

"Right, then," Jack said. "Give the nag a pat if ya like."

Rebecca moved to Chavive and rested a hand on her neck. "Good girl. You'll be all right." She circled the horse's neck with her arms. Rebecca knew she'd most likely never see Chavive again. "You take care, now." She pressed her cheek against the mare's sunbaked coat.

"That's enough," Jack snapped.

Rebecca startled and stepped away from Chavive.

Jack yanked on his reins and turned his horse toward the road. "Ya don't want us ta come back. If we do, we'll be forced ta take something more valuable." He laughed and then kicked his horse and galloped off.

The other two followed, leading Chavive and the colt away.

Daniel pulled a weeping Rebecca into his arms. "It'll be all right, luv. You'll see. We'll get her back and the colt too." He glared at the men's backs. "But I won't have you in danger. You and the children will be on the next ship out of Brisbane."

ⅅ

Rebecca tucked one of Audry's stuffed animals into her trunk. She wouldn't need it while traveling. She closed the lid, hooked the latch, and then stood staring at the dark chest. She could feel tears pressing.

She sat on the bed and gazed out the window. *I don't want to leave Daniel.* Rebecca was torn between protecting her children and supporting her husband. She couldn't bear the thought of Daniel facing Marshal and his men alone.

She closed her eyes to pray, but instead, she saw Daniel and the bushrangers. The men would come back. She knew it. Dread filled her, and she felt it choking her. *Lord, please keep him safe. Stand with him. And with Willa.*

A soft rap sounded at her door. "Who is it?" Rebecca stood, quickly wiping away tears.

"It's Willa."

"Come in."

Willa opened the door and stepped into the room. Her gaze swept over the trunks and settled on Rebecca. "Is there anything I can do to help, dear?"

"No. I've finished. Woodman said he'd take the trunks and bags down this afternoon so the wagon will be ready in the morning."

Heavy silence pervaded the room. Willa clasped her hands in front of her. Her eyes glistened with tears. "I know this is difficult, but it's the right thing to do."

"I just wish there was another way. I want to stay with my husband. This is my home."

Willa moved to Rebecca and pulled her close. "I recall your first day here." Her voice trembled slightly. "You and that snake . . ." An unsteady smile touched her lips.

"I remember," Rebecca said. "I hadn't expected to find a reptile sharing the dunny with me."

"Indeed." Willa sniffled and took a step away from Rebecca, pressing her daughter-in-law's hands between hers. "When you stepped out of the surrey that first day, you looked so out of place. But I loved you right off."

Rebecca managed a tremulous smile.

"All will be well. You'll come home to us soon. I'm sure of it. And I'm pleased for Mildred. She's thrilled at your coming."

"I do want to see her and to visit Boston, but not without Daniel . . . and you." Her throat ached from holding back tears. "Must I go?"

Willa wiped away a tear. "Joseph is so excited to see America. He's heard it's a grand place. This will be an adventure for him."

"I suppose."

"Callie will be with you. And although I think she's a bit frightened about going and sad to leave Koora, I know she'll have a grand time of it as well." Willa smiled. "And she loves reading so. The trip will allow time for that."

"I promised to buy some new books to bring home with us. We need some for the school."

"I'm so sorry I won't be able to oversee the school while you're gone."

"Oh, it's too much for one person, especially with all that you're already responsible for. The children will be fine until I return."

Closing the school was another reason Rebecca hated to leave. The students had been doing so well. She chewed on her lower lip, sorrow welling up. Suddenly she blurted, "I'm afraid for Daniel. I couldn't bear it if something happened to him." Her tears fell freely. "He'll be alone."

"No he won't," Willa said. "He has me and his friends. And I wouldn't be surprised if Bertram is watching over him as well. And we can't forget the Lord." Willa straightened her spine. "Daniel will be fine. He's a strong, young man."

"I know that." Rebecca pulled a handkerchief out from the cuff where she'd tucked it. She dabbed at her eyes. "I'm just frightened. I'm afraid I'll never see him again."

"Of course you'll see him again. Nothing's going to happen to him. You'll only be gone a short time, and then you'll come back to us."

Rebecca moved to the bed and lifted a satin pillow. She ran her hand over it and then held it against her abdomen. "What if Daniel's right and God holds him accountable? Do you think God will let him die?" She could barely get the words out.

"No. I don't. It might be different if Daniel had no desire to please God. But the Lord sees a man's heart. And he doesn't expect perfection. It's not possible."

Rebecca nodded. "I'll think of you every day."

"I know you will. I'll pray for you and the children, and it will be such a grand reunion when you return." Willa moved to the door. "I'll see you in the morning, then."

"Yes. In the morning."

"Good night, dear." Willa left the room, closing the door softly.

⫷

Rebecca folded the last of her traveling clothes and put them in her bag, then went to check on the children. When she stepped into the nursery, she found Daniel standing over the crib, gazing down at Audry.

He looked up, his blue eyes mournful.

Rebecca joined him, clasping his hand in hers. She looked down at their sleeping daughter. "She's a wonder."

"Bright little thing," Daniel said, his voice tight.

Rebecca leaned against him. "I'm going to miss you so badly. I wish you could come with me."

"Next time, eh?"

"Joseph will miss you."

"Right. But he'll have you and Callie. And I'm sure your aunt will win his heart in no time."

"Yes. I'm sure of that." Rebecca leaned on the crib railing. "Callie would gladly trade places with you."

"She's never been anywhere but the flats. I suppose traveling halfway 'round the world must feel daunting."

"It does to me, and I've traveled quite a bit."

"But you'll be home soon." Daniel kissed her temple.

Rebecca rested her head against Daniel's shoulder.

"When I was tucking Joseph into bed, all he could talk about was going on the big boat and all the adventures he was going to have in America. He's glad for an adventure. Course, what little boy isn't."

"I'm sure he'll have a grand time." Rebecca didn't want to have an adventure. She wanted to stay here with her husband. She looked up at him. "Isn't there any way we can stay?"

"I wish you could. But I can't think of a better solution than your spending time with your aunt."

"You're sure we'll be home soon? This will be resolved quickly?"

"Yes. I promise you."

Rebecca burrowed against Daniel's chest, wrapping her arms about him. "I pray you're right."

$\mathcal{D}$

Woodman tended the horses while he waited for Rebecca and the children. Looking miserable, Koora sat on the front seat of the wagon that carried the luggage and trunks.

Rebecca stepped out of the house, pausing for a moment at the top of the steps. Daniel stood at the barn door and watched, his face lined with misery. She took a quieting breath and started down the steps.

Willa stood with Rebecca while Joseph ran across the yard

to his father. Daniel scooped up the little boy. "Well, lad. You have a fine time, now."

"I will."

Callie moved to the surrey, Audry in her arms.

Willa grasped Rebecca's hand. "I'll keep you in my prayers, dear."

Rebecca couldn't speak past the lump in her throat. She squeezed Willa's hand.

"He can do all things. Nothing is too difficult for God."

Rebecca nodded, watching Daniel play with Joseph. "I believe you." She hugged Willa.

The older woman's eyes brimmed with tears. "It's going to seem awfully quiet without the children." She forced a smile. "You tell Mildred hello for me."

"Of course."

Using a lace handkerchief, Willa dabbed at her eyes. She took Rebecca's arm and walked with her to the surrey. "Have a wonderful time, dear. And don't worry about us. We'll be fine." She hugged her again. "I love you."

"I love you too." Rebecca blinked away tears.

Woodman helped Callie into the surrey. She settled herself on a seat. "So yer off ta America, eh?" Woodman said.

"Yais. Decided it was time ta see a bit of the world." She glanced at a mournful Koora. "I'll be back soon though."

Daniel lifted Joseph onto his shoulders and walked toward Rebecca. "You be a good lad." He handed him down to Rebecca.

"I will," Joseph said.

Daniel reached into the surrey and rested a hand on Audry's dark curls, then leaned in and kissed her cheek. Stiffly he straightened and then tousled Joseph's hair. "Take good care of your mum."

Joseph smiled brightly and nodded.

Daniel's eyes rested on Rebecca's. "This is for the best."

"I know. But I'll miss you terribly." Rebecca gazed at his

warm, blue eyes and gently laid her hands on his cheeks. "You be careful. Don't take any chances." She couldn't stop the tears. "I love you."

Daniel pressed a kiss to her forehead. "We'll see each other again soon, luv. I promise."

17

Rebecca stood at the railing as the ship steamed through the waters of Moreton Bay and moved toward the open sea. As the green shoreline grew smaller, Rebecca held the lush foliage in her vision, unwilling to let it go. When individual trees and plants and the place where the green and the aqua shore merged, her mind carried her back to the day she'd first seen this shoreline. It had been a time of fear and disquiet. Yet even then the beauty had calmed her unease.

Callie gripped the top of the balustrade with one hand and clasped Audry against her with the other. Joseph stood beside his mother, peering at the open ocean. "It's big, eh?"

"What's big, dear?" Rebecca asked.

"Water's big."

"Yes. It is."

Her brown eyes wide, Callie gently bounced a fussing Audry. She moved the infant to her shoulder. "I don't know 'bout this, mum. Never been far from home." She gazed at the quickly disappearing coastline. "I'm wishin' I was at the station."

Rebecca rested a hand on Callie's shoulder. "Try not to be afraid. We're absolutely safe."

"It's not 'bout bein' safe, mum, but I don't know what's comin'. On the flats I know the earth, the songs that it sings, but 'ere, well . . ." She gazed out over the widening sea. "I know nothin' 'bout this place."

"You'll get used to it. And I think you'll find the journey thrilling. You introduced me to your culture; now I get to share mine." With a smile, she took Audry and settled the little girl in her arms. "It's not easy to let go of what's familiar. I remember being quite anxious when I left Boston." She cuddled Audry close. "If only Daniel were with us, this would be an exciting journey to my first home."

"Home, mum? I think yer leavin' yer home."

"Yes. That's true. But not for long."

Audry whimpered and started to cry. "She's hungry," Rebecca said. "I'll feed her."

Joseph peered around his mother at a little boy who was blowing hard on a small tin trumpet. The sound coming out of the instrument whined, and Rebecca wished he'd stop.

Joseph clutched the top of the railing, watching the boy as he paraded back and forth. Rebecca rested a hand on his shoulder. "Would you like to go down to the cabin with me and your sister?"

He shook his head no.

"I'll stay up 'ere with him, mum." Callie's brown eyes warmed. "The lad needs ta walk 'bout a bit, especially after all the riding he's been doin'. The fresh air will be good for us, eh?" She ruffled Joseph's blond hair.

"Can I stay?" Joseph looked up at his mother, eyes hopeful.

"Yes. Have fun." She looked at Callie. "I'll feed Audry and put her down for a nap. I think I could do with one myself. Please come to the cabin anytime you like."

Callie glanced at a man who had fixed his eyes on her. He wore a scowl and talked around a cigar resting on his lower lip. "They'll let just about anyone on steamships these days," he told a woman standing beside him.

The woman was fashionably dressed and looked to be in her twenties. Raising a well-defined eyebrow, she pulled her coat closer about her. "It would seem so."

"No need to worry. Most certainly a servant," the man said.

Callie's mouth was set, and her brows looked pinched. "Maybe I ought ta come with ya, mum."

"Certainly," Rebecca said. She'd heard the conversation, and outrage roiled through her. *People have no manners at all,* she thought. *No respect.*

Without even a moment to consider what she was about to do, Rebecca strode up to the man. "The *person* you're referring to is called Callie, and she's my friend."

Callie's eyes widened.

"She's been kind enough to help me while I travel. Two children are difficult to manage on a long journey. I would appreciate it if you would keep your rude comments to yourself. I've always believed that people with class possess genteel manners and treat others with benevolence. It appears you have neither." With that, she turned on her heel and walked away.

"Come along, Callie. I think we'd be more comfortable in our room." She glanced over her shoulder at the couple. If she weren't so angry, she would have laughed at their outraged expressions.

ÐĐ

Callie was shocked. She'd never seen Rebecca behave in such a manner, not toward strangers, anyway. And no white person had ever stood up for her against another white.

189

She followed Rebecca to their room and said under her breath, "Mum, I *am* a servant."

"I see you more as a friend, Callie. That's how I'd like things to be between us."

"Thank ya, mum. But ya best be careful. Ya 'ave no need for enemies."

"And you have no need to worry. Everything will be fine."

Callie knew better. Her mistress was asking for trouble, and if things turned out as they usually did, the blame would somehow land on her.

𝔇

The sea changed from aqua to gray, and the swells grew larger. Wind tugged at Rebecca's coat, and she pulled it closed at the neck. "I do hope we don't have foul weather right off," Rebecca said as a strong gust threatened to relieve her of her hat. She pressed a hand down on top of it. "I suppose we ought to go in for dinner."

"I'm not hungry," Joseph said, skipping back and forth between the bulkhead and the railing.

"Stay back from the railing." Rebecca held Audry closer and rested a hand over the infant's. "Oh my. Your hands are like ice. We best get you indoors."

Callie was cold. She rubbed her arms. "It's chilly 'ere. Not like home."

"Yes. And it will be much colder by the time we arrive in Boston. Winter will have arrived. The leaves will have fallen. I wish you could see the fall colors. They are so vivid—dressing the trees up in gold and red."

"Why are the trees gold and red, mum?"

"The leaves change color in the fall. It's lovely."

"Yais, mum. I believe ya," Callie said, but she was unconvinced and was more inclined to believe that this trip might be a mistake. It seemed a long way to go to escape Marshal. Better to stand up to a man like that.

"Are you hungry?"

"No. Anyway, I'll not be welcomed in the dining room."

The couple who had been so disagreeable earlier strolled past. Making no effort to disguise their contempt, they glanced at Rebecca and Callie and then looked away. Callie hoped Rebecca wouldn't say anything more to them. They passed without a word, and she let out a relieved sigh. "I'll wait in the room."

"Are you feeling all right?"

"No. Not so good."

Swinging his arms and propelling himself forward with both feet together, Joseph leaped toward Callie. "You sick, Callie?"

"I'm all roight."

"Are you sure?" Rebecca asked. "You look a bit off color."

Callie nodded, but she wasn't well at all. Her stomach churned, and she felt dizzy.

Rebecca rested her hand on Joseph's blond head. "Shall we have some dinner?"

"Food tastes bad."

"How can you know that? You've only had one meal. I'm sure they'll be serving something scrumptious tonight."

Joseph shrugged and leaned against his mother.

"Whether you want to or not, you must eat." Rebecca gazed out over the ocean. It looked dark and rough. "Seems we're in for a storm. I was hoping for good weather." She glanced at Joseph and Audry. "I've always done well, even in rough seas. I hope the children don't have any difficulty . . . or you."

"What ya mean, mum?"

"Some people get . . . sick while traveling by ship. Some utterly."

191

"Roight." Callie swallowed hard. She must be one of them. "I'll be fine, eh?"

"I pray so."

The weather turned violent, and the seas raised large swells that sent the ocean liner rolling. Each time they climbed up a wave and reeled over the top to ride it back down, Callie suppressed a moan. She lay in bed and tried to remain silent, thinking about the flats and their quiet voice.

Rebecca laid a cool compress on Callie's forehead. "There, that might help a bit."

"Mum," Callie removed the compress and pushed up on one arm. "It's not roight ya takin' care of me."

"And why not? You're sick and I'm not."

Joseph knelt beside the bed and rested his elbows on it. "Why you sick, Callie?"

A knock sounded at the door, and Joseph charged across the room and opened it. "G'day," he said, looking up at a tall, skinny steward who himself looked a bit off color.

"I have your tea, ma'am," he said, peering in at Rebecca.

She took the compress and dipped it in a bowl of cool water, then gently laid it on Callie's forehead again. "Could you put it on the bed stand here?" She looked at Callie. "I want you to try some tea. Perhaps it will settle your stomach."

"No, mum. I couldn't." Callie turned onto her side.

"You must try," Rebecca said gently. She glanced at the steward. "Would you pour a cup please?"

The man looked at her, confusion on his face, then did as he'd been asked and handed the cup to Rebecca. He stared at Callie a moment.

"That's all for now," Rebecca said, dismissing him.

The steward nodded and left the room.

Rebecca helped Callie sit up and held the cup to her lips. Callie stared at it, her dark complexion turning pale.

"Try," Rebecca urged. "I think a little something in your stomach might help."

"The only thing that will help is if the boat stops movin'," she said weakly.

"I can imagine how terrible you must feel. I remember the queasiness I had in the mornings when I was expecting Joseph. Tea seemed to help." She held the cup close to Callie's mouth. "Just try it."

Obediently Callie sipped. "I hope yer roight, mum. 'Cause I never felt so sick before."

⚶

The storm finally left them, and the steamer moved across quiet seas. As the days passed, Rebecca and the children explored the ship or Rebecca relaxed in a deck chair and read while Joseph played on the promenade deck. Callie remained in the cabin most of the time, except in the evening. Then she'd step out onto the deck and allow the breeze to swirl the smell of sea air about her. Sometimes the expansive ocean reminded her of the flats. She rather liked it and had to admit that its openness was especially grand.

One evening while she and Rebecca shared a meal, she asked, "Why ya keep ta yerself so much, mum? A young lydie like yerself ought ta be havin' some fun. Ya shouldn't be stuck with me."

"I don't mind your company. I prefer it, and I like solitude."

"Ya've seemed roight sad, mum."

"I am. I'm looking forward to seeing my aunt, but I can't seem to find any enthusiasm for this trip. I can't stop thinking about Daniel and Douloo. I keep wondering about Mr.

Marshal and those men. They're awful. I worry about Daniel and Willa." She blinked back tears.

"I don't know that leaving Douloo was the right decision, but I felt I must obey Daniel." Using a handkerchief, she dabbed at tears. "What if I never see him again?"

"Of course ya will."

"I want to believe that. But Mr. Marshal is a very determined and very evil man."

"Look, Mum! Look at me!" Joseph called as he leaped from one board to the next, moving along the promenade. He grinned at her.

Rebecca offered him a smile. "Well done."

Moving up and down the deck, Joseph continued practicing his jumps.

Rebecca set aside her book and moved to the railing. She gazed out at the sea. They'd come so far; in only two days they'd dock in San Francisco. She looked westward and wondered what Daniel might be doing at that very moment.

The breeze picked up and carried moisture into the air. Rebecca pulled her shawl closer. Since marrying Daniel, this would be her first Christmas away from him. Most likely there would be snow and ice in Boston. Before moving to Queensland, she'd expected Christmas weather to be cold. Now sharing Christmas breakfast on the veranda at Douloo seemed more fitting. A longing for home wrapped itself about Rebecca.

Tears stung. They came so easily these days. Dabbing at them, she glanced down to see Joseph standing beside her.

"You miss Daddy?"

Rebecca nodded and bent to hug her little boy.

"Me too. I want to go home."

"We'll go home soon. This visit is just for a little while." Rebecca smiled, but worry stirred inside. "We have an adventure ahead of us. There's so much to see and do in Boston. And your great aunt Mildred will be so happy to see you."

"But Daddy's missing us."

Rebecca hugged him again. "Yes. He is. But he's very busy working, and I'm sure he doesn't think about our being gone too much."

Callie approached, Audry in her arms. "Mum?"

"Why, hello. How good to see you out and about." Rebecca studied Callie a moment. She seemed preoccupied. "What is it? Is something wrong?"

"I was just needin' some air."

"I'll take the baby." Careful to keep Audry bundled inside her blanket, Rebecca cuddled her against her chest.

Callie leaned on the railing and looked out over the sea. "Was wonderin' 'bout Boston. What's it like?"

"Are you frightened?"

"No. Just wonderin' is all."

Rebecca suppressed a smile. "Boston's a fine city. A bit like Brisbane, actually, but larger. It's quite green, not like the flats. However, by the time we arrive, the weather will be cold. San Francisco's much warmer than Boston. We'll be taking the train from there across the country."

"How far is it ta Boston from San Francisco?"

"More than three thousand miles, I should think. A great distance."

"Is that like the trip from Thornton Creek ta Brisbane?"

"Oh no. Much farther. It will take us more than a week by train."

"I like riding trains." Callie closed her eyes and breathed deeply. "Smells good, eh?"

"Yes."

Callie opened her eyes and gazed at Rebecca. "Is it much different in America than in Australia?"

"Yes. I would say so. But different isn't bad. It's quite nice. In fact, the trains are much nicer and more comfortable than the one we took from Toowoomba to Brisbane."

"Nicer how?"

"The seats are more comfortable and newer. And there's no dust. The passenger cars are always kept clean. Plus, full meals are served in the dining car. And we'll have a private room for sleeping, plus toilet facilities."

"Yer 'avin' me on, mum." Callie grinned.

"No. We'll be staying in a sleeping car. Daniel insisted." Rebecca wondered if the sleeping car was too great an expense for the family's present situation. "And indoor plumbing is something you'll have to get used to." Audry whimpered, and Rebecca gently bounced her.

"How's that, mum?"

"We don't use a dunny in Boston. There are indoor lavatories with flushing toilets and running water."

"Sounds strange."

"Not really." Rebecca pulled the blanket up over the top of Audry's head. "I've never seen Thomas's home, but I'm certain it will be quite comfortable." Feeling a rush of pleasure, Rebecca continued, "I can't wait to show you the city. It's a fascinating place. We'll go to the symphony and the ballet. Would you like that?"

"I never been. What's a symphony and ballet?"

Rebecca chuckled. "Well, a symphony is a group of musicians who play instruments like violins, flutes, and cellos. They play music for an audience."

Callie nodded but still looked confused.

"And a ballet is an elegant style of dancing usually performed to symphonic music. The dance tells a story."

"I'd like ta see that." Callie grinned. "America is a fine place, eh?"

"Yes. Very."

"I wish Koora could see it. I'll tell him all 'bout America

when I get home. Or I'll write ta him. He can read some now."

"Are you and Koora serious about each other?"

Callie's color deepened. "Yais, mum. We plan ta wed when I get back."

"How wonderful! We'll have a party."

"Maybe, mum. I don't know that Koora would like that much."

✺

Rebecca, the children, and Callie spent one full day in San Francisco. They traveled the city, mostly on foot, looking inside shops and walking along the seashore.

The ocean was cool and the sandy beaches a darker color than the ones in Queensland, but it felt good to stroll along the shoreline. At the end of the day, they were grateful for comfortable beds.

Callie climbed into a bed across the room from Rebecca's. "Night, mum."

"Good night," Rebecca said, pulling the blanket up under her chin and staring at the ceiling.

She was exhausted but not sleepy. The sounds of the city spilled in through an open window. A man's tenor voice carried from somewhere nearby. He sang a lyrical tune unfamiliar to Rebecca, but she liked it. The song ended, and the clomping of horses' hooves passing on the street below replaced its lilt.

"I never seen nothin' like this place, mum. It's grand, but I don't think I fit 'ere," Callie said from the darkness.

"You must give it time. When I moved to Douloo, it took me quite a long while before I became accustomed to life there."

197

"Yais. I remember. Ya didn't fit. And now yer goin' where ya came from."

"Yes. Boston." Rebecca's melancholy returned. Douloo was home to her now, not Boston.

"We won't be stayin' long enough for me ta get comfortable though, will we?"

Rebecca rolled onto her side and tucked her pillow beneath her cheek. "I hope not."

The city sounds that had once comforted now seemed dissonant to Rebecca. She preferred the yelp of dingoes and the thump of kangaroos or the soft whisper of a dry breeze. The grasslands were tranquil and unhurried. She missed them.

⌘

The following morning passed in a blur of activity. After rising, breakfasting, preparing for the journey, and finally catching a hansom cab that took them to the train station, Rebecca was thankful to board. She carried Audry against her shoulder and kept a hold of Joseph's hand as they climbed the steps. Callie carried two bags, which contained just enough necessities to provide for their needs.

Rebecca moved down the aisle, searching for their compartment. Finally spotting it, she opened the door and stepped into the small room, then wearily dropped onto a seat.

Still hanging on to the luggage, Callie looked around the compartment. "Roight nice. Like ya said." Callie sat facing Rebecca.

"Yes." Rebecca didn't feel much like talking. Her thoughts were with Daniel. If only he was with her—then things would feel right.

"Mum, ya look sad."

"Guess I am."

"We 'ave a saying. There's a reason for all things. Nothin's on accident."

"Why, Callie, that sounds like it came right out of the Bible."

"No, mum. I remember me mum telling me ta trust whatever come me way, that there was good reason for it. And if ya accepted what was happenin', then good would touch ya." She smiled.

"I agree," Rebecca said. "It's just that I don't always easily accept my lot."

The train whistle blew, and the coach jerked and then slowly moved forward. Joseph sat on bent knees and pressed his face to the window. He remained there as the train picked up speed and the station dropped away behind them.

$$\mathcal{D}$$

Hours and then days passed. Rebecca's body was sore, and she longed for the comfort of her own bed and the security of Daniel's arms. The thought of him made her feel tense and lonely.

Lord, please take good care of him.

Callie watched open countryside slide past. "This is a grand place. As big as Australia, eh?"

"Yes. It startles me, actually."

Callie gazed out at plains that stretched to the horizon. "Looks like the flats, I'd say."

"It does at that."

"Is Boston like this?"

"Oh no. Nothing like this. It's green and hilly, and of course, there's the Atlantic Ocean. Its beaches aren't as spectacular as those in Queensland, but they're lovely all the same. The city is busy and sometimes a bit brash, but it has a special charm." She moved a sleeping Audry to her other shoulder.

"We may have already had our first snowfall. It can get quite cold this time of year."

"Don't like the cold much."

⁊⁊

By the time the train arrived at the station in Boston, Joseph was barely able to restrain his excitement while he waited for his mother to disembark. He ran up and down the aisle, then stepped back into their compartment, all the while talking about everything he had seen while the train approached the city.

Finally he asked, "Are we there, Mum?"

"Yes." Rebecca wasn't sure what she'd expected to feel when she arrived, but it hadn't been numbness.

Callie gazed at the city. "It's big. And there's so many people comin' and goin'."

"Can we get off?" Joseph asked.

Rebecca looked out at the bustling city, feeling a flush of anticipation. She suddenly couldn't wait to see her aunt.

"Mum," Joseph said.

"In a moment, Joseph. The train hasn't stopped completely."

Rebecca could see Mildred and Thomas standing on the platform. Mildred gripped a handkerchief in her hands, and Thomas had placed his arm protectively about her narrow shoulders. The heavy weight Rebecca had been carrying suddenly lifted. All she could think of was finding her way into Mildred's arms.

"Mummy, where is she?" Joseph asked.

"There. See? Right there." Rebecca pointed at Mildred.

"In the funny hat?"

"Yes. She's wearing the funny hat."

Obviously Mildred had been to the millinery shop and

200

purchased the latest Paris fashion. It didn't quite suit her, but it was grand to see her wearing the stylish hat with its large feather drooping down in back.

Callie carried Audry, and Rebecca held Joseph's hand as they moved down the aisle and stepped from the train. Unable to contain herself, Rebecca picked up Joseph and ran. "Auntie!"

The small, frail-looking woman stepped toward Rebecca. "Oh my! How wonderful to see you!" She pulled Rebecca and Joseph into her arms. "Oh, my dears, I've missed you so." She stepped back and studied Rebecca. "I wondered if I'd ever see you again."

"Of course you would. Even without the difficulties, I would have come to visit."

"Difficulties. You didn't say what was wrong, but I did wonder when you said Daniel was remaining at Douloo." She reached out and caressed Joseph's cheek, then looked at Rebecca. "Is everything all right between you two?"

"Yes. Everything's fine for us. But there is trouble. We'll talk more about it later. Right now I just want to enjoy your company."

18

Rebecca arranged her dark hair in a stylish coiffure and then secured it with a comb made of mother-of-pearl. She pinched each cheek twice and then stepped back from the mirror. Dark smudges stained the skin beneath her eyes, telling of sleepless nights.

Her mind wandered to Douloo and to Daniel. She could see him sitting atop his stallion with his hat down in front to shade his eyes. Her heart ached at the thought of him.

She moved to the window and gazed out on a white world. Snow had started falling that morning. However, the tranquillity Rebecca usually felt at the first snowfall was absent. Taking a deep breath, she gladly allowed her mind to return to the heated Queensland flatlands, with their grazing cattle and sheep, and the silence found in an empty meadow.

The doorbell chimed, dragging Rebecca back to Boston. With a sigh, she returned to the mirror. She didn't feel up to company. Why had Mildred invited dinner guests just now? She smoothed the collar of her heavy satin gown. If only Boston society allowed more practical dresses like the ones she'd grown accustomed to in Queensland. This gown was bulky and too tight at the waist.

"Being sensible is not a Boston attribute," she told her reflection.

Images of primping women and pompous, cigar-smoking men sprang to Rebecca's mind. She'd been in Boston only a few days, but already she'd had her fill. She'd forgotten how much she detested the pretentious behavior of many of Boston's upper class. Australia had its elite groups, but they didn't seem quite so ostentatious.

Rebecca gathered up her heavy skirts and hurried to Callie's room just down the hall. She'd insisted Callie sleep in one of the guest rooms rather than staying in the servants' quarters. Thomas and Mildred were agreeable but had expressed concern over the staff's possible negative reaction. As it turned out, they were right to be uneasy. Some of the servants had been miffed over a black Australian receiving preferential treatment.

I don't care what any of them think, Rebecca thought as she knocked on Callie's door.

"Who is it?" Callie asked from inside.

"Rebecca. May I come in?"

The door opened. "G'day, mum."

Rebecca looked at Callie, who was still dressed in her day clothes. "Why aren't you dressed?"

"I am dressed."

"No. I mean why aren't you dressed for the dinner party?"

"Not goin'," Callie said, moving to her bed and sitting down.

"Why? Are you ill?"

"No." Callie glanced at the window, then looked at Rebecca. "I don't belong, mum. Ya know that. Servants don't eat with family and never with guests."

"You're my friend, and I've invited you."

"Yais, and I thank ya for bein' kind, but it's not roight. And I can't do it."

Rebecca moved to the armoire and pulled out a cream-colored gown. "I had this cleaned and repaired just for you. It's one of my older gowns, but it's quite nice." She held it up against Callie. "It will look lovely on you. Please put it on and join us."

"Are ya tellin' me to, mum?"

"No. I won't order you about, but I'd truly enjoy your company. And I believe it's time some of the formalities in Boston were challenged." Rebecca handed Callie the gown.

Callie pressed it against her and looked down at its flowing skirt. "It's a grand dress. Roight pretty. But I don't want ta be changin' anything 'ere in Boston. This place doesn't mean anything ta me. I'll be glad ta go home ta Douloo."

"Me too. But right now we're here, and I thought you might like to be part of the family."

"But I'm not, mum. I know ya mean well, but yer helpin' is makin' things harder."

"How?"

"The cook and one of the housemaids is mad. I ought ta be sleepin' in the servants' quarters, not in this elegant room."

Rebecca moved to a straight-backed chair and sat. "I understand, but I want better for you."

"Mum, back at Douloo I live in me little cabin, and that's fine by me. And ya don't mind either."

Rebecca was taken aback. She stared at Callie. She was right. She'd never given Callie's position a thought. "You're right. I haven't minded. I'm sorry. I've been insensitive, and I'd like to make it up to you. Things will be different when we get home."

"I don't want them no different, mum. Things were roight fine."

"All right, then. But I'll do my best to be more considerate."

"Fine, mum. But I like ya just as ya are." Callie smiled.

Rebecca met Callie's gaze. "I like you too. Would you mind joining us for dinner? I understand if you don't want to, and

I won't be hurt if you choose not to. Perhaps you could come down for just a few minutes. I'd hoped the reverend and you might become acquainted. He's a fine man, and Thomas said his friends were thrilled at having an opportunity to learn more about Australia from a real Australian." Rebecca could see Callie's resolve falter. "Please, would you join us? I met Mr. White, and he seems quite nice." She smiled. "You might actually enjoy yourself."

With a sigh, Callie said, "All roight. But I'll need help. This dress is stiff and heavy. Don't know why ya wear such things." She looked down at her bare feet and then at a pair of shoes sitting beside the bed. "And the shoes ya gave me hurt. I don't know how ya manage."

Rebecca grinned. "I must admit there are times I've longed for the freedom you have."

"Yais, well since I left home, me feet 'ave 'ad little freedom."

Rebecca smiled. "I'm sorry, Callie. But here if you don't wear shoes your feet will freeze."

"Roight. Not used ta that." Her expression turned whimsical. "Been thinkin' 'bout Douloo. Do ya think we ought ta go back?"

"I wish we could, but I'd be going against Daniel's wishes. And I don't want the children in danger." Rebecca touched a strand of pearls about her neck, running a finger over the smooth orbs. "You miss it badly, don't you?"

"Yais. This is no place for me. And I got friends at Douloo."

"You mean Koora?"

A blush showed on Callie's dark face. "Others too."

"But it's Koora you think about mostly, right?"

"Yais, but no more than ya miss Daniel."

A pang of loneliness swelled beneath Rebecca's breast. Now was not the time to think about him and home.

Standing, she said matter-of-factly, "We'll have to talk about that another time. Right now we need to get you ready for Thomas and Mildred's party."

⳩

It was a small dinner party. Mildred had invited only three guests—Rev. Dalton Jones and Thomas's friend Bradley White and his wife, Heloise.

After checking on Audry, who slept in an upstairs bedroom, Rebecca moved down the hallway, her mind preoccupied with thoughts of the upcoming dinner. She would have preferred spending the evening alone in her room, but she couldn't lock herself away until it was time to return to Douloo.

She walked down the staircase, which led from the upper floor of Thomas and Mildred's modest home. Callie followed close behind.

In comparison to the open, bright living space of Douloo, this house felt almost tomblike in the winter darkness. No matter how many lanterns were lit, gloominess seemed to win out over the light, and cold penetrated every room in spite of well-tended fireplaces.

Mildred met Rebecca and Callie at the bottom of the staircase. A flicker of surprise lit her face when she saw Callie dressed for dinner. "You look lovely," she told Rebecca, kissing her cheek. "And you, Callie . . . that dress makes you look quite beautiful."

"Never seen meself that way."

Mildred rested a hand on Callie's arm. "I have some people I'd like you to meet."

Joseph, who stood beside Mildred, gazed up at Callie. "You look grand!"

Callie smiled. "Ya think so, eh?"

"Yep."

Mildred led the way into the parlor, where Thomas and

206

the guests waited. Joseph walked between his mother and Callie, holding their hands.

Rev. Jones pushed out of his chair, smiling warmly. "Good evening, Rebecca. How wonderful to see you again."

"It's good to see you, Reverend," Rebecca said. She meant it too. She'd always liked the reverend.

A rotund gentleman sat on the divan beside a plump woman who looked as if she'd squeezed into her velvet gown. Bradley White stood. His wife, Heloise, remained seated.

"Callie, I'd like to introduce Rev. Jones," Mildred said.

The short, slight man smiled. "A pleasure."

"Good ta meet ya, Reverend."

Mildred turned to Bradley. "And this is an old friend of Thomas's, Bradley White, and his wife, Heloise."

Thomas stepped into the room and joined Mildred, dropping a kiss on his wife's cheek. "You look pretty in that dress, Callie."

"Thank ya." Callie turned back to Bradley. "I've seen ya 'round before."

"Yes. I believe when I was here yesterday, I saw you . . . dusting the office."

"Roight." Callie held her body stiffly and stood close to Rebecca.

"She insists on keeping busy," Mildred said. She turned to Rebecca. "And, Bradley, you've met Rebecca."

"Yes. Delightful to see you again."

"It's good to see you."

"Rebecca, this is Heloise White. Heloise, this is my niece Rebecca Thornton."

Heloise's lips tightened, but she didn't smile as she gave Rebecca a slow nod, as if she were royalty of some kind.

"It's a pleasure," Rebecca said, glancing at Callie, whose natural tranquillity was absent.

Rebecca suddenly felt badly as she realized she shouldn't

have persuaded her to join them. *And I just promised to be more considerate*, she thought.

Bradley turned to Callie. "I've heard a lot about you. I've read some on Australia, and I figured one day I might like to visit."

"It's a grand place."

Perhaps it won't be so bad. Bradley's pleasant enough, Rebecca thought.

Heloise ignored Callie altogether.

"Well then, shall we go in to dinner?" Thomas asked. "Mildred's been cooking all afternoon. I'm sure we're in for a rare treat."

As Heloise was seated, she commented quietly that she'd never shared a meal with a servant. Her husband shushed her, but the words were out, and it was too late to take them back. After that the dining room atmosphere was strained. Between bites Rev. Jones made attempts at small talk. They fell flat. Thomas and Rebecca both made similar tries, but finally the group settled for rigid, polite conversation interspersed by long silent patches.

Joseph was the only relief. In a continuous discourse, he recounted the day's adventures of sledding and snowman building. More than once he nearly toppled off a pile of books he'd stacked up to boost him high enough at the table.

Once after nearly falling, he proudly stated, "I piled them. Aunt Mildred said I'm big enough."

"He's quite precocious, isn't he?" Heloise said, making his intelligence sound like something naughty.

"I'd say yes. He's quite exceptional." Rev. Jones smiled at Joseph and then at Rebecca. He studied Joseph's precarious seat. "It looks like you've done a fine job of stacking."

"Right," Joseph said. "I'm good at it."

The reverend chuckled and took a bite of roast beef.

"We've a special chair on order. It should arrive any day," Mildred explained.

"His stack of books seems to be working out fine." The reverend took another bite of beef and chewed slowly, savoring the flavor. "Delicious, Mildred. Thomas said you did all the cooking. Did you spend the day in the kitchen?"

"Not the entire day, but yes, I cooked the meal. It's a hobby, actually." Mildred beamed.

"I'll have to send my cook over for the recipe," the reverend said.

"My Mildred's a fine cook and insists on preparing meals when we have guests." Thomas reached across the table and patted her hand.

Still smiling, Mildred said, "Our cook, Agatha, is quite proficient, but I do enjoy being in the kitchen."

Quiet settled over the table while the guests turned their attention to their food. Rebecca noticed that Callie was being careful to use the proper utensils, and her table manners were impeccable. While serving at the Thornton household, she'd obviously been paying attention to decorum.

The aborigine kept her shoulders up and slightly back and her spine straight. She gripped her knife and fork tightly and hadn't uttered a word since sitting down.

I should have listened to her, Rebecca thought.

Heloise buttered a roll and set her knife on her plate. She glanced at Callie and then turned her attention to Rebecca. "I must say, I've always been a supporter of the abolitionists, but I've never actually known a Negro personally, other than as a servant, of course."

"Callie isn't a Negro. She's aborigine. They're not the same."

Heloise studied Callie, who kept her eyes down. "Oh yes, of course."

"Negroes are from Africa," Thomas explained, his voice touched with irritation. "Aborigines are from a completely different part of the world."

Callie set her knife and fork down and studied her plate

while she chewed. She glanced at Joseph, and when he grinned at her, she smiled.

The reverend asked, "Callie, can you tell us a little about yourself and your life in Australia? I know nothing of aborigine culture."

Callie looked at the reverend, her black eyes wide. "Not much ta say, sir. I live on Douloo and work for the Thorntons as a housemaid."

"And she also helps me with the school," Rebecca said. "She knows how to read and write."

"Really?" Heloise asked. "I didn't think Negroes were allowed to read."

"I'm not a Negro. And I read," Callie said evenly. "Most blacks don't know anything 'bout books. It was Rebecca who taught me. I like books roight well."

Rebecca smiled. "Callie's a good student. She's quite intelligent."

"Is that so?" Heloise took a bite of her roll. "I understand there's been trouble at your ranch. Is that why you've come all this way to Boston?"

The room suddenly felt overly warm, and Rebecca searched for a way to redirect the conversation. She wasn't prepared to discuss Douloo's difficulties. She hadn't even told her aunt the entire story.

The room turned silent. Rebecca cleared her throat. "There's been a drought. And then we had a fire. It was quite fierce and destroyed almost the entire station. We're rebuilding now. By the time I return home, everything should be in order."

"Is that why you've come to Boston?" Heloise pressed.

"No. Not really," Rebecca said. "It had been far too long since I'd seen my aunt. And she hadn't seen Audry. That's why we're here." She picked up her cup and took a sip of tea.

"Oh?" Heloise lifted a brow. "I thought there was more to it." She dabbed at her mouth with a napkin.

"No. Not at all," Rebecca said.

"Oh!" Callie cried. She pushed away from the table.

The Negro housemaid, Corliss, had spilled tea down the front of Callie's dress.

Callie stood, pulled the soggy, hot gown away from her, and wiped at the spill with her napkin. "Oh, yer dress, mum! It's ruined!"

"No. It's fine. It will come clean." Rebecca glanced at Corliss. She didn't look the least bit sorry.

Their eyes met, and immediately Corliss said, "So sorry. I'll get you something to clean that with."

"No. I'll clean it meself," Callie said. She turned to Mildred. "Roight fine meal, mum. Excuse me." With a quick nod, she hurried out of the room.

Mildred looked at her house servant. "I've never known you to be clumsy, Corliss."

"I'm real sorry, ma'am."

Mildred stared at Corliss as if unconvinced of her innocence. Finally she said, "Please make sure it's cleaned up properly. I don't want stains in the carpet."

When Corliss left the room, Heloise picked up her tea and sipped coyly, wearing a look that reminded Rebecca of a cat with a mouse trapped beneath its paws. "What a shame. I'd hoped to find out more about Australia."

Rebecca wanted to give her a verbal thrashing but bit back angry words. Heloise wasn't worth the energy.

Corliss returned with a washcloth and bucket of water and proceeded to clean up the spill. She worked quietly.

"You'd think you and that Australian were friends," Heloise said, as if accusing Rebecca of wrongdoing.

"She's our friend," Joseph said. "Right nice. And brave. She saved me . . . from the fire."

"How nice." Heloise folded her napkin and stood. "I have a terrible headache," she told her husband. "Would you call the carriage around?"

"I was just getting into the spirit of the evening," Bradley

211

said. "Thought we'd stay a while longer. I'd hoped to talk with Mrs. Thornton about Australia."

"You may do as you please, but I'm leaving." Dramatically she rested the back of her hand on her forehead. "I believe I'm ill."

"Oh dear," said Mildred. "I hope not."

Bradley almost smiled. "I'm sorry, dear. I'll have the driver take you home, but I'll stay a bit longer."

Surprise touched Heloise's face. "Fine." She turned to Mildred. "Thank you for the meal. However, I must say, it would have been more pleasant if there had been suitable dinner companions."

Mildred's eyes turned cool. "I found the company quite suitable. I'm sorry you can't see that." She stood. "I'll see you to the door."

Heloise glanced at those around the table, nodded stiffly, and then walked out of the room with Mildred and Bradley following.

When Mildred returned, she asked, "Shall we have our dessert in the parlor?"

"The parlor will be just fine," Thomas said.

"I'll have Corliss serve in there, then." Mildred walked toward the kitchen.

The reverend, Bradley, and Rebecca moved to the parlor. Thomas excused himself, explaining he'd left his pipe upstairs.

"I'm sorry about Heloise's display," Bradley said. "She's always been a bit high-strung."

"You needn't apologize for her. You're not responsible."

"Thank you for that." He patted his oversized belly. "I think I'll go in and see if your aunt needs any help with the dessert. It's one of my favorite parts of a meal." With that, he headed for the kitchen. Joseph skipped after him.

"I like him," Rebecca said, sitting in a straight-backed chair opposite Rev. Jones, who had settled on the settee.

"He's a good man." Resting an arm over the back of the

sofa, he took in a slow breath. "I think I overate. Mildred is too fine a cook."

"And if you hadn't eaten well, her feelings would have been hurt."

The reverend nodded. "I suppose. So I'm excused, then?"

"Absolutely."

He leaned forward and rested his arms on his thighs. "I don't mean to pry, Rebecca, but Thomas said there were some difficulties at your home in Queensland. Is there anything I might do to be of help?"

Rebecca had hoped the conversation would take a different tack. "There are some problems, but things will soon be set right."

"Do you mind if I inquire as to the nature of the trouble?"

"It's a bit complicated." Rebecca glanced toward the kitchen and wished Mildred would reappear with dessert. "With the drought and then the fire, we've been left in a bit of a financial bind. We're in a predicament, but my husband is doing all that he can."

"I see."

Rebecca clasped her hands and considered how much more to tell the reverend. "I love my husband very much. He's a fine man. However, he did get involved in a bad business arrangement."

"Does that have anything to do with why you're here?"

Rebecca longed to share her hurt with the reverend, but to do so would shame Daniel. He'd not want her to share his failings with a stranger.

"Thank you for being concerned, Reverend, but I'd rather not say more. However, I do ask for your prayers."

"You certainly have those."

19

Daniel swung a rope above his head and whistled at the cattle ambling along in front of him. The dust was thick, and the sun baked the earth and anyone unlucky enough to be out in the open. He'd always taken pleasure in driving a herd south, but this time he felt no satisfaction. Too much depended on his making good money.

The days felt long, and the heated, deserted land only fed his sense of emptiness and drained what little energy he possessed. The beauty of Queensland's expansive landscape, with its indomitable plants and trees, and the blue, hazy-looking mountains that sprawled along the distant horizon went unseen. He felt and saw only bleakness. The expansive lands no longer fed his soul.

He watched a goanna scuttle across a patch of open ground and disappear into a dry thatch of grass. Still gazing at the place the reptile had disappeared, he heard a screech overhead. Looking up, he spotted a wedge-tailed eagle. The bird soared, its broad wingspan carrying it easily on heated air currents. Daniel watched until the eagle disappeared. When it was gone, the sky seemed empty.

Daniel turned back to the cattle in front of him and resumed his work. His thoughts turned to Robert Marshal. *I shouldn't have made the deal. It was foolhardy.* He stared at the back of a heifer plodding along in front of him. *I've got to make a good deal on this mob. I need your help, Lord. They're in good shape, but there aren't enough of them.*

His gaze moved to the scene around him. Dust filled the air, blanketing the cattles' backs. Drovers, looking like apparitions in the swirling brown grime, whistled and called out to the moving, mooing herd.

Daniel's heart carried him to Rebecca. He missed her and the children. If he could make good money at the sale and pay off Marshal, he'd be able to bring them home.

"They'll be 'ere soon," he said aloud, as if speaking the words would make it happen.

Jim loped up to Daniel. "You need any help along here?" He scanned the ridge of an embankment that dropped off toward a river.

"Yeah. We need to move the cattle down to the water." Daniel lifted his hat, wiped his forehead with his shirtsleeve, and then resettled the hat. "Murderous hot, eh?"

"It's hot, all right."

"There's a good spot about a mile south of 'ere." Daniel sat up high in his saddle and lifted the lasso above his head, swinging it. "Hep, hep, hep," he called, following the herd.

Jim rode beside him.

"Tell the drovers to start moving them closer to the riverbank."

Jim nodded but didn't ride off.

"You needing company?" Daniel teased.

"Gets lonely working by yourself all day." Jim grinned.

"That it does. But we'll have time off soon enough."

"Heard there's an outbreak of typhoid down south. Might want to warn the blokes."

"Right," Daniel said. "I'll leave that to you."

Jim continued to ride alongside Daniel. Solemnly he said,

"You don't seem yourself. Been down in the mouth for weeks now."

Daniel nodded. "Right. I have been at that." He couldn't trust himself to say more. How would it look if he started blathering over his fears about Douloo and his missing Rebecca? He peered at the blue sky, then lowered his gaze to his friend and asked, "What if I lose Douloo?"

Jim didn't answer right away, then said, "You won't. I can't see it happening. You'll find a way."

"It's only a matter of time before those bushrangers find their way back to the station. They've shown what they're willing to do. No telling what we'll be facing next time."

"We've time. They took the horses as payment. No need to worry. After we sell off this mob, there'll be plenty of money."

"The herd's small. What if we don't get enough for it?"

"My mother would have said you're borrowing trouble."

"That might be."

"If there's not enough money to satisfy Marshal, then we'll stand up to him. There are plenty of blokes who'll lend a hand."

Daniel took a deep breath and let it out slowly. "Don't want it to come to that."

A gust of wind grabbed at his hat. He captured it and pressed it down more securely.

"Things don't always turn out the way we want. They are what they are. And then we have to do what's necessary," Jim said flatly.

"Know that. Don't like it though." Daniel whistled at a balky calf. "It would be easier if Rebecca were 'ere. She makes me stronger."

Jim leaned on his saddle horn. "Women are that way. Don't know what I'd do without Cambria."

"You're doing without her right now." Daniel winked.

"Yeah, well, we'll be home in a couple weeks."

Daniel nodded. "Rebecca's only been in Boston a few weeks. It'll be a long while before she sees home." The wind sighed and dust swirled.

"She'll be back before you know it."

"Yeah," Daniel said. "I just pray she has a place to come back to." He looked toward the northwest, and his heart thumped. A dark wall of dust moved toward them!

"We've a dust storm! Get the mob down the bank and into the gorge!" Daniel looked out over the herd and yelled at his men, "Dust storm! Move! Into the ravine! Now!"

He knew that if the drovers and cattle didn't find protection, a lot of the herd and maybe even men's lives could be lost. He'd seen bad dust storms before where men and animals had suffocated, choking on air thick with dirt.

He whistled and called, "Hep, hep, hep!" while he twirled his lasso, sometimes allowing it to stretch out and trace the hairs along the backs of nervous animals. "Come on, now. Get on down there." He steered them toward the steep incline. He'd hoped for a safer route, but there wasn't time. Reluctantly the animals surged over the rim and lunged down the embankment. Most kept their feet under them. A few stumbled and bawled as they tumbled toward the river. Daniel followed, leaning back against his saddle. It was steeper than he'd thought.

One rider went down, his horse tumbling and rolling over the top of him. For a moment all Daniel could see was dust and hooves. Frantic, bawling cattle swelled around the downed horse and rider. The drover stood and amidst the melee managed to grab the hand of another drover, who pulled him up behind him and onto the back of his horse. Daniel turned his attention to the mob in front of him.

The wind grew stronger. He could taste dirt. *We better find shelter quick*, he thought. Already he could see only a few feet in front of him. He sucked in thick, dry air. His throat felt like it was coated in coarse sand. He coughed, but that didn't help. He pulled his handkerchief up over his face. It cut some of the dust, but he still huffed as he sought oxygen for his lungs.

At the bottom of the ravine, the cattle bunched together. *That's the best we can hope for*, Daniel thought and turned his horse toward the embankment, searching for a place of refuge. There were no caves. The only protection was a hollowed-out spot in the bank. *That'll have to do. It would be enough for Woodman.* He moved toward it, searching for his men. The only one he could see was Jim. He pointed toward the opening in the hillside and kept moving. Jim followed.

Daniel dismounted and tied his horse to a scrub bush close to the embankment. Crouching against the dirt wall, he tightened his handkerchief, pulling it securely over his mouth and nose. Jim hunkered down beside him. Neither man spoke. There wasn't enough oxygen for that. And even if there had been, Daniel's throat was too dry to do anything more than croak.

His eyes met Jim's. He could see fear in his American friend. He offered a nod of reassurance, although he felt none himself.

Pulling his hat down over his eyes and face, he hunkered down. Wind and dirt pellets pummeled him. His thoughts turned to Rebecca. If he didn't survive, what would she do? What would happen to Douloo?

Keeping her back straight, Rebecca stared at the heavy curtains onstage. She could barely breathe. Mildred had pulled her stays too tight, saying the Paris fashions required she be securely cinched. Anything less would be inappropriate. Rebecca cared little about the latest fashions but hadn't wanted to disappoint her aunt, who had paid a considerable amount for the elegant gown.

"Oh," Mildred said. "Look there. Isn't that Mrs. Fullbright?"

Rebecca looked in the direction Mildred pointed. "Yes. I believe so."

Mildred gave Rebecca a secretive look. "I heard her daughter is back from Europe, and that her husband remained behind. I understand they're still married, but word has it—"

"Auntie! How can you gossip about something like that? I'm in a very similar situation, and I feel utter distress. We should think kindly toward her. We're in no situation to judge."

Mildred looked contrite. "You're absolutely right. I apologize. I just thought it might make you feel better to know that you're not the only one who had to return home without her husband."

Rebecca patted her aunt's hand. "I know your intentions were honorable. I'll be going home soon, I'm certain of it."

Mildred settled serious eyes on her niece. "Rebecca, just why are you here? I know you haven't told me everything."

"I told you, there was the fire, and all the work still to be done, and it had been far too long since I'd seen you, and then with Audry . . ."

"I know that's not the entire story. In truth, Audry is too young to travel so far. There's more to this visit than you're telling me." She smiled. "I wish it were just because you longed to see me, but I know that's only part of it. Why won't you tell me?" When Rebecca didn't answer right away, Mildred said, "That's all right. You don't have to share your secrets. You'll tell me when the time is right."

"It's a long story. And now's not the time," Rebecca said.

She didn't want to worry her aunt, and she couldn't bear for Mildred or Thomas to think poorly of Daniel. However, if he didn't send for her soon, she'd have to give them more of an explanation. She turned her gaze back to the stage. If only the ballet could chase away the loneliness and worry. She wished they'd hurry and turn down the lights so the dancers could begin. She yearned for music that could lift her out of the maelstrom of anxiety she'd been caught in.

Rebecca saw a woman staring at her and knew she ought to smile politely, but instead she looked away. What were people saying? That she'd become a loose woman or that she was seeking to divorce her husband? Were rumors flying like the ones about Mrs. Fullbright's daughter? Embarrassment and frustration welled up in Rebecca.

Let people think what they like, she decided, glancing about. She didn't belong in Boston anyway. This wasn't her life. In truth, she didn't want to be here among the "best" of Boston. She longed for quiet evenings on the veranda at Douloo. She needed Daniel beside her.

So did Joseph. He asked nearly every day how long it would be before they could go home. He talked about his father and all the things he couldn't wait to do—milking cows, riding, and fishing.

This isn't fair to him, Rebecca thought sadly. *I'm sorry, Joseph. I pray we'll go home soon.*

She leaned close to Mildred. "Auntie, I'm sorry if I was sharp with you. I didn't mean to be. It's just that I have a lot on my mind."

Mildred rested a hand on Rebecca's arm and gave her a gentle squeeze. "Perhaps if you shared some of your worries, you'd feel less burdened." She gazed at the stage, and Rebecca could see tears well up in her eyes. "We've never had any secrets, Rebecca."

"I know. And it's not about us. It's . . . well, I'll explain to you later. I promise."

"If you and Daniel are having marital difficulties, I can understand."

"Oh no. It's not that. Not at all."

Mildred smiled. "Well, thank the Lord for that."

"Daniel and I are fine. I love him so much, this separation

is squeezing the life out of me. You are so dear to me, but I long for home."

"Then why don't you go?"

"It's not so easy as all that."

Mildred nodded and concentrated on the stage.

From the beginning Rebecca had prayed, and yet God had not acted. He seemed far away; she felt alone.

"Excuse me." A tall gentleman stood in the aisle. "I apologize, but I do believe you're sitting in my seat."

"Oh," Rebecca exclaimed. She could barely catch her breath. For a moment she'd almost thought Daniel had been standing there. The man was tall and blond like Daniel, and his eyes were almost the same shade of blue.

"I am?" she managed to stammer and looked down the row. "Aren't these our seats?"

"Oh, it's my fault," Mildred said. "I sat down too quickly I'm afraid. My seat is the next one."

The man smiled warmly. "Then perhaps I could take that one."

"No. No." Mildred stood. "It's my error. I must have been distracted. I apologize . . . sir."

"Daniel Martin." He bowed slightly.

Daniel! Rebecca's mind shrieked. *His name is Daniel.*

"I'm Mildred Murdoc, and this is my niece Rebecca Thornton."

"A pleasure to meet you both. Please, sit. I'm sorry to have disturbed you."

Mildred and Rebecca took their new seats. Mildred looked across Rebecca at Mr. Martin. "Should I move down one more? Are you expecting someone?"

"No. I'm unaccompanied this evening. My companion became ill suddenly and was unable to attend. I rather enjoy the ballet, so I decided to come alone." He smiled. "Perhaps you can be my companions this evening." His eyes rested approvingly on Rebecca.

She felt panicked. Did he think she was single?

"My husband is at home," Mildred said. "He has no appreciation for the ballet. My niece was kind enough to accompany me. She's visiting from Australia."

"Australia, the land of mystery." Mr. Martin's blue eyes turned warm. "I've never been, but I've heard it's an extraordinary country."

"That it is," Rebecca said, feeling uncomfortable under his approving eye.

"It's not possible you left a husband so far behind?"

So here it is, then, Rebecca thought. "I did leave my husband at home but not permanently. I'm here to visit my aunt and her husband."

"Will you be staying long?"

"I don't actually know just yet."

"Then I presume your husband will be joining you?"

"No." Rebecca wished the ballet would begin.

"Perhaps I'll see you about, then."

"Perhaps." Rebecca gazed at the stage.

"I hope I'll have the pleasure of your company again before you leave."

Rebecca glanced at Mr. Martin. "You're very kind, but I doubt we'll have another encounter, sir."

Rebecca settled back in her seat and leaned as close to Mildred as she possibly could. She didn't feel comfortable sitting beside the bold man with the same look and name as her husband. She wished there were some way to exchange seats with her aunt without appearing rude or silly.

Finally the lights were turned down, and soft, lyrical music filled the theater. As the sound of the orchestra swelled, ballerinas glided onto the stage. Rebecca turned her attention to the performance, but only her eyes were on it. Her mind was in Queensland.

20

Worn out and lonely, Daniel rode across the yard and to the barn. None of his men had died in the dust storm, but that was about all he could be thankful for. He'd lost a good number of cattle. Lifting his hat, he shook off lingering dust. Dirt caked his hair, his clothes, and his shoes. A bath would do him good.

Woodman met him with a smile. "Ya look a bit done in. Ya 'ave a rough time of it?"

Daniel replaced his hat, dismounted, and handed the reins to Woodman. "It was bad."

"The dust storm?"

Daniel nodded. "How was it 'ere?"

"Roight unpleasant, I'd say. But we managed ta hang on ta most things. House was filled with dust, and we lost a few animals, but we done all roight."

Daniel nodded. He felt so weary that even the walk to the house seemed too much. He loosened the handkerchief around his neck and slipped it off. The inside was caked with dirt and sweat. Daniel glanced at the filthy cloth, then wadded it up in his hand.

"You don't suppose Mum's got any lemonade, eh?"

"I'd bet on it." Woodman smiled, and his brown face rounded.

"Good. Been thinking about Lily's lemonade for the last twenty miles." Daniel walked toward the house.

"I'll make sure yer horse is brushed and fed."

Daniel kept moving.

Willa met her son at the top of the steps. Ignoring the dirt clinging to him, she pulled Daniel into a motherly embrace. "So good to have you home. When that storm came through, I knew you'd be out in it. Did you lose any men?"

"No. Everyone made it."

"And the herd?"

"Didn't fare so well. Managed to get what was left to the stockyards though."

A crease of worry crossed Willa's forehead. "Is there enough to pay Mr. Marshal?"

"No. Can't keep on living and pay him." He frowned. "Course, if we don't pay him, we might not live anyway." Misery choked him.

"Come on, then. Have a seat. I'll get us something to drink."

"You have lemonade?"

"As a matter of fact, Lily made some this morning." Willa smiled. "I was hoping you'd show up."

Daniel dropped into a chair. "Thanks, Mum." He removed his hat and fanned himself with it. "Right hot."

"That it is," Willa said and stepped inside the house.

Daniel stared at the dirt yard. Renewed heartache swept over him as prior homecomings played through his mind. Joseph always rushed out to greet him, calling, "Daddy! Daddy!" The youngster would lift his arms, and Daniel would sweep him up and lift him over his head. Joseph would giggle and then hug his father about the neck.

Thinking of Rebecca, he dragged in a slow breath. Brown eyes radiating pleasure, she'd always meet him with Audry in her arms. After a kiss and a kind word, her questions about his well-being would begin.

Daniel returned to the present. Wind gusted, and heat radiated off the empty, quiet yard. There were no children now, no wife, and no idea of when they would return. Douloo felt bleak.

His mother stepped onto the porch. Handing Daniel a glass of lemonade, she said, "Perhaps this will give you a boost."

"I've been dreaming of it. Lily makes the best this side of the Great Dividing Range." He sipped, then took a large swig and downed nearly half the glass. "Good." He leaned back in his chair.

Willa took a few sips from her glass and then set it on the table between them. She studied Daniel, then asked gently, "Are you all right?"

Daniel didn't answer right away. What could he say? He nudged his hat up. "I'm tired, Mum. It was a long trip."

"And . . . ?"

"And I'm full of grief. I miss Rebecca and the children. And what am I going to do about Marshal? I promised to pay him after this run. We could lose Douloo."

"I don't know what to do about Mr. Marshal." Willa picked up her lemonade and studied the glass for a moment. "But I know about grief. Sometimes I think if only I could bring back your father, then everything would be set right again. Only, it's not possible for him to return, and even if he were here, life would still not be just right. This side of heaven it never will be. We'd be struggling; we always did."

Letting out a slow breath, Daniel leaned forward and rested his arms on his thighs. "This is bad, Mum. Don't know how we'll keep going. And I want Rebecca home."

"Then you should send for her." She smiled softly. "If only I could send for your father."

Daniel straightened. "I can't. If Marshal or his men show

up and something happens to Rebecca or the children . . . well, I couldn't live with that."

"I'm not sure I don't agree with you, but it doesn't feel right having them gone. And it's at times like this that families need each other." She ran a finger along the rim of her glass. "There's a fine line between being practical and being faithful. Sometimes it's not easy to make the right choice." She crossed her legs at the ankles.

Daniel stared at his mother. "I feel selfish bringing her back. Especially when I figure we'll be having another go 'round with Marshal. Soon as he finds out I can only pay a portion of what I owe, he'll be having a go at us." He shook his head. "Can't risk it. I'll have to do this without her." Daniel rotated his hat in his hands, then looked at his mother. "Don't know just what to do."

"You start by praying. Then you wait, and God will show you."

"I've been praying and waiting." Daniel thrust his feet out in front of him and leaned back into his chair. "I'm waiting to hear from God, but . . . I don't hear him talking."

"It'll come. He'll speak through his Word and through circumstances as well as wise counsel. And then you'll have peace when you know his will." Willa was quiet for a long moment, then added, "I think you ought to speak to Rush Linnell. He and your father were mates a long while. Maybe he can help."

"He's been mad ever since I brought Rebecca home. You know he wanted Meghan and me to marry. Don't think I can count on any help from him."

"I should think he has some loyalty to Douloo."

"Rush? No. His loyalty was to Dad." Daniel took another drink. "And that won't carry far. He's a businessman before he's anything else." Daniel set his glass on the table. "No. We can't rely on him."

"Daniel," Willa huffed. "Don't be so stubborn. Ask him.

It won't hurt to ask." She studied him a moment. "Well, it won't hurt anything but your pride. Can't you lay that aside to save Douloo?"

Daniel felt the sting of her words. He *was* being stubborn and prideful. "I'll talk to him."

"Good." Willa pushed out of her chair and moved to the porch railing. Resting her hands on it, she gazed out over the open prairie. "I've been thinking about poor Dusty and what happened to him. It would be a tragedy if something like that were to happen again. We can't allow it."

"What do you think we should do?"

"Accept help from the men in the district. We must unite and stand against Marshal."

"I thought you were against violence."

"I believe in avoiding it when possible. But there are times when it's all a man will hear." She turned and looked at Daniel. "If Rush won't give you the money, I think you need to challenge Mr. Marshal."

"How do I do that? We can't storm his office. He's got the whole constabulary in Brisbane on his side."

Willa chuckled. "I don't think it has to be all that dramatic, but you must do something. Rebecca, the children, and Callie need to come home." A breeze caught her skirts, and she smoothed them down. "You're not the only one missing your family, you know. Just this morning Lily was telling me how bereaved Koora is over Callie's absence."

"He's a good roustabout, that one," Daniel said. "He'll make a good husband to Callie one day."

"He has hopes and dreams bigger than that. He's counting on Rebecca returning to teach, and one day he hopes to know enough to do business with the men in the district. He's planning on having his own station one day."

"That's a big dream for a black man."

"Maybe so, but I think he can do it." Willa smoothed her

hair back off her face. "And Callie would be just the one to be at his side. Wouldn't it be grand?"

"He's a fine bloke."

Willa turned her gaze toward the corral. "Chavive and her colt belong here. We need to bring them home too."

Daniel let out a sigh. "Don't know that we can do that, Mum."

✑

When Daniel rode into Thornton Creek, he could still see his mother standing on the veranda, her soft features touched with hope. He'd also noticed more gray in her hair. The troubles were taking a toll on her. The time for waiting and praying for a solution was past. It was time to do something.

Rush Linnell and his daughter, Meghan, rode toward Daniel. He hadn't planned on speaking with Rush so soon, but it seemed God had other plans.

The Linnells slowed and stopped their horses. Facing Daniel, they waited in the street. "Ya look a bit done in," Rush said.

"Just came off a drive."

"Bad timing. Ghastly storm."

"Too right."

"Heard Rebecca's gone off ta America."

"Yeah. She's visiting her aunt."

Rush glanced up the street and then said, "Also heard there was more to it than that. Ya having trouble?"

Daniel wasn't ready to ask Rush for help. He hadn't even thought over what he ought to say. "I'm in a bit of a scrap, but we'll work things out."

"What, a scrap between you and Rebecca?" Meghan asked, unable to mask the hope in her voice.

228

"No. It doesn't have anything to do with Rebecca."

The light in Meghan's amber eyes dimmed.

Daniel turned his attention to Rush. "I did want to speak to you though."

"Well, I suppose this is as good a time as any, eh?"

Daniel watched dust whirl up in a wind gust. The current of warm air carried debris down the street. He looked at Rush. "I'm in a bad way, what with the drought and then the fire."

"Drought's easing. The rivers are coming up."

"Right. But I had to rebuild the house, the cottages, and the barns. I went to the bank for a loan . . ." Daniel hated to go on, loathed exposing his weakness. "Anyway, I got turned down, and Charles Oxley gave me the name of a man who might help. I went to see him—"

"Marshal? Robert Marshal?"

"Right. How did you know?"

"Word gets out." Rush scratched at a day's stubble. "He's a bad one."

"He's that, all right. He's been giving me a hard time. Killed one of my roustabouts. I figured on making enough on the sale of cattle to pay him, but the dust storm ended that. Killed more than half the herd."

"And what is it ya want from me?"

"I was hoping for a loan. I'm good for it. You know that."

"I do know that, lad. And I wish I could help. But we've been hard pressed by the drought. Just getting back on our feet."

"No worries, then. I'll manage."

"Don't know that you will." Rush spit, then looked up at Daniel. "Couldn't abide yer dad's place going to the likes of Marshal. If ya need me for anything else, I'm ready ta help."

Daniel's hopes of an easy answer evaporated. "Right, then."

Rush nodded, and he and Meghan moved on.

Daniel headed for the pub. It had been too long since he'd had a pint with the blokes.

⏝

Daniel pushed open the pub door and stepped inside. The room was poorly lit and smelled of stale cigars and ale. There was only a smattering of men. Women weren't allowed. Two men Daniel had never seen before sat at one end of the bar, smoking cigars and drinking ale. They were most likely waiting for the stage. John Oliver, one of the local ranchers, and Stephen Burstow were playing a game of cards.

A bushie sat at the far end of the room, his chair tipped back, his feet propped on a table. His head rested against the wall, and his eyes were closed, his mouth slack. *Good a place as any to sleep*, Daniel thought.

Patrick O'Brien, the man who owned the mercantile, sat at a small wooden table with Charles Oxley. Each had a pint in front of him. Deep in conversation, they didn't notice Daniel.

Most likely working out some sort of deal, Daniel decided, hoping Mr. Oxley didn't notice him. He wasn't in the mood to make polite conversation with a man who could have saved him a lot of trouble if he'd had a mind to.

Daniel walked to the bar. Resting his foot on a rail just above the floor, he leaned on the countertop and studied notices posted on a board on the back wall—there were herding pups for sale, someone needed a drover, and there was a piece of land for sale up north—nothing of interest.

Davis Crawford, the bartender, finished cleaning up a portion of the bar and then slung his towel over his shoulder. "Haven't seen ya in a while. How ya been?"

"Good," Daniel said, keeping his voice reserved. He didn't want to visit.

"What can I get you?" The bartender smoothed his red beard.

"Whiskey will do me fine." He laid down his money.

Davis took it and then filled a small glass. Daniel stared at the counter.

"Figure yer missing the wife, eh?" Davis set the drink on the bar.

Daniel nodded. "Yep." He stared at the whiskey, contemplating the wisdom of drinking it while feeling miserable. *No better time*, he reasoned and picked up the glass. Downing the fiery liquid, he choked back a cough.

"Who we got 'ere?" a booming voice asked from across the room.

Daniel didn't look up, hoping the voice wanted someone else.

"Come on, now. I never knew you to be unfriendly," John Oliver said. He crossed to Daniel, then slapped his back and draped an arm over his shoulders. The reeking odor of beer and foul breath descended on Daniel.

John grinned broadly. "Long time since I seen ya. Ya been good?"

"Fine."

"Not what I heard." He slapped Daniel's back again. "Come on over 'ere and join us. We could use another player to make the game interesting."

Before Daniel could object, John tightened his arm about his shoulders and hauled him across the room. When Daniel moved past Oxley, the banker smoothed his mustache and nodded at Daniel. He couldn't hold his gaze. "Daniel."

Anger rising, Daniel stared at the man. He wanted to tell him what he thought of his loaning practices.

"Daniel. Good ta see ya," Mr. O'Brien said. He glanced at John. "Seems he's had a bit too much grog, eh?"

231

"A bloke can never have too much," John said.

"I just came in for one drink. I've got business at home." Daniel tried to walk to the door, but John's grasp was too tight.

"Stay for a game of cards, eh? Heard ya been having a hard time of it. A little fun would be good for ya."

"Another time." Again Daniel took a step toward the door, but John held him fast.

"Heard yer having trouble with a snake from Brisbane. Figured it's time we showed him how we do business." John laughed, then looked around the room at the others. "What do ya say, eh? How 'bout we give our mate 'ere a hand."

"You got my help any time," Mr. O'Brien said.

"And mine," Stephen added, leaning so far back in his chair that he fell over backward. Wearing a sheepish grin, he quickly jumped to his feet.

"Ya 'ave my help too, lad," Davis said. "Heard what's been going on at your place." His eyes went to Mr. Oxley. "Crying shame, I say. Too bad no one could give ya a loan."

The room turned quiet, and every eye went to Mr. Oxley. He stood. "I've got a business to run. Can't be making bad loans, no matter who it is." He grabbed his hat off the chair next to him and pressed it down on his head. Without another word, he strode out of the room.

"Got no money, but we'll help ya any other way," John said. "Ya can count on me. I'm a pretty good shot." He grinned. The others added their assent.

"Well, I hope it won't come to that." Daniel moved toward the door. "Have a fine night, eh?" He tipped his hat. "I'll be on my way." Daniel stepped outside and breathed deeply of the early evening air. He felt stronger. He wasn't alone.

"You're quiet this evening, Callie," Rebecca said.

"Got nothin' ta say, mum." Callie carried a gown to Rebecca's closet and hung it up.

Rebecca returned to her embroidery, then watched Callie tidy the room. "I can take care of that."

"I like ta keep busy." She smoothed the skirt of another gown that had been draped over the back of a chair. "Roight pretty. I remember when ya wore this. It was the first night ya came ta Douloo." Her voice sounded sad. "It was a hot one, that day. The dress was too heavy, but I figure ya wanted ta look grand for Mr. and Mrs. Thornton."

"Yes. I remember. It was hot, and I was certain they hated me. Well, not Willa, but Bertram. And he did, actually."

"He was roight unhappy." Callie grinned.

"Oh yes, Bertram was fit to be tied. He'd had Meghan in mind for Daniel." Rebecca thought back to her early days at Douloo. She'd been miserable.

Callie stared at the gown. "I thought Mr. Thornton might send ya packin'." She looked at Rebecca. "Glad he didn't."

"I was afraid of him. He was rather intimidating. Even in the beginning, it wouldn't have taken much to convince me to go. Everything is so different there than here." Rebecca pushed her needle through fabric stretched across an embroidery hoop. "Of course, it wasn't long before I was devising a plan to escape. I thought Douloo was ugly and desolate."

"I remember when ya asked me 'bout life there. I was shocked ya wanted me ta answer yer questions."

Rebecca smiled. "Now all I do is dream about Douloo. I miss it so."

"Maybe ya ought ta think 'bout goin' home, mum?"

"I want to, but I'd be disobeying Daniel." She let her embroidery rest in her lap. "I wonder if he would be terribly angry with me if I went against his wishes."

"It takes a while for a post ta reach us. There's probably a letter on the way roight now askin' us ta return."

"And what if there isn't?"

Callie shrugged.

"You received a message yesterday."

"Yais."

"I can guess who wrote to you," Rebecca teased.

A soft smile touched Callie's lips. "Koora wrote it 'imself."

"He must have sent it the day we left."

"He wants us ta come back. And I'd like ta be home again."

"Hopefully, everything will be settled soon."

Callie compressed her lips, and the brown in her eyes looked almost black.

"What is it?"

"Nothin'."

"Yes. It is something."

"None of this is me business." Callie turned to leave. "I best get ta bed."

"Wait. Please, Callie. I need your opinion. It's important to me."

"It's not me place, mum. I'm no more than a servant."

"You know better."

Callie didn't speak.

"I want to know what you think about my going home."

Callie stared into the mirror on the bureau.

"Callie?"

She turned and looked at Rebecca. "Ya ought ta be with yer husband. Husbands and wives should be together in bad times."

"I agree, but if I return, I'm going against Daniel's wishes. And I endanger my children."

Callie glanced at the floor, then looked back at Rebecca. Finally in a hushed voice, she said, "Ya speak 'bout God and how great he is, and then ya don't trust him ta help.

Daniel, he went out and borrowed money from a bad man, and then he stands by and lets the man run yer life. That Mr. Marshal's tellin' ya what ta do. He killed off Dusty, and then he takes yer horses." She shook her head. "I don't understand. If ya believe and are prayin', then why ya here hidin'?"

Rebecca felt as if the wind had been knocked out of her. She didn't know how to reply.

"I shouldn't 'ave spoke," Callie said.

"No. You said what you thought. And what you said is right." Rebecca crossed to the window, pushed a heavy brocade drapery aside, and looked down on the street. Snow had turned the city white. Three boys had built walls of snow and now hid behind them while they pummeled each other with a stockpile of snowballs.

"It's true, we need to stand up to evil, not run from it."

Callie's eyes widened. "Mum, I'm confused. I've seen ya strong and brave, and I've seen ya act scrawny too. Sometimes it seems as if ya don't believe the things ya say 'bout God. Daniel needs ya now, and yer 'ere instead of there. I don't understand."

Guilt deluged Rebecca. She leaned her head against the cold glass of the window. "I'm sorry. I guess it must seem confusing." She turned to face Callie. "I do believe in a great and powerful God, and I know he loves me. Still, there are times when I lose sight of him and I'm afraid. It's human, I guess." Rebecca placed a hand on Callie's arm. "Please don't judge God by my weaknesses or Daniel's."

"I don't see ya as weak, mum. But yer scared when ya shouldn't be."

Rebecca took a deep breath. "I've been a poor example to you. I'm sorry." Rebecca walked to the bed stand and picked up her Bible. "This must be your truth, Callie. Not me. Not Daniel. The Word of God is the only truth."

"I can't get hold of it all. 'Ere people have so much—big

houses, fine clothes, lots of food. But people aren't happy. The aborigine way is better."

"But aborigines aren't always happy either. Nor are they without hardship. They experience hunger and sickness, hatred and evil."

Callie nodded slightly. "I don't know what ta believe."

Rebecca gazed at her Bible, ran her hand over the black leather, and then looked at Callie. "God will speak to you. He always speaks to those who search for truth."

21

Rebecca stood at the window and looked out on the street. Wind swirled snow into heaps that piled against buildings and fences. Feeling the chill, she pulled her shawl closer.

November had rolled into Boston with uncommon force and hadn't relented. Icicles hung from eaves, and fresh snow piled on top of frozen heaps left from previous storms. Rebecca's mind roamed to Queensland and Douloo, where the summer season was upon them. The idea of sunshine and heat was appealing. Dust seemed more tolerable than the icy cold of Boston. No matter how well tended the fires were, cold seeped into the house.

The front door whooshed open with a swirl of snow and cold air. Thomas stepped inside. "Brrr. It's freezing out there. And it's not yet Thanksgiving."

"Thomas, you look absolutely frozen," Rebecca said. "You must be careful. Weather like this can be treacherous."

He smiled at Rebecca and unwrapped his neck scarf. "I'm being careful." He removed his hat and hung it on a stand just inside the door. He smiled. "But thank you for caring."

Footsteps clicked across the vestibule tiles. "I was beginning to worry," Mildred said, stepping up to Thomas and planting a kiss on his cheek. "Oh, you poor dear. You're freezing." She pressed her palms against his cold cheeks.

His brown eyes warming, he said, "I'm feeling warmer already." He pulled Mildred close and kissed her.

"Thomas," she reprimanded playfully, pulling away and then helping him remove his coat. "I thought all you intended to do was purchase a turkey."

"Oh. I did that, all right. But I ran into a business acquaintance, and the next thing I knew, we were talking about mergers and the shortage of goods coming into the city. This weather isn't helping matters."

"Well, it would seem best if you did your business indoors on such a day."

"We did. But it wasn't far, and I decided to walk home."

Mildred smiled and then studied her husband. "Where is the turkey?"

"A delivery boy will bring it around tomorrow morning. That should give you enough time to prepare our feast." He chuckled and patted his stomach. "As if I need more food."

Watching them made Rebecca feel almost happy. It was grand to see her aunt and Thomas so content and in love. They'd found each other late in life, but that seemed to only intensify their enjoyment of one another. Remembering Daniel, she sighed. She'd be spending Thanksgiving without him.

"Oh. I nearly forgot. I have a letter for you." Thomas reached into his breast pocket and took out an envelope. He handed it to Rebecca. "Hope it's good news."

Rebecca's heart jumped. "From Daniel?" She glanced at the postal address. Cambria had sent it. Her expectations evaporated. Looking at Thomas, she said, "It's from my friend Cambria."

"Oh. Well, perhaps you'll hear from Daniel soon." Thomas offered Rebecca a compassionate smile.

"Perhaps," she said, walking into the parlor.

Dropping into a chair close to a stone fireplace, she unsealed the envelope, removed the letter, and opened it.

"Dear Rebecca," Cambria began. "It seems so long since you left. I've missed you and our afternoon rides. Sometimes I ride to Douloo and visit Willa. It makes me feel better, but as much as I love her, she's not you. The church feels rather empty without you and the children.

"I'm getting maudlin. Sorry. I do have grand news. Jim and I have actually set a date for our wedding—July 25. He finally found a piece of land. It's a fine place, and I'm sure we'll have a grand station one day. It will take a lot of work, but I don't mind. The property is east of Thornton Creek and not far from Douloo. We'll still be able to visit regularly. That is, when you come home. I pray that will be soon."

Cambria moved on to Jim and the house he was building. "He's already started work on our home, and he promises it'll be completed by July. That's why we're planning our wedding on July 25.

"I consider you my closest friend and can't imagine your not being here for my wedding. If you're to be my matron of honor, you must return."

Rebecca let the letter rest in her lap. July was months away. It wasn't possible that she wouldn't be home by then.

Rebecca closed her eyes and prayed, *Lord, please resolve this matter soon. Don't allow Mr. Marshal to take Douloo. Provide a way for us.*

She returned to reading the letter.

"Enough about the wedding. I saw Willa at my aunt's dress shop last week. She looks well and said she'd started a letter to you. She did admit that she misses you and the children terribly. Don't mention that I told you. She'd be unhappy with me if she knew."

Rebecca smiled. *Dear Willa.*

"Daniel joined Jim and me for dinner last week. I could tell you he's doing well, but that wouldn't be true. He looks

239

tired and is still trying to scrape together enough to pay that Mr. Marshal. A dust storm destroyed a great deal of the herd he was taking to the sale, and Mr. Marshal won't wait for payment."

Poor Daniel.

"I'd like to have a go at that man," Cambria continued. "I'm not feeling very charitable right now. But if you ask me, I don't see that Mr. Marshal deserves anyone's charity, not even God's."

Rebecca smiled. She had to agree with Cambria.

"Figure Daniel's getting lonely enough that he'd do almost anything to get you home. I'm praying he doesn't do anything foolish. I've known him a long while, and I've seen him unruly a time or two."

Again Rebecca prayed. *Father, help him to be strong and wise.* She rested her head against the back of the chair and closed her eyes. Envisioning Daniel, she could nearly hear his tender voice and catch the scent of him and his cotton work shirt. An ache, like a wave, flowed through her and pooled in her eyes. *I need to go home, Lord. Please, make a way.*

She wiped away the tears and then went back to reading the letter.

Cambria told her about the hot season and the summer storms they'd had. There'd been a grand party at one of the stations. She shared church happenings, including some of the sharp-tongued monologues by Elvina Walker. There'd been tiffs between Mr. Oxley and some of the people in the district. Others who'd suffered from his tightfisted business practices were more than happy for a reason to lay into him. Daniel, to his credit, had done all he could to quiet the antagonism. Cambria explained that there were some who had pledged to shoot Marshal on sight if they had the opportunity.

Rebecca pressed a hand against her abdomen. Her stomach ached. How had Daniel's attempt to help his family become

240

something so ugly? *Lord, he's a fine man. You know that. Why are you punishing him so?*

She looked back at the letter. Cambria finished with advice. "I know God wants you here with Daniel. He meant for you to be together. No matter what the obstacles, you can overcome them if you're together.

"That's all I have to write for now. I'll look for a letter from you, but I hope I see you in person before a letter can arrive. It would be grand if you could help me pick out my wedding gown. I admire your good taste. You're so elegant. Miss you. Come home soon."

If only I could go home, Rebecca thought, slipping the letter back inside its envelope. How would Daniel feel if she simply packed up and steamed home without his permission?

Mildred walked into the sitting room. "Rebecca dear . . ." Her words fell off. "Are you all right? Is it bad news?"

"No. Everything's fine. Cambria and Jim have set the date for their wedding—July 25," she said more cheerily than she felt. Taking a handkerchief from inside her cuff, she added, "I do need to talk with you though." Rebecca gently blew her nose.

Mildred sat in a chair beside her. "What is it?"

Rebecca took in a slow breath. "Cambria wants me to be her matron of honor."

"Oh, how nice. Cambria's a lovely girl, and Jim's a fine young man. They'll make a splendid couple."

"I agree. The wedding isn't until July. That's months away. You don't think it's possible I'll still be here, do you?"

"Oh, my heavens, I wouldn't think so. I'm sure whatever's troubling you and Daniel can be resolved by then." She turned quiet, then asked, "What is the trouble? You've been very vague about it."

"I know, and I'm sorry. You've been gracious in not asking. But I guess you do have a right to know."

"I'm not so certain I have any rights in this, but I would like to help if I can."

"I wish you could." Rebecca folded her handkerchief and tucked it back inside her cuff. "I haven't said anything to you because I didn't want you to worry, and I don't want you to think badly of Daniel. He's a fine man." Her eyes stung, and she quickly swallowed away the hurt. "You know how bad the drought was."

"Yes. It was dreadful," Mildred said.

"And then how much damage the fire caused."

"You told me, but I can only imagine how awful that must have been."

"It was frightful." Rebecca pressed a closed hand to her mouth. "We were in a bad way financially before the fire, and then after, well, things became worse. Daniel went to the bank and asked for a loan, but Mr. Oxley wouldn't give us a loan while the drought was still so bad. He told Daniel about a man, Mr. Marshal, who might be able to help."

"Help? In what way?"

"Mr. Oxley said he could give us a loan."

Mildred nodded but remained quiet.

"Daniel went to Brisbane to speak with Mr. Marshal . . . he's an American. He agreed to loan Daniel the money. But . . ." Rebecca could barely continue. "Mr. Marshal turned out to be a horrible man. Daniel agreed to pay high interest, but he never imagined what would happen if he missed a payment."

Understanding touched Mildred's eyes. "He's unable to pay on the debt?"

"No." Now that she'd decided to share, Rebecca needed to tell Mildred all of what had happened. "Mr. Marshal wasn't willing to wait for the money. He's done some terrible things."

"Oh dear. What has he done?"

"He sent some men to the station; they threatened Daniel,

and then when he couldn't pay what Mr. Marshal wanted, they came back and threatened me while I was teaching." Rebecca managed a smile. "I must say, Willa was quite a surprise that day. While keeping them in the sights of her rifle, she ordered them off the station, even threatened to kill them."

"Oh my!"

"Not long after that, they returned. That time they took one of the roustabouts and hanged him."

Mildred blanched.

"Daniel and Woodman tried to save poor Dusty, but the men shot them."

"Shot them! You never said anything about Daniel or Woodman being shot. Are they all right?"

"Yes. The wounds weren't serious, but they could have been."

"Why didn't you tell me?"

"I didn't want to worry you."

"Were the men jailed for their hideous actions?"

"No. Dusty was an aborigine. The law doesn't protect the aborigines. Actually, there isn't any law in Thornton Creek anyway."

"It sounds just dreadful. I must say you've done the right thing by coming here. I only wish Daniel would come to his senses and join you."

"Oh, Auntie, Daniel will never move here. I don't want him to. He loves Douloo, and so do I."

Mildred looked shocked. "You can't mean you want to go back with people like that roaming about?"

"Yes. I do. It's home. You know how we love it."

Mildred's expression turned soft. "I do. Even I have affection for Douloo."

She moved to the hearth. Picking up a cast-iron poker, Mildred nudged burning logs and coals into a more efficient stack. New flames flickered. She straightened and looked at

Rebecca. "But even you must admit that this is a terrifying state of affairs. Just the idea of you and the children being there under such circumstances is enough to make me shudder."

"I was frightened too, but now all I want is to go home."

"Is everything settled with Mr. Marshal?"

"No. He took Chavive and her foal as partial payment."

"Chavive. Oh, what a pity."

"I pray he'll return her when we've paid the balance, but I have little hope. He's an evil man."

"So what does Daniel intend to do?"

"He was going to pay off the debt with the last batch of cattle he sold, but they were caught in a dust storm and we lost a lot of them, so I don't know what he plans now."

Mildred moved to Rebecca and rested a hand on her shoulder. "I'm so sorry. I had no idea."

"I don't know what to do. I feel like I need to be with Daniel. I want to be with him, but I don't want to put the children in harm's way." The tears came freely now. It felt good to release them.

Mildred gave Rebecca's shoulder a squeeze. "We must give God time to work. He knows all about your trouble, and he will set it right."

"You don't think I should go back?"

"Well, that's a difficult question. I'm afraid my answer is tainted by my need to keep you safe. But if Daniel told you to wait, then that's what you ought to do. Honor your husband. He has enough to worry about. At least with you here, he knows you and the children are safe."

Rebecca nodded. "Willa said the same. It's just that I miss him so badly. And I know he misses us." She took out her handkerchief again and dabbed at drying tears. "Do you think God is punishing Daniel?"

Mildred thought and then said gently, "No. I don't believe that. It's possible the Lord is allowing circumstances to follow a natural course so Daniel will learn a very important lesson."

"But isn't that punishment?"

"Not really. If Daniel went to this man knowing he was an unsavory sort and that he shouldn't do business with him, and he went because he was unwilling to wait on the Lord, and then all had gone well—then what would he have learned?"

Rebecca could see the wisdom of her aunt's words. "You're right."

Mildred smiled. "When you've worked through all this trouble, you'll both be much wiser."

"I just wish it were already part of our past. I'm certain Daniel has learned the lesson."

"Oh, adversity is hard to bear, but this experience will become a building stone for you two. You'll see."

Wind gusted against the window, carrying a flurry of snow. "Even so, I'm still frightened, Auntie."

22

Weary, Daniel and Jim walked toward the barn. It had been a long day, and Daniel was glad to be done with it. "Better get this scrubbed off." He glanced down at bloodied hands and arms and blood-splattered clothes.

"Cambria said she'd be stopping by this afternoon."

"You figure she'll take kindly to calves' blood?" Daniel grinned.

"She's a country girl, but there's a limit. Castrating's not my favorite job either."

"If it was, I'd be a bit worried about you," Daniel teased.

Stripping off his shirt, he headed for the water barrel. He dropped the shirt on the ground. Jim's landed on top of Daniel's.

Dipping a bucket into the barrel, Daniel filled it and then set it on a bench alongside the barn. He grabbed a bar of soap off a shelf above the barrel and started scrubbing away the blood on his arms and hands. Jim did the same.

Woodman stepped out of the barn and watched. "The two of ya are a roight fine mess."

"We are at that," Daniel said.

Woodman filled another bucket with clean water and set it out. He picked up the shirts. "I'll 'ave the pants too."

"And what will you give us in return?" Daniel asked, scooping clean water and splashing it over his head. Sweeping back wet hair, he straightened. "I'll not be caught running 'round in my drawers."

Woodman grinned. "No faith in me, eh?" He nodded toward the interior of the barn. "There're clothes for ya in the tack room. Ya'll 'ave all the privacy ya need." His dark eyes glinted with mischief.

"Right, then." Daniel stripped off his jeans and handed them to the servant.

"Yer gettin' forgetful. Where's yer mind, eh? As long as ya been castratin' young bulls, I've made sure ya had somethin' ta wear afterward."

Daniel shrugged, unwilling to confess that his mind was on Rebecca. The longer she was gone, the more he longed for her.

⫶

Dressed in clean clothes, Jim and Daniel sat side by side on a wooden bench in the tack room. Jim pushed his foot into a boot and then pressed the sole against the floor. His foot slid in. "What you gonna do about Rebecca?"

Daniel shoved his foot into his own boot. "I miss her, but things aren't any better than they were. She'll have to stay put."

"You saw Marshal?"

"Yeah. Well, not him. I couldn't get past his bushrangers. Said he wouldn't see me. Took my money though. I didn't have enough to pay him all I owe. Figure we'll be getting a visit any day."

Involuntarily Jim glanced toward the door. "You think so?"

"Yeah. He's not going to give up."

"Wonder what they'll throw at us next."

"Can't say, but it won't be good." Daniel pulled his belt tighter. "You're free to go. This isn't your affair." He rested his forearms on his thighs and pressed his palms together. "No need for you to be in harm's way. Especially with your getting married."

Jim pressed his foot into his other boot. "It's bad timing, all right. But none of it is your fault. Could have been different if Oxley had given you a loan." He folded his arms over his chest. "And I'm not budging. You've got me, and that's the way of it. I won't desert you." He stared at Daniel. "Figured you'd know that."

"Guess I do at that." Daniel patted Jim's back. "Thanks, mate." He turned thoughtful. "But you're wrong. It is my fault. Oxley gave me Marshal's name, but then he told me not to contact him and threw the name and address in the trash." Daniel shook his head. "I dug it out."

"So you're saying that while we've all been mad at Oxley, this whole business has been your fault?" Jim winked.

"Right. And it's not funny."

"Too right, it's not funny." His expression turned hard. "Oxley should have given you a loan."

"Right. But I'm the one who went to see Marshal. I knew his sort right off, and I made the deal anyway." Daniel rested his elbows on his thighs, covered his face with his hands, and then slowly kneaded his forehead. Finally looking at Jim, he said, "I deserve what I get, but Dusty didn't deserve to die. And Rebecca and the kids and my mum don't deserve any of this." He blew out a quick breath. "My grandfather and my dad, everything they worked so hard for, I tossed it all away."

"I understand you're feeling bad, but there comes a time

when a bloke's got to let go of his guilt and move on. My grandmother used to say, 'No use crying over spilt milk.'" He stood. "Time to do something about it."

Daniel leaned against the wall, folding his arms over his chest. "I've tried to get Marshal to deal with me, but he won't budge. And I can't figure out what else there is to do. I've prayed, and I've worked hard. Every time I get close to having the money, something happens . . . like the dust storm. Feels like I'm swimming upstream."

"Pray more and listen better."

"You sound like the reverend. But I can't remember the last time I saw you in church."

"I'll be there. Cambria's not about to let me avoid that one much longer." He pushed his hands into his pockets. "Used to go when I was a kid. We never missed Sunday services. I figure it'll feel good to go."

"There's rejoicing in heaven!" Daniel grinned.

"Don't know about that, but Cambria will be happy." Jim picked up his hat off a stool and pressed it down on his head. "She makes me better. Women have a way of bringing out the best in us."

"They do. I'd be better if Rebecca was 'ere."

"You ought to send for her. She'd be a help. She's quick-witted and determined. Have you written to her?"

"I started to, but I've never been very good about that sort of thing. Mum's written though."

"As much as Rebecca loves your mother, I figure it's you she'd rather hear from." Jim stepped to the door. "How much longer you think it'll be before she comes home?"

Daniel shrugged. "Can't say."

"Wire her. Tell her to get herself and the kids back here." Jim grinned.

Daniel nudged up his hat. "I've been thinking on it. Even considered going to Boston after her."

"You don't have money for that. Need to hang on to all you can. And she's got Callie to help her."

"Hello. Anyone here?" Cambria called.

Jim smiled. "That's my gal." He leaned out the door. "We're back here," he called.

"Ah, there ya are," Cambria said, stepping up to Jim.

He hugged her. "Didn't expect you so soon."

Cambria pulled away and looked him over. "Yer all cleaned up? Don't want yer bloody mess on me."

Jim held his arms away from his body and made a slow turn. "Clean as a whistle."

"Good, then." Cambria crinkled up her nose. "Ya still smell of blood."

"Sorry. Can't do anything about that. It'll take a day or so."

"He'll be fresh as a field of flowers in no time," Daniel teased.

"I can hope, eh?" Cambria grinned.

"I'm right thirsty. Who's ready for something to drink?" Daniel asked and headed for the house.

"Sounds good to me," said Jim, who fell into step beside Daniel. Cambria walked alongside Jim.

Lily met the threesome on the porch. She was carrying a pitcher of water and a tray with glasses. Setting them on the table, she said, "Figured ya'd want something ta drink."

"Thank ya, Lily," Cambria said. "I'll pour." She filled three glasses and handed one to Jim and one to Daniel. She kept a glass for herself.

Daniel dropped into a wicker chair and downed half the glass. He rested one leg on the other. "You want to stay for supper? Lily always makes enough for a crowd."

Jim sat on the top step, and Cambria settled beside him. "Sounds grand, but me mum's counting on me tonight. She's baking pies for the church social." Cambria smiled at Jim. "Ya want ta help?"

"Me? Bake? No, you wouldn't want that." He drank some of his water, then set the glass on the step and rested his arms on his thighs. "Besides, I've got to get out to the house. There's a lot of work to be done. Daniel's given me a few days off, and I figured I'd stay out there and work straight through."

"Maybe I'll stop by." Cambria's blue eyes shone with delight. "I can help. I'm right good at carpentry."

"What do you know about building a house?"

"You'd be surprised at what I know. Being raised on the station with nothing but brothers for company, I learned a lot."

"You're a prize all right." Jim smiled.

"We'll have a grand house, eh?"

"Don't know about grand, but it'll be sturdy." Jim pushed a strand of hair off his face. When he looked at Cambria, his brown eyes turned tender. "It'll be small, but we can add on later."

"You'll have to," Willa said, joining the three on the porch. "One day there'll be babies, and you'll need the space."

Cambria blushed.

"Sons first, I figure," Jim said with a grin.

"And if not?" Cambria challenged.

"If we have a daughter, I'm sure she'll be like you, and that would suit me just fine."

Daniel's mind went to Rebecca and his children. His mood deflated. Jim was planning his future, and Daniel was about to lose his.

His distress must have shown, because Jim turned a challenging gaze on Daniel and asked, "So you bringing Rebecca home?"

"Ya goin' ta Boston?" Cambria asked.

"Can't afford to go, but I'm thinking of sending for her. What do you think I should do?" His eyes moved from Cambria to his mother.

"She ought ta come home," Cambria said.

Willa reached into her apron pocket. "A wire came today. It's from Rebecca."

Daniel took the envelope and tore it open. "Why do you think she wired me?"

"Can't say, son. You'll have to read the message."

Quaking inside, wondering what could be so urgent that she'd wire him, Daniel looked down at the short note.

"All is well," Rebecca wrote. "Children are fine. Want to come home. Soon. Love. Rebecca."

"So what does it say?" Cambria asked.

"She wants to come home," Daniel said, his voice breaking with emotion.

"I dare say, it would be nice to have them here." Willa looked at her son. "Maybe the payment you made to Mr. Marshal will see him through for a while."

"Wish I believed that."

"She can't stay away forever, son. And we haven't had any trouble for some time."

"I don't think ya should have sent her off in the first place," Cambria said. "She's tough, and she wanted to stay." She settled her eyes on Jim. "I wouldn't leave. Ya couldn't make me."

"No. Don't figure I could," Jim said with a grin.

"It would be nice to have the school open again," Willa interjected. "Koora keeps asking about it and about Callie."

"He's been moody ever since she left," Cambria said.

"And what if Marshal's men show up?" Daniel asked. "What about Rebecca and the children?"

"They can stay close to home and not go anywhere without you or one of us," Jim said.

"A lot's happened, and more will," Daniel cautioned.

"She wants ta come home." Cambria set a challenging gaze on Daniel. "Ya have ta think of her too and how hard this is for her." She clasped a knee in her hands. "It would be grand ta have her 'ere." She looked at Daniel. "I've a wedding ta plan, and she would be a fine help."

"I care about you, Cambria, but I won't bring Rebecca home to be a help to you."

"Course not," Cambria said. "I was just teasing."

Daniel moved to the railing and let his eyes travel from the cottages to the barn and beyond. "We wouldn't be in this predicament if it weren't for my poor judgment."

"Enough of that," Willa said. "You've said all that needs to be said and more. What's done is done. No reason to be bringing up the past. It's time to make things right."

"The grass is greening up, and the rivers are running again. The herds will grow," Jim said.

"Marshal won't wait. And I don't know where to get my hands on the money I owe." Daniel gripped the top rail and smiled wryly. "I suppose the place is just right for someone else to take it over."

"Feeling sorry for yourself won't help." Willa stepped up to Daniel. "You can't look at this problem through your human eyes. If you do, all you'll see is the trouble and not the solution. The Lord has the answers."

"And what if God takes Douloo?"

"If he does, then that's his choice. We either trust him or we don't." Willa smiled softly. "After all we've been through, I thought you'd learned that lesson."

"I should have," he admitted. He couldn't let go of either his fear or his sense of failure.

"Remember the day of the fire when you thought Joseph had died?" Willa asked.

"I'll never forget."

"What was it you said when you discovered he was still alive?"

Daniel thought back to the dreadful day. He'd believed Joseph and Callie had perished. He'd been angry and bitter. But when he saw his son and held him, joy was all he knew.

And then he remembered the words he'd uttered. "I had no faith, but he remained faithful," he said.

"That's right," Willa said. "God was faithful then, and he is faithful now."

Daniel looked at his mother. "I remember, but that was different. I brought this trouble on us."

"Either way God is the one in control."

"And if Marshal takes Douloo?"

"We'll begin again. I'm not so old that I can't do that. Are you?" Willa challenged.

"No. I could give it a go."

Willa smiled.

Daniel studied the open plains. He could see his father and remembered his respect for the land and for this station. How would he have felt about risking Douloo? *Dad would have trusted.*

Daniel turned to his mum. "There's someone living across the sea who's waiting to hear from me." He smiled. "I'll send the wire."

23

Wind drove cold air beneath Rebecca's collar. Shivering, she huddled deeper inside her coat and wondered why she'd decided a walk across her childhood estate would be a good idea.

She gazed at the frozen grounds. Sorrows cold as the frigid air settled inside her. The estate seemed untouched, and yet it wasn't at all the same. Without her father nothing was the same. And Tom and his son, Jimmy, were gone. Tom had died, and Jimmy had set out to make a life for himself. Even the housemaid, Flora, had moved on to another post.

The house looked in good repair, and the barns seemed to be as they'd always been, but the family living in the house no longer belonged to Rebecca. Mr. and Mrs. Fortier seemed nice enough, and their three young sons were well mannered, but they were strangers. It felt odd to have people she didn't know in her home.

Her eyes moved from the empty pastures to the barn, and she was reminded that Tomlin and Chavive were no longer tucked warmly inside, munching hay. After her father's death, Tomlin had been sold off, as had Chavive. An ache squeezed her heart as she thought of Chavive. She'd been elated and thankful when Daniel had purchased her mare and had shipped her to Queensland. Now what had become of her? Was Marshal seeing that she was well cared for? Rebecca doubted it. *Lord, please bring her back to me.*

She remembered the days when Chavive had carried her over the lush estate. So often they'd gone to their favorite spot, the place that overlooked the valleys. They'd often stood and gazed at the view that reached all the way to Massachusetts Bay.

The wind blustered, and dry snow sifted into the air, exposing patches of frozen ground. Rebecca had celebrated Thanksgiving with Mildred, Thomas, and the children, but it hadn't felt festive, at least not the way she remembered it. Without Daniel it had seemed an empty ritual. She needed him; she needed Douloo.

Again her eyes lingered on the estate. How and when had it happened? When had this place ceased to be home? The dry, open lands of Queensland called her now. *I'd never have believed Douloo would feel more like home than this place*, she thought. Tears burned. *What shall I do?* She'd hoped for an immediate response from Daniel, but she'd not heard from him.

Swiping at stray tears, she straightened her spine and set her jaw. "That's enough of feeling sorry for yourself," she said. "Your children are counting on you. And Daniel needs you to be strong. Crying will change nothing. You'll be going home when the Lord sees fit."

Her mind settled on Daniel. What was he doing at this very moment? She could envision him on the back of his stallion. Then her thoughts carried her to more frightening possibilities. Had he faced more confrontations with Marshal? Surely Cambria would have mentioned them in her letter.

Rebecca remembered the last time she'd seen Daniel—the set of his shoulders, the weariness in his step, and the uneasiness in his eyes. So much had been placed on his shoulders.

Lord, you promised to carry our burdens. Remind Daniel to give you his.

Why hasn't he written? Fear pressed down on her. Was he safe, or had something happened to him? Had Marshal done something awful?

Thomas's carriage rolled up to the house. Mildred was driving. Alarm charged through Rebecca. Something must be wrong. Mildred wouldn't travel all the way out here without cause. Lifting her skirts, Rebecca hurried over the frozen ground toward the drive.

Mildred pulled back on the reins and stopped the carriage. Cautiously she stepped down.

"Auntie!" Rebecca called. "What's happened?" She ran to her aunt. Gasping for each breath, Rebecca met her at the gate. "Is everything all right?"

"Yes. Yes." Mildred said. "Well, I believe so."

Rebecca rested a hand on her chest. "You frightened me nearly to death. Why are you here?"

"A telegram," Mildred said, extending an envelope. "From Queensland. I knew you'd want to read it right away."

Rebecca stared at the envelope but didn't reach for it. What if it was bad news? She looked at her aunt. "You open it."

"It's not for me to read."

"If everything was all right, wouldn't Daniel have sent a letter?"

"Open it."

Rebecca reached for the envelope. With trembling hands she removed one of her gloves and tucked it into her coat pocket. Then she tore open the telegram and lifted out the message. "Rebecca. I am well. Miss you. Please come home."

"Oh my! He wants me to come home!"

"I knew it was good news." Mildred hugged Rebecca.

Pressing a hand against her chest, Rebecca reread the short message. "I pray everything has been settled with Mr. Marshal." She slipped the note back inside its envelope. "I must start packing immediately. I wonder if I can make it home in time for Christmas?"

"Oh, I don't think that's possible. But of course you can celebrate after you arrive." Mildred smiled kindly, her eyes tearing. "I shall miss you, but I'm so glad you're going home. Do you think the trouble has passed?"

Rebecca looked at the telegram again. "Daniel says he's well, but he doesn't mention anything else." She placed the envelope in her pocket. She didn't care about what kind of trouble she and Daniel had to face. All that mattered was that they would be together.

"Well, I'd best get to that packing, and I'll have to make arrangements for travel."

🜨

Joseph was dressed in his traveling clothes. He'd been instructed not to get dirty; however, while he waited for the carriage to be brought around, he climbed up and down the staircase on his hands and knees, dirtying his pants.

At the top of the stairs, Rebecca picked him up. "Oh dear. Look at those knees." She dusted him off and sent him downstairs to wait.

She changed Audry's diaper and then smoothed the little girl's dress. Hefting her into her arms, she stood at the mirror and stared at their reflection. "You ready to go home?"

The infant smiled and cooed and then clapped her hands. Rebecca ran a baby's brush through her dark, fine hair. It was beginning to curl like her mother's.

Rebecca kissed her cheek. "Not long now. We'll be home soon."

Rebecca walked to the door, then stopped and looked around the room before stepping into the hallway. It was time to go. She felt a swell of sadness. Returning home meant saying good-bye to her aunt.

Mildred met Rebecca at the bottom of the stairway. "Ah, let me have that little girl," she said, reaching for Audry. She took the baby and held her up in front of her. Audry smiled. "What a love you are."

Audry's smile broadened.

"You are a beautiful child," Mildred said, cuddling her. "I'm going to miss you."

Rebecca watched, realizing that her happiness would bring her aunt sorrow. "I wish you were going with us."

"Ah, we'll come for a visit just as soon as we can." She gently patted Audry's back.

"Oh, Auntie. I'm going to miss you."

Mildred's eyes were kind but concerned. "I'll miss you too, but you've more to think about than an old woman in Boston. You need to take care of that husband of yours."

"I know. And I can hardly wait to see him."

Callie walked in from the kitchen. "I've got me things packed, mum. Is there anything I can do for ya?"

"No. Well, you could see to Joseph. Make sure he doesn't get dirty. I'd hate to have people thinking I have unruly children."

"Roight, mum." Callie smiled. The light in her eyes told of her anticipation. "It'll be roight nice ta be home, eh?"

"I don't suppose you'll be glad to see Koora?" Rebecca teased.

"He's waitin' for me, that's for sure."

Thomas stepped into the room. "So you're nearly ready to go, then?"

"Yes." Rebecca faced Thomas. "I can't thank you enough for allowing me and the children to stay. You've been a great help to us."

"It was Mildred's and my pleasure. We've loved having you here. And you're welcome to visit anytime." Thomas hesitated, seeming a bit ill at ease. "Here, this is for you," he said, offering an envelope to Rebecca.

"What's this?" she asked, taking the envelope.

Thomas glanced at Mildred. "It's a loan, actually. Mildred and I want to help. Over the years I've managed to set aside a fair amount of cash. I had a bank draft made out to Daniel. It ought to be more than enough to cover your debt."

Rebecca looked at the envelope, then back at Thomas.

Mildred laughed. "Why, Rebecca, I don't know that I've ever seen you speechless."

"I . . . I don't know what to say." Her eyes stinging from unshed tears, Rebecca turned the envelope over in her hands.

"Don't worry about paying me back right away. There's no rush." Thomas said.

"I had no idea." Rebecca was breathless.

"When Mildred told me about your predicament, I knew I had to do something."

"But this is far too generous."

"Not at all. It's the least I can do."

Joy bubbled up inside Rebecca. "It's possible Daniel has already settled the debt."

"If so, all the better."

Rebecca moved to Thomas and hugged him. "Thank you so much. I'm forever grateful."

Thomas stepped back. His face was flushed. "My pleasure."

Holding Audry against her shoulder, Mildred moved close to Thomas. "We're grateful we can help."

Rebecca couldn't control her tears as they brimmed over and spilled onto her cheeks. "This is a miracle, an answer to prayer. I can't wait to tell Daniel."

"Well, you'll have to surprise him. There's no time to send a wire now," Mildred said. "We'd best get you to the depot. You don't want to miss your train."

Joseph stood up in the dory, grabbing hold of Callie's arm to steady himself. "Daddy!" he called.

"Joseph, sit down," Rebecca said.

Callie picked up Joseph and set him in her lap.

While the oarsman maneuvered the boat toward the dock, Rebecca forced herself to remain seated. She stared at Daniel. He looked wonderful!

Daniel smiled at Rebecca. When the boat was close enough, he grabbed a rope thrown by one of the crewmen and tied it, then grabbed another tossed from the rear of the boat and secured it.

"Daniel," Rebecca said in a hushed voice. Her heart pounded hard.

"Daddy," Joseph said, stepping toward the edge of the boat.

Daniel grabbed him and hauled the lad onto the dock and into his arms.

"Grand to see you, lad." He hugged the little boy, then held him away from him. "You've grown. I barely recognize you."

"I'm big now," Joseph said proudly.

"Right you are."

Callie remained seated, her brown eyes bright with anticipation. "You go ahead, Callie," Rebecca said.

The servant stood and grasped Daniel's hand, allowing him to haul her onto the dock.

"Welcome home," he said.

"Roight good ta be 'ere." She reached for Joseph. "I'll take him for ya."

Daniel handed off the boy and turned to Rebecca. He took her hand and helped her and Audry out of the boat. Lifting the little girl out of Rebecca's arms, he held her up. "You've gotten so big." He looked at Rebecca. "She's changed so much." He smiled in such a way that Rebecca's heart did a little flip. "She's beautiful. Just like her mother."

"Oh, Daniel," Rebecca said. Unable to restrain her joy any longer, she wrapped an arm around his neck and buried her face in his shoulder. "Oh, how I've missed you." She held on to him tightly. "I love you." She couldn't restrain her tears.

"I love you," Daniel whispered against her hair. He sucked in a deep breath and stepped back, looking into her eyes. "You look fine. Right fine."

"So do you." Rebecca wanted to kiss him but restrained herself. It wouldn't be proper. "I'm never leaving you again."

"I'll never let you go." He grinned. Tucking Audry in close to him, Daniel looped his free arm through Rebecca's. "I've a room here in Brisbane, not far from 'ere. Figured you could use a night's rest before we set off for home."

"That sounds just right to me." She leaned against Daniel as they walked toward the hotel.

$\mathcal{D}$

"The bybies will be just fine," Callie said. "Ya 'ave a good time." She smiled, and her white teeth looked bright against her dark skin.

"Thank you, Callie," Rebecca said, moving toward the hotel door.

"Roight fine bein' back in Queensland, eh?"

"That it is," said Rebecca, allowing Daniel to escort her out the door.

They walked the one flight of stairs down to the main lobby and crossed the room, stepping outside. It was a short walk to the eatery. Rebecca wanted to take her time. She enjoyed every sight and smell, and she especially liked being on Daniel's arm.

262

She took his hand. "I feel like I'm in a dream. It's so wonderful to be here."

Daniel squeezed her hand. "I'm a lucky bloke." His smile faded as he added, "But we've still got troubles, luv. I've not been able to pay off Marshal yet."

"Oh yes. But I have a surprise for you. I've been so giddy I nearly forgot."

"What is it?" Daniel asked as they stepped into the restaurant. The smell of roasted chicken and freshly baked bread greeted them.

"It smells heavenly," Rebecca said, only now realizing how hungry she was.

Daniel steered her toward an empty table and pulled out a chair for her. She sat, and he took the seat across from her. "Now, what is the surprise?"

"I wanted to send you a wire, but there was no time, and then I thought how grand it would be to surprise you." She reached into her bag and took out the envelope Thomas had given her.

A waiter approached their table. He handed them each a menu, then stood and waited.

Rebecca set the envelope on the table while she and Daniel looked over their options. "I think I'll have the roasted chicken with carrots and some of that delicious bread I smell."

The waiter wrote down her choices, then turned to Daniel.

"Figure I'll have the steak and potatoes. And make the steak rare, eh?"

After noting Daniel's selection, the waiter said, "I'll have some water brought to the table for you." He retrieved the menus and walked away.

Rebecca clasped her hands on the table in front of her and looked about. The room was large, and it looked bright even though darkness had settled over the city outside. There were ample wall lanterns, and a candle lit up each table. A row of windows at the front were draped with green and white curtains. Tablecloths matching the curtains were laid over small tables set with crystal goblets, fine china, and silver flatware.

"This is very nice," Rebecca said.

"They've good food too. I've eaten 'ere before." He gazed at Rebecca. "Now, what is this about a surprise?"

"I have something for you." Rebecca picked up the envelope and handed it to Daniel.

He studied it a moment.

"Open it."

He smiled and then slid a finger under the seal, careful to open the envelope without tearing it. He lifted the flap and took out the bank note. After studying it a moment, he turned a questioning look on Rebecca. "What's this?"

"A loan. From Thomas. He wants to help."

Daniel smiled. "Well, this will help. It's more than we need."

"He wanted to include enough just in case we had other expenditures."

Daniel shook his head. "Can't believe it. I've been worrying and praying. Mum kept telling me to believe and to trust, and I just kept worrying. And 'ere you arrive with more money than we need." He closed his eyes a moment. "I thank the Lord."

Rebecca smiled. "He's answered our prayers. We can clear the debt, and Thomas said he's in no hurry for us to pay him back."

Daniel returned the note to the envelope and placed it in his jacket pocket. "We'll see Mr. Marshal in the morning."

🖉

Daniel and Rebecca stepped into Marshal's front office. The same secretary who had greeted Daniel on his first visit sat at the front desk.

She looked up. "Mr. Thornton? You don't have an appointment."

"Right. But I'm 'ere in town, and I need to see Mr. Marshal."

The secretary clasped her hands in front of her. "He's busy at the moment."

"I can wait."

"Well, it could be a long while."

"How long?" Rebecca asked.

"I'm not quite sure, but . . ."

Voices carried from down the hallway. Soon Marshal and a man nearly wider than he was tall emerged. Marshal glanced at Daniel and, offering his hand to the rotund man, said, "Fine. We'll meet next week. Good doing business with you, Mr. Jones."

With a quick nod, Jones moved to the door and stepped outside.

Marshal set his gaze on Daniel. "What are you doing here?"

"I've come to pay my debt."

"Bit late for that." He turned and started down the hall.

Daniel and Rebecca followed.

"I've got the money. All of it," Daniel said.

Marshal didn't look at him but kept walking. "I don't want your money."

Daniel grabbed his arm. "I said I've got your money."

Marshal stopped. He looked at Daniel's hand and lifted it off his arm, then turned a glare on Daniel. "The time for payment is past. I told you—thirty days to vacate. You've lost the station, lad. You might as well accept it."

Rebecca pressed a hand to her chest. "Lost the station? How can that be? We have the money."

Marshal moved his small, hateful eyes to Rebecca. "Your husband signed the station over as collateral. He didn't make his payments as promised. The station belongs to me."

"What about Chavive?"

"Chavive? Oh, your horse." Satisfaction touched his eyes. "Sold her."

"You what?" Daniel exploded.

Wearing a satisfied smirk, Marshal continued down the hall and disappeared into his office.

24

Rebecca walked as fast as she could and still couldn't keep up with Daniel.

"He'll get his," Daniel muttered. "He'll not get away with this."

"Daniel. Please. Slow down."

He glanced at Rebecca and stopped. Swiping aside a wisp of blond hair, he said, "I'm sorry. All I could think of was to get to the constabulary as fast as I could. My mind is there, not with you." He circled an arm around her waist. "He won't do this to us. And we'll get Chavive back too."

At the mention of the mare's name, Rebecca could feel tears press against the back of her eyes. "How? We don't even know who has her." She managed to contain her tears but couldn't control the quivering of her chin.

Daniel caressed her cheek. "I don't know just how, but we will, luv. I promise." Taking Rebecca's hand, he moved on, only more slowly this time.

"I can't bear the thought that she might be with someone who would mistreat her."

"We'll tell a constable about that too. They'll see to it that she's found. You'll see."

"I thought you said that when you spoke to the police before they wouldn't help you."

"Right, but maybe it was just the bloke on duty at the time. Doesn't hurt to try again."

Rebecca wasn't at all convinced that this visit would turn out any different from the first. According to Daniel, the Brisbane policeman he'd spoken to had made it clear that Marshal was to be obeyed. *He bought them*, Rebecca thought, unaware that she was clenching her teeth.

Daniel stopped in front of a brick building. "This is it." He stared at the windowless front door. A man wearing a smart-looking uniform stood on a small porch. "We'll get some assistance now," he said, striding up the steps. The officer nodded and moved aside, allowing them to pass.

He seems cordial, Rebecca thought, following Daniel inside. Perhaps this time would be different.

Daniel kept a hold of Rebecca's hand and led the way to a man sitting behind a desk. "I want to report a murder and a theft."

The man lifted his eyebrows. "You better sit." He nodded at a wooden chair.

"We'll stand, thank you."

The officer grabbed a pen and piece of paper. He dipped the pen into ink. "Tell me what happened."

Sucking in a deep breath, Daniel began, "Four months ago one of my roustabouts was hanged by thugs hired by Robert Marshal."

Rebecca could see an instantaneous change in the officer's demeanor. He looked aggravated and instead of writing, he set down the pen.

Daniel pushed on. "Marshal threatened my wife and children and took our best mare, and now he refuses to accept payment for a loan and insists my station belongs to him."

The officer clasped his hands together and rested them on the table in front of him. "That's a ridiculous complaint. Mr.

Marshal would never do something like that. You're mistaken."

"Mistaken? I ought to know when a man hangs one of my workers!"

"I'm sure Mr. Marshal had nothing to do with it. Probably the blokes that hanged him just got carried away and it wasn't Mr. Marshal's intention to kill anyone."

"I told you—"

"And I'm telling you I want you to go on your way." His eyes narrowed. "Robert Marshal is an upstanding businessman in this town, and I don't like blokes bad-mouthing him." He stood. "You'd be right smart to go back to where you came from."

Daniel looked the man straight in the eyes. "I want to speak to your superior."

"I am my superior." The man smiled maliciously. "Now, on your way."

Daniel stared at the man.

"There's no help for you 'ere."

Rebecca was afraid the officer would get angry enough to arrest Daniel. She took his hand. "Come on. We'll find another way."

Daniel glared at the constable.

"You best listen to your wife. Seems she's the intelligent one in the family."

Daniel stared at the man a long time, and then he glanced at Rebecca.

"We'll find another way," she repeated.

"You tell Marshal we'll settle this and that he'll wish he'd been reasonable."

The constable's gaze remained fixed, and he folded his arms over his chest.

Rebecca nudged Daniel, and he finally turned and followed her out.

When Rebecca stepped off the stagecoach and onto the walkway in front of the Thornton Creek Hotel, *elation* was the only word appropriate for what she felt. The weariness from travel evaporated. She was home.

Mr. O'Brien stepped onto the porch in front of his mercantile and waved. "G'day," he called.

"Good day, Mr. O'Brien."

"Grand ta have ya back." Wearing a smile, he turned and walked into his store.

The bank president, Mr. Oxley, wasn't so friendly. He peered out of the bank window but didn't wave or smile. A scowl was firmly planted on his face.

"Don't figure he's happy with me. Word's out about his not giving us a loan. There are some unhappy blokes around town." Daniel set a suitcase on the wooden sidewalk.

"I suppose he deserves some criticism."

With Audry in her arms, Callie joined Rebecca. The baby whined and squirmed. "I think she's hungry, mum."

"Oh, there's nowhere for me to feed her right now." Rebecca rummaged through a travel case. "Perhaps this will satisfy her for now," she said, taking out a bottle with water in it.

Callie took the bottle and offered it to Audry, who seemed content with it.

"Woodman!" Joseph hollered and ran toward the black man.

Wearing a smile, Woodman hefted the little boy. "Roight fine ta see ya lad."

"Right fine ta see ya," Joseph echoed.

Woodman carried Joseph back to his parents. "Sorry I'm late. Got held up at the livery." He gave Daniel a friendly slap on the back. "Grand ta have ya home."

"It's good to see you," Rebecca told Woodman and spontaneously hugged him. "It's wonderful to be here."

Woodman held Rebecca lightly and quickly let her loose. "Douloo hasn't been the same without ya, mum."

Callie looked beyond Woodman to the street.

He grinned. "Ya lookin' for someone?"

"No. Just lookin' 'round the town."

"Roight. Well, there's a bloke waitin' for ya at the house."

"Really?" Callie smiled. "He's waitin', eh?"

"That he is."

"I suppose we ought to get home," Daniel said, unable to find any enthusiasm at the reunion.

"Yer soundin' a bit down in the mouth," Woodman said. "Somethin' wrong?"

"Marshal's set on taking the station."

"Can he do that?"

"Figure he can, but I don't plan to let him."

Rev. Cobb stepped out of the hotel. "May the Lord be praised. I heard you were returning." He smiled broadly. "Grand to see you." He took Rebecca's hands in his. "So happy to have you back."

"It's wonderful to be back," Rebecca said. "And so nice to see you again. I've missed you and your uplifting sermons."

"I would think with the fine churches to choose from in Boston, you'd not have missed me for a moment."

"They're fine indeed, but I did miss you."

"Well, I hope you had a splendid journey."

"It was quite nice. The weather was calm most of the way."

"I saw a whale," Joseph said, grasping a post and leaning as far back as he could. "It was big."

"A real whale?" The reverend smiled.

"Right." Joseph skipped down the sidewalk toward the mercantile.

"I'd best let you be on your way. I'm sure you're anxious

to get home." The reverend tipped his hat. "I look forward to seeing you this Sunday."

"Of course. But before you go, Daniel and I have something we want to discuss with you."

"We need advice," Daniel said, "and prayer."

"Sounds serious."

"It is."

"Shall we talk at the church? We'll have privacy there."

"Yes." Rebecca looked at Daniel. "Is that all right with you?"

"Right."

"Callie, can you stay with the children?" Rebecca asked.

"Yais, mum."

Rebecca dug into her purse and took out several coins and handed them to Callie. "Take them to the eatery. Joseph's probably hungry and thirsty. And please treat yourself as well."

"Will they serve me, mum?"

"If not, maybe you could all eat outdoors?"

With a nod, Callie called Joseph, and she and the children headed for the café.

"Woodman, would you load our bags? We won't be long," Daniel said.

"Right," Woodman said.

Rebecca and Daniel walked alongside the reverend. Rebecca sensed resolve and determination in Daniel. He'd been downhearted since his meeting with Marshal; it was good to see a bit of spark in him.

"Rebecca!" someone hollered from down the street. It was Cambria. She ran toward Rebecca, holding her skirts up out of the dirt.

"Cambria." Rebecca hurried toward her friend.

When the two met, they grabbed each other in a tight hug. After a few moments, they stepped back and looked at each other.

"I can't believe my eyes," Cambria said. "I heard ya were coming home, but I was afraid ta believe it until I saw ya." She hugged Rebecca again. "I've missed ya."

"And, oh, how I've missed you."

"I prayed ya'd return soon."

"Why are you in town?"

"I'm helping me aunt with a fitting."

Cambria's aunt Elle walked down the street toward them. As she approached, she said, "Rebecca. Grand ta see ya home at last." She held her arms out and pulled Rebecca into a sturdy hug and patted her back.

"You look wonderful," Rebecca said, looking at Elle's short blond hair. "What have you done? Have you cut it?"

Elle's hand went to her hair. "Right. I did. It's the latest fashion. Do you like it?"

"Yes. It suits you, but I don't recall seeing this style before."

"I'm sure you haven't. It's *my* latest fashion." Elle winked. "I got mad one morning and just chopped it off. Everyone was quite shocked." She grinned. "I did see a cut very much like this in a magazine."

"Really?"

"What, ya don't believe me?" Elle smiled.

"Of course I do. And I think it makes you look quite youthful."

"Thank ya."

"I like it too," Daniel said.

"Is that so? I believe yer the first bloke who's said he likes it."

"Like Rebecca said, it suits you."

"I like you just the way you are, long hair or short." Rebecca smiled. "How has business been?"

"Right fine. And we're in for a bit of fun, with Cambria's wedding. She's been waiting for you to help her decide about her dress."

"Yes. I can't wait."

Elle looked at Daniel. "So ya get things sorted out with that Mr. Marshal?"

"No. We've some business to take care of yet."

"Let me have a go at him. I'll set him straight." She watched a dried bit of weed tumble in the wind, then looked back at Rebecca and Daniel. "'Ere I am blathering on, and ya must be tired. Would ya like ta come in for a bite and something ta drink? I always keep refreshments in the shop with me."

"I'd love to," Rebecca said, "but we've got business with the reverend, and then we really must get home."

Elle smiled. "Right, then. We'll have to picnic after church on Sunday, eh?"

"I'd like that," Rebecca said.

"See ya Sunday, then."

☞

Once inside the church, the reverend sat on the front pew and waited for Rebecca and Daniel to sit. He clasped his hands, then asked, "What is it you need?"

"You know the reason Rebecca went to Boston, right?"

"My understanding is that you wanted her and the children safe in case that man in Brisbane got violent."

"Right. But things never got resolved, and . . ." Daniel looked at Rebecca.

She warmed under his loving gaze.

"We decided she ought to come home."

"Good," the reverend said.

"My aunt's husband, Thomas, loaned us the money to pay Mr. Marshal," Rebecca said.

"Excellent."

"Yes, except that when we tried to pay him, he refused to take the money, saying it was too late and that Douloo belonged to him and we had to leave."

"What?" The reverend's eyebrows peaked.

"We went to the constabulary in Brisbane, but the police won't help. I'd say they've been paid off," Daniel explained. "We're on our own."

"You're never on your own," the reverend said. "But you are in a predicament."

"We are that." Daniel took a deep breath. "Some of the blokes 'round the district want to have it out with Marshal, kill him if need be. Said they'd stand with me to defend Douloo. What do you think about that?"

The reverend was quiet for a long moment. Rebecca wondered if he might be praying.

Finally he looked at Daniel. "Seems to me if you did all you could to pay the man and actually had the money and he refused to take it, then you're right to defend Douloo. But I don't advocate killing."

"We won't go after him, but if he tries to take Douloo, well, then I figure we'll do what we have to. We might not have a choice about killing him or not."

"Perhaps the Lord will provide one." Rev. Cobb stood and walked to the window. He folded his arms over his chest and gazed out. "We'll call people in to pray. Let the Lord decide this one, eh?" He turned and looked at Daniel and Rebecca. "He's our strength."

$\mathcal{D}$

Sunday morning Rev. Cobb announced that there would be a prayer vigil during the week and explained that he'd be at the church every day to meet and pray with anyone who wanted to come in to pray for the Thorntons. Immediately several women offered to provide food and drink for those who would be coming and going.

Rebecca felt enfolded in the love of her neighbors and whispered a prayer of thanks. Her faith in the premise that good wins out over evil was strengthened. The Lord would care for her, Daniel, the children, and Douloo. She even prayed for Marshal. She decided that he must be a very unhappy man to be so cruel. Perhaps God would see to him as well.

⌘

The next day when Rebecca headed for the church to pray, Callie asked if she could join her. "I thought you didn't believe in God."

"Roight, but I believe in ya, mum." Her eyes went to Willa. "And in ya too."

Rebecca took Callie's hand. "Well, you come along with us, then. We would be grateful for your prayers."

Willa hefted a basket. "I helped Lily make some biscuits, and we added some fine apple butter too." She climbed into the surrey and sat beside Callie. Rebecca clambered onto the driver's seat. "Are you going to drive, dear?"

"Yes. Woodman's with Daniel and Jim. They're making preparations for Marshal and his men in case they show up." She felt a stir of anxiety. "I pray he and his men stay in Brisbane. I don't want Daniel or any of the other men hurt, and I'd hate to run into them while traveling to town."

"I've been praying, and I'm sure there are already people at the church praying. I dare say, we'll be safe."

The muscles in Rebecca's body were tight. She knew what Marshal was capable of. She glanced at the house, suddenly afraid for the children. *Lily will look after them*, she told herself. *She'd give her own life if she had to.*

"Everything will be quite all right," Willa continued. "We needn't waste our energy on worry."

"Mum," Callie said hesitantly. "Sometimes I read the Bible,

276

and there are places where God's people are hurt. Don't see that we're safe."

Rebecca turned so she was facing Callie. "It's true, even God's people suffer. And I'm frightened. But we can't let someone like Mr. Marshal have power over us. We're obliged to stand up to him, and we must trust God to look out for us."

"I'll do me best, mum."

"We *can* trust that God is in control of all that happens and that he'll see us through any hardship. We don't have to be afraid."

"I hope yer roight, mum," Callie said.

25

Rebecca closed the church doors and turned to look down the street. She was tired but spiritually refreshed.

Callie sat on the bottom step of the porch. She seemed anxious to be on her way. Rebecca smiled, guessing Callie's need to hurry had something to do with Koora.

Cambria moved down the stairway. "I'll continue ta pray. Jim and I both will."

"Thank you." Rebecca blew out a quick breath and again scanned the street. "I know they're here. I can feel it. I just wish they'd do whatever it is they plan to do."

"Just remember, you have friends."

Rebecca walked down the steps. "Yes. I know." She hugged Cambria. "Thank you."

"We'll not let anything happen ta ya. Jim and I will stand with ya, and so will a lot of folks from 'round the district."

Rebecca smiled, taking comfort in her friend's loyalty. "I'm praying it won't come to that."

"I'll be back tomorrow," Cambria said. She glanced around. "Are Jim and Daniel at the house?"

"Yes. Daniel wants to stay close to home, just in case."

"Right." Again Cambria glanced down the street. "Is Willa all right?"

"She's fine. Elvina Walker and her husband offered to take her home. She had some things there to take care of." Rebecca straightened her hat. "Elvina was probably hoping to find out if there's anything she doesn't already know about our dilemma." Rebecca grinned.

Cambria looked at Callie and then at Rebecca. "I don't like the two of ya traveling from 'ere ta home by yerselves."

"We'll be fine. And we're supposed to pick up Koora. He's working at the livery today."

"All right, then. I've got to stop by me aunt's shop, then I'll be on me way."

"See you tomorrow, then." Rebecca watched Cambria stroll across the road toward Elle's shop. "Time we were headed home too," she told Callie.

"I was goin' ta meet Koora. If ya need us, we'll ride, but we were wonderin' if ya'd mind us walkin'."

"It's a long way."

Humor touched Callie's eyes. "I've walked a lot farther. But if ya want, we'll ride with ya."

Rebecca gazed down the street toward the mercantile and the pub. "I haven't seen any strangers in town. You go ahead." A pang of apprehension moved through Rebecca. "Be careful."

"Roight. I will." Callie walked down the street toward the livery.

Rebecca climbed into the surrey. Picking up the reins, she scanned the partly cloudy sky. Suddenly feeling alone and frightened, she wished she hadn't agreed to let Callie and Koora walk. She glanced at Callie. It would take only a word. But she knew the two had planned this, and she hated to spoil their time together.

Well, Lord, it's just you and me, she thought and slapped

the reins. The horses plodded forward and away from the church.

𝄞

Callie stepped into the livery. It seemed dark after being outside. She breathed in the aroma of hay and horses. She liked the smell. The beat of her heart picked up at the sight of Koora. He leaned against a horse, its leg braced between his thighs as he examined the animal's hoof.

"Ya still workin', eh?" Callie said.

He glanced up. "Roight. This horse come in a bit ago. Owner said it's actin' lame. Looks like he picked up a stone." He pried out the offending pebble, flicked it away, and then set the animal's foot down.

Callie leaned against a stall door. "Why ya workin' 'ere, anyway? Ya 'ave plenty ta do at the station."

"I got ta learn all I can if I'm gonna 'ave me own place one day. And I need the money. I'm puttin' some aside every week." He smiled. "Don't mind the work."

"Will ya be comin' with me?"

"Can't. Not yet."

Callie watched the young man. She liked the way he moved, smooth and easy. He never seemed to be in a hurry. "I'll go along, then," she said with regret. "Lily will be needin' help with dinner." She hesitated, hoping Koora would decide to put off his tasks. "I guess we can walk another time, eh?"

"Roight." Koora studied her and acted as if he might say more, but then he led the horse back inside a stall and grabbed a pitchfork and moved on to the next stall.

Callie watched a moment longer, then turned and walked outside. Maybe she could catch up to Rebecca. Gazing down the road toward the edge of town, she didn't see the surrey. She started walking.

Elle swept dirt out of her store. She stopped and waved. "Hey, there."

"G'day," Callie said.

"Ya have a fine prayer meeting?"

"Roight fine I guess. Never gone ta a prayer meetin' before."

Elle rested an arm on the top of the broom. "Yeah. I don't go ta such things much meself." She smiled. "Figure I can talk ta God right where I am, and he'll listen."

Callie nodded, but she didn't really understand what people meant by talking to God. Sometimes, though, like today when she was praying with the ladies, something stirred inside her. It was like a longing, but she didn't know just what it was that she yearned for.

"Ya be careful, now, eh?" Elle said. "Thought I saw a couple of strangers ride in earlier. Got distracted, though, and don't know what happened ta them. Could be nothing, but ya have reason ta be watchful."

"Roight. I'll be watchin'." Callie moved on, scanning the street.

Everything appeared to be in order. However, she knew how quickly circumstances could change. She'd not forgotten the threats made by Marshal's men, nor the fire or Dusty's hanging. She supposed she had cause to be afraid, but she didn't feel any fear. Walking always soothed her. She enjoyed the touch of the earth beneath her feet and the sounds of the open land. It would feel good to be alone on the flats.

Two women strolled along the wooden sidewalk. Callie didn't know their names, but she recognized their faces. They continued chatting and acted as if they hadn't noticed her, which was just as well. Callie wasn't much interested in them.

A sharp breeze caught at her cotton dress and swirled up dust from the street. Thornton Creek seemed quiet. But then she liked things quiet. Once away from town, Callie breathed more deeply. The freedom she felt stirred up a renewing energy.

As if cleaning house, wind gusted, sweeping pieces of brush and dirt ahead of its hearty tide. A hawk screeched from overhead, swooping and then circling as it searched for a meal. Callie watched until it glided away.

She picked up her pace slightly, swinging her arms at her sides. The air was warm, and she could taste the sharp flavor of eucalyptus and the moisture of the greenery growing alongside the stream at the edge of the road. She glanced back at Thornton Creek. The town seemed to huddle beneath the sun as if afraid to stretch out its arms and embrace the sprawling world.

People are like that, Callie thought. *Afraid and closed up*. She had to admit that sometimes she was afraid too and that there was a lot inside she kept hidden. Many things in life taunted, and there was so much she didn't understand. She'd been puzzling over the ideas in the Bible Rebecca had given her. She wanted to understand. In fact, she longed to understand.

The town faded into the afternoon haze, and Callie felt the quiet of being alone with the land. A desert quail scampered from a bush and quickly hid beneath another.

Smiling, Callie told the bird, "Ya got no reason ta be afraid of me." She glanced at the empty sky. "Course, that hawk might still be 'round, eh?"

Strips of white clouds rested like torn bandages across the sky as if it needed mending. She wondered about the God Rebecca believed in.

"Are ya real, eh?" she asked. "I read 'bout ya in that book, the Bible. But I don't know ya. Would like ta talk with ya though."

She listened, wondering if she might hear him speak. Was he looking down on her?

The idea of a God and his Son, Jesus, loving and caring for people was foreign to Callie. She'd read many of the holy words, but they felt like a mystery to her, although some of the stories were soothing. She considered the assurance of a

God so great that he could set mountains in place, bring rain to thirsty places, and take care of people's needs all over the world, even remote places like Douloo.

Even though the idea gave her peace, she also felt guilty. It wasn't right for her to think on such things. To do so was to deny the insights and knowledge of the wise ones who had taught her. Aborigines knew about everything that mattered. She could trust the teachers and the storytellers.

Whites don't know what they believe. Every one of them thinks something different. And they're always tearing at each other. They don't honor the earth. Instead, they try ta conquer it.

There were some people she respected though. Rev. Cobb was a good man, and he seemed wise. And there was Willa. She was kind and fair to everyone. And Willa loved her garden, tending it with care. Rebecca and Daniel were courageous, and they trusted and believed in God.

Were all these fine people deceived? Or should she consider more carefully what they believed? What if the Holy Book was true? Callie felt as if her breath had been snatched away as truth swept through her. Hope, like cool water, washed over her. Stretching out her arms, she tipped her head back and looked at the sky. *I want ta believe.*

It was then she heard riders. Her heart quickened, and instinctively she searched for a place to conceal herself. There were bushes along the creek, but she had no time to scramble down the bank and hide. She gazed down the road behind her. Two riders were galloping toward her. They were two of the men who'd been at Douloo, the ones from Brisbane. Turning her eyes ahead, she kept moving.

The men slowed and walked their horses alongside Callie. "What ya doing way out 'ere on yer own?" one asked.

"Just walkin'," Callie said without looking up.

"Ya must be walking somewhere. Where ya going?"

"To me house. Just a ways up."

"Don't remember no houses out 'ere," the man said.

Callie didn't reply but glanced up at the man she knew to be Jack.

"Figure ya could get there a lot faster if ya had a horse, eh? Instead of yer dirty, black feet." Both men chuckled.

"They carry me just fine," Callie said, doing her best to keep the quaking in her body from affecting her voice.

Jack rode his horse around in front of her. "When I talk ta someone, I expect them to stop and listen."

"I got ta get home. Got work ta do." Wishing she'd gone with Rebecca, Callie stepped around his horse.

She heard the sound of the rope before she felt it. It circled over her head and dropped around her shoulders. Then quickly it was pulled tight, and she was yanked off her feet. Her back hit the ground hard, and the air was pushed out of her lungs. Rolling onto her side, she fought for breath. She could feel coarse dirt against her cheek.

"So how's those feet working now?" Jack taunted.

Callie managed to sit up. Her arms were pressed tightly against her body, held by the rope. She pushed to her feet and stared at Jack. He had the coldest blue eyes she'd ever seen. Had he been the one who hanged Dusty? Would he hang her too?

"Got some questions for ya," the quieter one, Wade, said.

"Don't know nothin'." Callie kept her eyes on the ground.

"I think I saw ya at Douloo before. That's where yer heading, right?"

"No. That's not roight. Ya must 'ave me mixed up with someone else." She glanced at Wade. "Ya' goin' ta the Thorntons?"

"Right. We 'ave business there." Wade leaned on his saddle horn and pushed his feet into the stirrups, pushing himself up out of the saddle. He studied Callie. "I seen ya. It was ya."

"Ya can keep denying ya work there, and we'll haul ya 'round this place, or ya can take a message ta yer boss."

Callie met Jack's ruthless gaze. "Tell Thornton he's out of time and we're comin'." A vicious grin tightened his lips.

A zinging sound flashed, and all of a sudden Jack reeled sideways. He clapped a hand against the side of his head and fell from his horse, landing hard on the ground. Stunned, Callie stared at him. He didn't move, and blood leaked from a place near his temple. The earth beneath him turned red.

"Go on! Be on yer way!" Koora shouted, swinging a leather sling over his head. "It'll go hard on ya if ya don't!" Like a wild man, he strode toward Wade.

Wade grabbed his rifle out of the saddle holster but fumbled, dropping the weapon to the ground. His eyes went from the gun to his injured cohort and then back to Koora. Yanking on the reins, he turned his horse toward town. Without looking back he galloped away.

Koora ran to Callie and loosened the rope from around her arms. "Ya all roight?"

"Yais. But . . ." Callie bent over Jack and felt for a pulse. "There's no life in 'im." Alarm surged through her. "Ya killed 'im. What we gonna do?"

Koora stood over Jack. "He deserved it. For what he done ta Dusty."

"Roight, but no one's gonna care 'bout Dusty."

He grabbed Jack under the arms and started to drag him off the road. "Come on, give me a hand."

With a glance toward town, Callie grabbed the man's feet and lifted. "They'll come for ya. Why'd ya do it?"

"Ya think I was gonna let 'im hurt ya?" He gazed at Callie, then added, "I'd rather be dead."

Callie wanted to cry, but she couldn't allow it.

"All roight, now. Let's get 'im hid," Koora said.

Together they carried Jack to a large bush along the creek bank and pushed him underneath it. "No one'll see 'im 'ere," Koora said.

"That man, Wade, knows ya killed 'is friend. Him and his friends will come for ya."

"I figure. But we gotta tell Mr. Thornton 'bout them." He scrambled up the bank. "Come on," he called, climbing onto the back of Jack's horse.

Callie sprinted to the horse and grabbed Koora's extended hand while her foot found the stirrup. Koora pulled her up behind him, and before she was settled, he kicked the horse and they set off.

Neither spoke for the first few minutes. Callie knew Koora would meet a white man's justice. She probably would too. She rested her head against Koora's back and hugged him more tightly.

"Ya think God's angry with ya for killin' that man?"

"God? What do ya mean God?"

Callie realized she was talking about the God she'd been reading about in her Bible. "Ya know, God, the one the whites believe in."

"Why ya care 'bout 'im? He's not for us." He settled back in the saddle. "What ya know 'bout 'im anyway?"

"I know 'im." Callie figured she shouldn't say more, but something inside prompted her to speak. "Rebecca give me a Bible. I been readin' it, and I understand what it says."

"Ya believe in that book?"

"Yeah, maybe." Callie glanced at the sky and remembered how she'd felt God's presence while praying with the ladies and when she talked with God while she was walking. "The Book says God loves everyone."

"Not everyone, just whites."

"No. I read 'bout how no matter what yer people are or yer religion, God loves ya. And he wants ya ta be 'is child."

"And what 'bout color?"

"I don't think that matters."

"Callie, yer no gal. Yer grown-up. How can ya believe in that religion?"

"Mr. Thornton, Mrs. Thornton, they believe, and they're grown-up."

Quiet settled over the pair. Callie loved the Thorntons, and she trusted them. If they loved God, then maybe she should too.

Koora leaned forward and kicked the horse, and they broke into a gallop.

26

Rebecca had just finished changing Audry when she saw Koora and Callie ride into the yard. Callie swung off the horse and leaped to the ground before the horse stopped moving.

"Mr. Thornton! Mrs. Thornton!" she hollered, running toward the front steps. Koora followed.

Something was terribly wrong. Clutching Audry, Rebecca ran to the front of the house and pushed through the front door.

"What is it?" Willa asked, stepping onto the veranda.

Callie clutched the top of the balustrade.

"What's wrong?" Rebecca asked.

"Mr. Marshal's men. We had a run-in with 'em." Callie took a quick breath. "They're on their way." She looked at Koora. "There was trouble."

"I killed one of 'em, mum," Koora said soberly.

"What?" Rebecca exclaimed.

Willa pressed a hand to her mouth. "Lord, no. What happened?"

"I was workin' but got worried 'bout Callie, so I decided ta walk with 'er. When I caught up ta 'er, those men had 'er tied up. I thought they might kill 'er. So I used a sling and hit one of 'em with a rock. Didn't mean ta kill 'im." Koora dropped his arms to his sides.

"Of course not," Willa said kindly. "Who was it that you . . . killed?"

"The one called Jack," Callie said. "The other man with 'im was the quiet one. He got scared and rode off."

Rebecca looked toward town. "They're most likely on their way here," she said, unable to keep the tremor out of her voice. "We have to tell Daniel."

"First," Willa said firmly, "we need to collect ourselves. There's no need to speak about what happened to anyone outside our family." She drew in a slow breath, closed her eyes a moment, then looked at Koora. "You did what was necessary. Nothing more will be said about it."

"But the—"

"Nothing more need be said."

"Roight, mum."

Willa turned to Rebecca. "You take the children to Elle's. She said she'd look after them if we needed her to."

"I don't think that's a good idea. I'm likely to meet those men between here and town."

"Right you are." Willa walked to the balustrade and looked toward Thornton Creek. "If they show up, I want you and the children to hide in the root cellar."

She moved toward the stairs. "Now, where is Daniel? I thought he was going to stay close."

"Roight. I think we might 'ave seen him when we was ridin' home," Callie said. "Didn't know it was 'im, though."

At that moment riders were heard, and everyone looked to see who was coming up the road. Daniel, Jim, and Wood-man appeared. They were riding hard. Daniel didn't stop until he'd reached the staircase.

"I saw you two riding like there were demons after you," he said. "What happened?"

"I seen those men," Callie said. "They stopped me on the road. Said ta tell ya that yer out of time and they're comin'."

"How many of them were there?"

"There was just two, but . . . Koora killed one, and the other man rode away. Figure he went ta get help."

"The roustabouts and drovers are working down on the south section," Jim said.

"So it's just us?" Daniel asked, looking from Jim to Woodman to Koora. His eyes rested on Koora. "You know how to use a gun?"

"I do."

"I'll see that you get one, then." Daniel's eyes stayed on Koora. "How did you kill that man?"

"Sling and a rock."

"They had rifles?"

"Roight. They did."

Daniel looked toward town. "Figure there'll be extra men this time, probably more bushrangers. If we're to take a stand, we'll need help."

"The men won't be back 'til the end of the day," Jim said.

"I could go after them," Rebecca offered. "I know the area, and I'm a good rider."

"No," Daniel said. "I'll not have you risk your life."

"But . . ."

Daniel raised his hand, palm out. "You've got to think of the children. Where would they be without a mother? Marshal's men could be out there anywhere. And I . . . I don't want to think what they'd do to you if they got hold of you."

"What 'bout me?" Callie asked.

"You?"

"Roight. I can ride. I could get help, eh?"

"And what will you do if those men find you?" Rebecca asked. "They'll blame you for what happened to the man who was killed."

Callie leveled a serious gaze on Rebecca. "Yer fine people. I care 'bout ya. I want ta help." Her eyes teared. "And . . . and God will look after me." She smiled. "Yer God is a big God, roight? That's what ya always say, and I believe it."

"Oh, Callie." For a moment Rebecca could think only about how her years of praying for Callie had been answered. "You believe?"

"Roight. I do." Callie moved toward the horse. "I best be on me way, eh?"

"Be careful." Rebecca caught hold of Callie's hand. "I couldn't stand it if something happened to you."

"You keep your eyes open for trouble," Daniel said, helping Callie up into the saddle.

"I'll be watchin'."

Koora stood beside the horse, his hand resting on the animal's shoulder. "Watch yerself, eh?"

"I will."

"Ya'll find the blokes down on the south end, along the deep draw, beyond the river," Woodman said.

Callie nodded.

"God be with you," Willa said.

"He is, mum." Callie turned the horse and kicked it and galloped toward the road.

Rebecca stepped close to Daniel and took his hand. "She'll be fine, right?"

"Right." He looked at Rebecca. "I want you to take the children to the root cellar. I don't want them 'round when those bushrangers get 'ere."

"But—"

"Rebecca," Daniel said sternly.

"I'll have Lily watch them. I won't leave you." With a challenge, Rebecca met his eyes.

Daniel smiled and pulled her close. "You're a one aren't you." He smoothed her hair. "You stay hidden though."

"All right."

"You promise?"

"Yes. But I know a little bit about using a gun. I might be able to help."

Daniel gazed at her, then cupped her cheek in his hand. "I'm so sorry. This is my fault. All of it." He turned then and stared at the distant prairie.

Rebecca pressed in close to his side. "Daniel. Please, no more regrets. You did what you thought you had to."

"No. I did what was easiest." His eyes glistened. "I didn't have enough faith to wait. And now you and mum and the children . . ." He shook his head. "If Dad could see me—"

"If your father could see you, he'd be proud," Willa cut in. "You're a brave man and an honorable man. And you've done your best to protect and care for this station and your family." Willa's eyes were filled with pride. "Your father couldn't have asked for a better son."

Daniel smiled. "Thanks, Mum." He looked over the small group. "Probably be right smart if we prayed, eh?"

Woodman stepped up to Daniel. "I don't mind prayin' with ya."

Jim and Koora joined them.

Rebecca grasped Daniel's hand.

The family stood beneath the hot sun and bowed their heads. For a few moments no one said anything.

The heated earth and air felt good to Rebecca. A breeze touched her like a caress, and she envisioned the blue sky with its tattered clouds and felt as if she were standing beneath a grand cathedral—a place where God waited to meet with her.

Willa spoke first. "Our heavenly Father, you are ever faithful to your people. You see us here, weak and helpless and dependent upon you. It is only because of you that we dare accept this task.

"We have no doubt that you are the creator of all things, the protector of us all, and the provider of all we need for life. You are a great and mighty God. We bow to you and to your will. On this most weighty juncture, I pray that our hearts are brave and strong and yet that we shall still know compassion and mercy."

Again quiet settled over the group. Rebecca felt the Lord's presence, yet she couldn't speak. Still, she was confident that her voice was heard by the one who listened.

Finally, Daniel prayed. "God, it's my doing that we're 'ere now needing your help. I ask for your forgiveness. I was foolhardy and sinful. May you be merciful toward me. But even more so, to my family and friends. I know that whatever happens 'ere today, you are still God and my life belongs to you."

Rebecca was breathlessly proud of Daniel. She couldn't remember loving him more than at that moment.

"Lord, I have people 'ere I love. I pray for your protection. Amen."

Rebecca couldn't stop the tears. She looked up to see Willa pull a handkerchief from beneath her cuff and dab at her eyes. Even Woodman and Jim blinked back tears. Koora had an expression of appreciation and understanding.

Daniel placed an arm about Rebecca's shoulders and gently squeezed. "Everything will be fine, luv."

He smiled down at her, and the dimple in his cheek appeared. She leaned against him. "I love you. Oh, how I love you."

❦

Two hours passed, and no one came. Daniel, Woodman, Jim, and Koora kept watch, each armed with a rifle. Willa and Rebecca sat on the veranda, their rifles at their sides. Lily kept the children entertained indoors. The servants and their children had taken refuge in their cottages. The estate was quiet and felt as if it were waiting to take another breath.

"Willa, do you think we'll have to use these?" Rebecca asked, referring to the guns.

"I pray not. But if we must, then the Lord will help us."

"I've never killed anyone. Never even considered it."

"I doubt today will be the day we're forced to take a life. But whatever comes, I pray for the Lord's strength."

"I thought some of the men from the district would be here."

"Yes, I'm sure they meant well. But how would anyone know they're needed?"

Rebecca watched the plains, wondering what had become of Callie and praying that she and the men would return soon.

Joseph pushed open the front door and marched onto the veranda. Holding up a wooden sword, he tromped back and forth in front of his mother and grandmother.

Carrying a sleeping Audry, Lily stepped out of the house. "I'll get him roight back inside," she said.

"Oh, let him play for a bit," Rebecca said.

Lily smiled down at the little girl in her arms. "She's such a lamb. I'll put her to bed, eh?" She walked into the house.

A swirl of dust appeared in the distance, and Rebecca stood. "Someone's coming!" She stared at the cloud, praying it was Callie and the rest of the workers.

Willa stood next to Rebecca, her arm circled around her waist. "All will be well," she said.

Rebecca silently repeated the words. *All will be well. All will be well.*

There were several riders, but Rebecca couldn't tell who they were. Was it Callie, or was it Marshal and his men?

"Will you look at that!" shouted Jim with a broad grin. He was the first one to recognize the riders.

They were men from the district—Davis Crawford, the bartender; Patrick O'Brien from the mercantile; Rush Linnell;

Rev. Cobb; even Charles Oxley, the banker; and a handful of others—plus Cambria.

"Oh, my heavens!" Willa exclaimed. "Praise be to God! He's provided us with an army." Her eyes glistened with tears.

"What is Cambria doing here?" Rebecca asked as she followed Willa down the front steps and into the yard.

"Cambria Taylor," Jim almost shouted. "What are you doing here?"

"I came ta help. I'm a good shot, and I figured ya could use me."

He took hold of her arms, acting as if he would scold her. "I ought to tan your hide." A smile broke out on his face, and he scooped her into a hug.

"I just couldn't not come," she said. "I love ya. I'm going ta be yer wife soon, and figured I belong with ya."

"All right, then," Jim said. "You're a ringer for sure."

"Oh, Cambria," Rebecca said. "You are something. I wish you'd stayed home where it's safe, but I'm so glad to see you."

"Couldn't stay away." She grinned.

"Got word those blokes Marshal hired were in town and figured ya'd need some help out 'ere," Rush said.

Mr. O'Brien climbed down from the back of his small, sturdy paint. He smiled. "Knew if I needed help, ya'd be there." He shook Daniel's hand.

Mr. Oxley approached Daniel. "This is my fault. I owe you."

"Thank you. But this isn't your fault. I had a choice, and I made the wrong one."

The men put their horses in the barn, out of sight, and the waiting resumed.

Mr. O'Brien stood beside Daniel, resting a foot on the corral fence. "Where's yer crew?"

"They're down the south end today. Callie's gone for them."

He kept his eyes on the endless plains. "You see how many men Marshal had?"

"Not exactly, but there's a number of new faces in town. I saw a mob of them at the pub downing their grog. Figure we'll have our hands full."

Another group of riders approached. They weren't Daniel's men.

"Lily, take the children to the root cellar," Rebecca said, trying to quiet her thumping heart. "Please. Hurry."

"Roight, mum. I'll fetch the bybie. Come along, Joseph." Lily took Joseph's hand and led him inside.

Rebecca, Cambria, and Willa moved indoors and stood at the windows. The men took up places in the barn and cottages.

Daniel, Woodman, Jim, and Koora stood in the yard and waited.

There were a dozen men riding with Marshal. When they rode up to the house, the horses raised dust and stirred up the chickens, who started squawking and carrying on as if they were expecting to become the evening's meal. Rebecca thought she could hear Audry crying.

Marshal sat upright on his horse, looking pompous and overconfident. Rebecca wasn't surprised to see him. He was most likely so sure of having his way that he couldn't resist being present to claim his prize.

She recognized the two men who'd visited before. The one she knew as Luke was riding Chavive. "Chavive," she whispered, feeling the sting of tears.

The mare didn't look her usual good self. She was thin and needed a brushing. She swished her tail again and again, chewed on her bit, and danced from side to side. Luke was heavy-handed with her.

Daniel moved toward Marshal, keeping his eyes on the man. "I see you felt the need to bring along help." He said, his tone light.

"Dangerous country," Marshal said. "Never know when trouble might arise. In fact, one of my men was killed today. Heard it was a servant of yours that did it."

"No one 'ere did any killing."

Marshal leaned on the saddle horn. "Oh? Well, figure we can sort that out later. I come to claim my property."

"Get down off that horse, and we'll do business."

"No need for business. Time for that's over." Marshal glanced from the house to the barn and then to the cottages. "Right fine property. It'll do nicely. Shame you and that lovely wife of yours didn't see fit to move your things out. Sorry to see you lose everything."

"We're not leaving. It's you who'll not be staying." Daniel walked toward Marshal. He took an envelope out of his front pocket. "Payment in full." He held it out. "Take it. Douloo's not for sale."

Marshal smirked and brushed it aside. "Don't figure you and your mates are any kind of challenge for my men." He glanced at the collection of bushrangers. "They're first-rate with a gun and don't mind killing when there's a need." His small eyes surveyed Daniel, Jim, and Woodman. "You'd be wise to take your family and move along. Don't think you'd enjoy seeing your friends and loved ones die."

"I told you; we're not going anywhere. You're a fool not to take good money."

"Some things are better than money." An evil smile touched Marshal's lips.

Daniel shrugged and tucked the envelope back into his pocket. "Have it your way, then."

Rush, Mr. O'Brien, Mr. Oxley, Davis, the reverend, and the others stepped out of hiding, their rifles trained on the intruders.

Surprise lit Marshal's eyes, but he quickly recovered. "You think this bunch of farmers is going to stand in my way?" He laughed. "You might get a couple of us, but every last one of you will be dead before we're done."

"These are good men, and we're not budging." Daniel tipped his head up slightly and looked at Marshal through lowered lids. "I don't want a fight, but I'll give you one if you insist. This station belongs to God, but he put it in my care. I'm about his business today." He smiled.

Rebecca pressed a hand to her chest. She could feel her heart pounding. It would be so easy for one of those men to kill Daniel. "Lord, please protect him," she whispered.

"I'm not going to tell you again," Marshal said. "You go, or my men will send you on your way."

The bushrangers dismounted, keeping their rifles pointed at Daniel and his friends.

"I'm a tolerant man," Marshal said, "but my patience has run out." His blue eyes looked like ice.

"I'd rather do business than kill one another," Daniel said.

"We'll do business, all right." Marshal rested his hands on his belt buckle. He moved his right hand closer to his holstered gun.

"Don't do that. You won't have time to draw."

Without warning one of Marshal's men shot Mr. O'Brien, hitting him in the arm. O'Brien yelled and grasped his arm as he dropped to the ground. The men with Marshal ducked behind trees and ranch equipment and started shooting. Daniel and his comrades ran and dove into hiding places. Mr. O'Brien managed to scramble into the barn. The two camps exchanged fire.

Rebecca dropped down below the window and pulled her legs in close to her body, pressing her back against the wall. When the explosions of guns stopped, she inched up and looked out the window. Three of Marshal's men lay in the dirt. She wondered how many of Daniel's friends had fallen.

Her attention was drawn to a swirling ball of dust moving

toward them. It was Callie and the whole mob of roustabouts and drovers. "Willa, look! They've come!"

"Praise be."

Rebecca could see Marshal crouching behind a gum tree very near the house. She placed him in her sights and gently put pressure on the trigger—she could shoot him if she liked. Her heart jumped, and she continued to study him through her sights. Could she actually do it? He deserved it after all he'd done to her family.

Rebecca caught a movement just behind Marshal. It was Woodman. He was moving up on the man. "Lord, make him invisible," she prayed.

"You're outnumbered two to one," Daniel called. "No reason to fight this out. I'm asking you to be on your way."

"When hell freezes over!"

"Don't think we'll have ta wait that long," Woodman said, pressing the barrel of his rifle against the back of Marshal's head.

Rebecca lowered her rifle and leaned forward, her eyes riveted on the rifle at Marshal's head. There was no need for her to do any killing.

"Tell yer blokes ta put down their guns," Woodman said.

Marshal hesitated.

Woodman pressed harder.

"Drop your guns," Marshal called, his voice quaking. "Do it! He'll kill me."

One gun at a time dropped in the dirt until all the bushrangers stood powerless.

"All roight. Let's walk, then, eh?" Woodman prodded Marshal with the gun. They moved into the center of the yard. Using the rifle, Woodman shoved the man into the dirt, and instead of lowering his gun, he stood over Marshal and glared at him. "Ya killed a friend of mine, hanged him. And ya hurt people I care 'bout. I ought ta kill ya. Lay ya down right where ya are."

Moments passed. "Please, no," Rebecca whispered.

Finally Daniel walked up to Marshal. "Get up."

Sweat soaked Marshal's shirt and dribbled down his face. He stood slowly, looking from side to side.

Daniel pressed a bank note into the man's shirt pocket. "That's the last of what I owe you. I don't ever want to see you 'round 'ere again."

Marshal stared at Daniel. Without his power he was nothing more than a second-rate crook.

"Get on your horse and go back to Brisbane. Then take the next ship to America."

Marshal climbed onto his horse, and so did his men.

"Take your dead and wounded with you," Daniel said.

Marshal nodded at Luke and Wade to load the bodies and help the injured. Luke bent to get his gun off the ground, and Daniel said, "Leave it."

Wearing a scowl, Luke headed toward Chavive.

"You can leave her too. She belongs 'ere," Daniel said.

Luke stared at Daniel, then looked to Marshal. "She's mine. I paid for her."

"Leave her," Marshal growled. "Wade, give him a ride," he snapped.

Reluctantly Luke climbed on behind Wade.

Daniel moved to Chavive and took hold of her bridle. Turning to Marshal, he said, "Be on your way." He leveled a hard stare on Marshal. "You'll do no more business with the people 'round 'ere."

Marshal used a handkerchief to wipe sweat from his face, then turned his horse and rode toward the drive. His men followed.

Rebecca, Willa, and Cambria moved onto the porch and walked down the steps. Rebecca ran to Daniel and hugged him tightly. "I was so frightened. You were wonderful."

Chavive nudged her, and Rebecca turned to the mare and

rested a hand on her face. "Hello, girl. Grand to have you home."

"I knew the Lord would find a way to get her here," Willa said.

Cambria tucked an arm into Jim's and kissed his cheek. "Yer a good mate."

Jim pulled her closer. "A mate forever, eh?"

Rebecca leaned against Daniel. "I was so proud of you."

"You did right fine, yourself."

"Callie, you were very brave to go and get the men," Rebecca said. "Thank you."

Koora rested a hand on Callie's shoulder. "She's a fine one, eh?"

"Yeah, well, this'll be a lesson to me—never go looking for help under a rock." Daniel bent and scooped up a handful of dirt. "The Lord's given me another chance." He sifted the soil through his fingers. "Douloo is the Lord's, but as long as he wants me to, I'll do my best to take care of her."

Rebecca reached out and caught some of the falling soil, then clasped Daniel's hand and pressed the earth between their two palms. "We'll watch over her together."

Bonnie Leon dabbled in writing for many years but never set it in a place of priority until an accident in 1991 left her unable to work. She is now the author of more than a dozen historical fiction novels, including *The Heart of Thornton Creek, For the Love of the Land,* and *Journey of Eleven Moons*. She also stays busy teaching women's Bible studies, speaking, and teaching at writing seminars and conventions. Bonnie and her husband, Greg, live in Glide, Oregon. They have three grown children and four grandchildren. You can contact Bonnie at leon@rosenet.net.